WHAT HAPPENED THAT NIGHT

A shocking and gripping psychological thriller

SUSANNA BEARD

Originally published as
Dare to Remember

JOFFE BOOKS

Revised edition 2021
Joffe Books, London
www.joffebooks.com

First published in Great Britain in 2017
as *Dare to Remember*

ISBN: 978-1-78931-757-2

To my sons Greg and Charlie
To my late parents, Bill and Marion Beard,
who I know would have been proud.

CHAPTER ONE

She remembered the first part of the evening well enough: the after-work crowd spilling onto the pavement outside the pub, the hum of voices, the smell of beer. They had sat by the open door where it was cool.

They were joined by the usual gang in ones and twos and by the time Fergus turned up there were no seats left. “Move up,” he said, squeezing onto the end of the bench next to Lisa. “Give a man some space.” As he sat down she caught a whiff of whisky mingled with a strange, earthy smell she couldn’t identify. Sweat glistened on his forehead.

“How’s it going, then, Lisa?” he said.

“Yeah, good, thanks,” she said, shifting her leg away from his, trying not to be too obvious. There were now four of them on a bench meant for two and she was hemmed in, uncomfortable and hot.

She was glad when someone found him a chair.

* * *

She and Ali left soon after to walk the short distance to the flat. There were plenty of people around; the corner shop still open, catering for late workers on their way home. Ali stopped for some milk.

As Lisa waited outside, someone tapped her on the shoulder. The old trick, tapping on one shoulder, but standing at the other, so you turn the wrong way. It was Fergus.

"Going home already?" she said.

He grinned at her. "Yeah. Not much happening, I'm moving on. What're you doing?"

"Waiting for Ali to get some milk."

He was standing a little too close. She could feel his breath on her hair, smell the alcohol. There were tiny trails of red in the whites of his eyes. He swayed slightly as he spoke. "Having your bedtime Ovaltine tonight, then?"

"Very funny. I actually hate the stuff."

Ali reappeared with the milk. They said their goodbyes and headed home.

For a while, that was all she remembered. By the time the rest came back, it was too late to tell the police; the verdict had been handed down and the sentence passed.

* * *

Her mum told her when she woke from the surgery. She was dazed for hours after regaining consciousness, drifting in and out of sleep, the sting in her neck interrupting dark dreams. She was dimly aware of a constant presence by her bedside, holding her hand.

Eventually she felt awake enough to speak. Her mum was stroking her forehead, and smiled a wobbly, crooked smile when she saw she was awake. "Mum. What happened?" Her throat felt like sandpaper, her voice deep and unfamiliar.

"Oh, my darling. How are you feeling?" Her mum's face was pinched with anxiety, her eyes puffy and red-rimmed. There was a nurse standing by the bed, fixing a line into a dangling plastic bag.

"I don't know. Pretty groggy. Why am I in hospital?"

"Don't try to talk now, darling. Just rest."

"But Mum . . ."

When she moved her hand, there was a tube attached. A piece of white sticking plaster pulled at the skin. With her free hand she explored the unfamiliar dressing on her throat, feeling the ache beneath her fingers. "What happened? I can't remember."

"Shh, darling, rest now. We'll talk later."

As she looked around her a dark mist fell and the shadows in the corners of the room grew together. There was something urgent, something important she wanted to ask, and she squeezed her eyes shut, trying to clear the fog. But her eyelids felt glued together and she drifted, falling softly into the blackness.

* * *

When she woke the next time, her head was clearer. The nurse poured some water and offered her a plastic cup, a yellow straw bobbing. She lifted her chin to drink, wincing at the pain in her neck. Her mum was still there by the bed, holding her hand as if she'd never let it go.

"Mum, please tell me. What happened? Why am I here?"

Her mum glanced up at the nurse, who gave a small nod, a black curl escaping the cap pinned into her hair.

"You were attacked, both of you, at the flat."

"Attacked? Who by?" A flush of panic ran through her. "What happened? Where's Ali?"

"I'm so sorry, darling, but . . ." Her mum's voice shook and she squeezed Lisa's hand tightly, her face close, tears in her eyes.

"Mum, what is it?"

"It's Ali, darling . . . she's dead. She fell from the window onto the steps outside. She hit her head . . ." Her mum's voice faltered as the tears came down. She wiped at them ineffectually with a crumpled tissue as Lisa struggled to absorb what she'd heard.

"Dead." It came out as a whisper. "Ali . . ." Lisa tried to sit up. The nurse came close and leaned across the bed, adjusting the line into her arm. "Don't sit up, you're still very drowsy. You need to rest."

"Mum . . ." But the nurse must have increased the sedation and she was drifting back into darkness, resisting, wanting to return to what she'd just heard. "Ali . . ."

It wasn't until later that her mother filled in what details she knew and she understood, with horror, what had happened to her best friend.

* * *

She never went back to the flat. Her previous life was reduced to a small bag of belongings. Lisa shoved it, unopened, under the bed.

She slept in the spare room, which had been cleared of the boxes waiting to go into the loft. She became used to the faded pattern on the thin curtains — always drawn, hiding the world outside — the pale blue of the walls and the single bed with its linen from her childhood.

She stayed in her room during phone calls, blocking out the sound of her mum's voice with a pillow. A police officer called in a few times, hoping that Lisa had remembered something from that night. He drank tea from their delicate bone china cups, his sausage fingers fumbling on the tiny handles, and probed for news. Lisa was glad she had no recollection of the event.

Then it started. One morning, as she lay in bed staring at the ceiling, there was a crash from the kitchen. She sat up with a start, heart racing, a memory striking her with blinding clarity. She saw Ali's face as she stood by the window in the flat, her eyes wide with horror. The curtains were open, the street light shining yellow in the darkness behind her. The smell of whisky was overpowering.

She sat on the edge of the bed, trembling, until the image faded. It was a long time before she felt steady enough to go downstairs.

She walked around the town as fast as she could, to tire her body and occupy her mind, but there were too many reminders of Ali. The bus stop where they used to wait every day, the shop where they'd bought sweets on the way home. In the park was the bench where they would sit for hours, wasting homework time, gossiping. Back at the house, she felt exhausted but she couldn't sleep. She needed distraction but couldn't find any.

She would have stayed longer, but the silent pressure from her mother, the unformed questions, felt like an ever-present weight on her shoulders. She was jumpy and bad-tempered. She couldn't confide in anyone for fear of making those around her even more worried. At times, her mum would ask how she felt, but without a word, tears welling, Lisa would shake her head, retreat to her room and lie on the bed, staring at the wall.

* * *

Her boss had been shocked and sympathetic when she heard what had happened; she'd understood immediately that going back to her job was out of the question for Lisa. The home-based work had come up later, and though she'd been reluctant, now wanting a complete break from her previous life, she realised that without some kind of income she'd have to stay at her mum's long-term and she didn't want that. She'd accepted the offer.

She took only her laptop and her old bike with her.

She'd have gone somewhere remote — the north of Scotland, maybe, or the distant reaches of Wales — but she didn't want to be too far from home, or from the psychotherapist she was seeing in the city. Though ambivalent about the weekly sessions — her stomach muscles clenched, her palms sweating — she knew she needed help.

So she'd looked at a map, drawn a virtual circle around the city and found a village with a reasonable train connection and not much more. She arrived one day, bought the local paper and trudged around looking for somewhere to live. Her criteria were simple enough: quiet, safe, affordable, furnished. 12 High View Cottages was the second place she saw and she took it immediately, moving in as soon as she was able.

* * *

It's comfortable in a shabby way, the sofas squashed and worn and the rugs on the wooden floor mismatched, like something her grandmother would have chosen. But it has all she needs and there's a cosy feel to it — mostly thanks to a small wood-burning stove in the sitting room, which adds a pleasant woody aroma and supplements the inefficient central heating. There's a small table and chair where she works each day and another in the kitchen where she eats. At night she can hear nothing. No cars, no people. The arrangement suits her.

She changes very little. Once she's made up the bed with new, plain covers, she manages with what's been provided or left by the previous tenant.

* * *

A few months in, she has fallen into a steady routine. Enjoys the silence, the isolation, the anonymity. The only person she has spoken to so far is her neighbour, John, a frail old man who lives alone with his dog, Riley. And, when passing his house, heading for one of the long walks she now takes religiously, Lisa was surprised when he asked if she would mind walking Riley at the same time. 'He's lovely really,' he said. 'Poor thing doesn't get much exercise. You'd be doing me a huge favour.' She was taken aback by her own prompt acceptance.

The wind bites her face as she walks and whips her hair into a tangle. She treads the frozen ground, forcing herself to march for warmth, her hands thrust deep into her pockets. She's glad of the cold; there are fewer people around and she can hide in her big coat and boots, a scarf wrapped securely around her neck. Riley trots happily alongside her.

A small group of walkers meet by the lake every day. They talk and throw balls for their dogs. She exchanges brief greetings with them but doesn't stop.

A little further on a woman falls into step, a golden retriever trotting alongside her. Lisa feels the intrusion but says nothing. Riley runs up to greet her, his tail wagging as usual. The woman stoops to stroke him. "Hello you," she says. "What's his name?"

"Riley."

"Great name."

"Yes. Not my choice."

"Was he a rescue dog?"

"Kind of. He belongs to my neighbour — he's old, and can't get out to walk him." This is the most Lisa has uttered in days. Her voice rings strangely in her ears, as if it's lost resonance through lack of use.

They approach the gate at the village side of the lake, a grey metal kissing gate straddling a large muddy puddle.

"I'm going round again," Lisa says, a lock of hair persistent in her eyes, hoping the woman will excuse herself, but she nods and plods on with her, their dogs loping ahead. Their boots stick in the mud and they skirt round the worst of it, treading down the grass at each side of the path.

"Have you lived here long?" the woman asks.

"Just a couple of months." She doesn't want to be rude, but she doesn't want to talk. Small talk was never her forte and now it feels so futile that she feels almost nauseous. There was a time when nothing much bothered her. But now her every waking thought seems shrouded in doubt. The unknown weighs on her.

"We're new to the area too, though my husband grew up round here," says the woman. "We live just across the road, over there. I'm Jessica, by the way."

"Lisa."

"Where do you live?"

"Just a bit up the hill, not far."

"Do you like it here?"

She shrugs. "It's fine."

"I didn't really want to come here, it's a bit quiet for me," Jessica says, with a sigh. "But it's a friendly place and it's great for walking. My husband's away a lot and we don't have children, so it's just me and Bobby here most of the time." She gives the dog's head a stroke as he walks along beside her.

Lisa nods, huddles into her coat. They walk on in silence. She still finds contact with new people almost unbearably painful. Though she knows it's not a way to live, she'd rather not know anyone at all.

When they reach the gate again, she makes her excuses and turns away towards her house.

* * *

A few days later, at the same spot, she realises she's lost Riley.

When she turns and he's not there, she's stunned. She'd been deep in thought, oblivious to her surroundings. She has no idea how far she's walked since he disappeared.

"Riley? Riley, come here. Where are you?"

She runs back along the footpath that borders the lake, calling and whistling, hoping to find him digging at a rabbit hole or waiting by the gate. She climbs over the fence on the far side and into the fields where horses sometimes graze, catching her clothes on barbed wire and thorns. She asks the few people out walking if they've come across a small black spaniel. Nobody's seen him. Frantic, she does an entire circuit of the lake, checking all the copses and footpaths which branch off the main track. There's no sign of the dog.

How could she have lost him? She looks at her watch. A whole hour has passed. He could be miles away, he could be on a main road, he could be running scared, or lying injured, unable to move. The panic rises. She's hot and sweaty from running and her heart's pounding.

Oh God, she thinks, where are you, Riley? I can't lose you. Where have you gone?

She's almost in tears as she reaches the gate for the second time and looks out onto the street, terrified that Riley might have reached the main road that runs beyond the village.

At the house opposite, the front door opens and Jessica appears with a watering can, her dog sniffing around her heels. Lisa runs across the road towards her, breathless with panic.

"Jessica . . . I've lost Riley . . . have you seen him?" She's panting so hard her throat hurts. She can barely speak.

"No, I haven't. Where did you lose him?"

"I'm not sure. I think I was by the lake, over the other side. I've looked everywhere, for ages. Nobody's seen him. He could be anywhere by now. Oh my God, what shall I do?"

"Hold on, I'll help you," Jessica says, putting down the watering can, which teeters on the uneven path. "Have you called the police or the vet? People sometimes take lost dogs there."

"No, I don't have a mobile. Could we use yours? I'm sorry but I'm really worried now."

Jessica hurries indoors and returns with a mobile in her hand. She's already dialling as she walks. After a brief conversation she cuts the call. "Nothing at the police station. Let's go round to the vet's, it'll only take a minute."

The vet's reception is empty except for a woman with a cat in a cage and a young girl working at a computer screen.

"I've lost my dog," Lisa says to the girl at the desk, still out of breath. "He's a small black spaniel, has anyone brought him in?"

"Nothing this morning, I'm afraid," the receptionist says. "How long's he been gone?"

"Over an hour now. I've looked everywhere. We were at the lake and he just disappeared."

"Probably chasing rabbits. They're all over the place, the dogs-"

Lisa interrupts. "Could you let us know if someone brings him in? His name's Riley. He is tagged."

"Is he chipped?"

"I don't know . . ."

Jessica writes her number on a message pad beside the computer. "My name's Jessica," she says to the girl. She looks at Lisa. "And the owner is Lisa . . ."

"Well, I'm the dog-walker, really. But he's my responsibility. Lisa Fulbrook."

The receptionist writes down their names and promises to call if she hears anything.

Back on the street, Lisa looks around and starts to run back towards the lake, not knowing which direction to take, but desperate to keep looking.

"Wait," Jessica says. "Wait, let's just think for a minute. You've looked everywhere around the lake and asked everybody. Nobody's seen him. Where might he go, if he can't find you?"

She stops for a minute and looks at Jessica, realisation dawning. "Home. I haven't been home. He could be there, or at my neighbour's . . ."

"Okay, you run home, I'll stay here and keep looking. If he's there, call my mobile. You do have a land line, don't you?"

She nods.

"Here, I'll write my number on your hand."

"Thank you, thank you." She runs as fast as she can, her legs weak, her heart thumping at the unfamiliar exercise. She's there in five minutes.

The gate is ajar and Riley is sitting at the front door.

When he sees her, he saunters towards her as if nothing has happened, tail wagging. Weak with relief, she collapses onto the path and hugs him, her cheeks straining at the unfamiliar sensation of a smile.

"Riley! Where were you? I've been looking and looking! Were you here all the time, you little monster? Don't scare me like that. Don't ever, ever do that again."

She ruffles his head and he runs around her excitedly. She stands slowly and ushers Riley inside. It's time to call Jessica.

* * *

"Lisa, hi! Come on in, have a coffee."

"I just wanted to say thank you for helping to find Riley." She hands Jessica the flowers she's clutching.

"You didn't need to do that. I was happy to help. Hello, Riley, you monkey, what got into you? You scared your mum half to death."

"He certainly did," Lisa says.

"Go on, have a quick cup of coffee with me," Jessica says, opening the door and beckoning her in. "I could do with some company."

Lisa checks her watch, in the pretence that she's busy. But her mind goes blank; she can't find a spur-of-the-moment excuse.

"Um, okay, then," she says, regretting it immediately. It's only a coffee, she tells herself. Don't panic.

They walk through into a small but immaculate kitchen. Everything looks clean and new and there's a faint smell of fresh paint.

"The dogs'll be fine in here," says Jessica. She indicates the kitchen table flanked by curved wood chairs, an invitation for Lisa to sit.

She inserts herself into the space between wall and table, feeling out of place and anxious. Jessica puts biscuits onto a plate and starts to make coffee, her movements neat and efficient. Riley makes himself at home on the dog bed in the corner; Bobby, unconcerned at the intruder, flops down by the cooker.

Lisa watches Jessica, noting the sparkle of an engagement ring on her finger, a wedding ring slotted neatly into the curve in the gold.

"So, how's Riley after his adventure yesterday? None the worse for it, I bet."

"No, he's fine. Probably had a great time exploring. I'm the one who nearly had a heart attack."

"We love our dogs, don't we? I'd hate to lose Bobby."

"I don't know what I'd have done if he'd been really lost, or run over." Though she tries to say it lightly, Jessica glances at her, a look of concern flitting across her face. She places coffee cups and milk on the table and sits down opposite Lisa. “What do you do for a living, Lisa?”

More small talk. She has to force herself to be friendly. It’s just a cup of coffee with a new friend, she tells herself, what could be the harm?

“I sub-edit technical documents, from home.”

“Is that interesting?”

She attempts a smile. “No, not really.”

But Jessica’s expecting more.

“It pays the bills.” Then, a little too fast, to shift the attention: “And you — what do you do?”

“I’m a teacher — lapsed. I had to leave my job when we moved here.” She plays with her hair, smoothing a flat section over her fingers. Lisa lets her talk and Jessica seems not to notice the shift in subject.

“My husband’s in the oil business,” she says. “To him, nothing else is important. He lives in a man’s world, travels a lot. Sometimes he’s away for a couple of months. I’m bored, to be honest, I need to get back to work.”

“Why don’t you?”

“He doesn’t like the idea. Thinks I need to be at home, looking after the house. Unfortunately, I disagree.”

“That must be difficult for you,” she says, trying to empathise, but the problem seems trivial and she’s already wondering how to get away.

“Oh well, it’ll sort itself out,” Jessica says, as if to finish the subject. “Anyway.” Jessica jumps up to clear the mugs. “Let’s have a drink one evening. I need to get out more.”

Lisa feels a flush sweep across her face.

“I . . . don’t . . . I mean, I’m not . . . I’ve been ill . . . I don’t go out very much.” Her voice trails away and she’s left staring awkwardly at her hands.

“Oh, I’m sorry.” Jessica pauses, clearly hoping she’ll fill in the gaps.

“It’s okay, it’s nothing really.”

"Maybe I could come to you one evening? If you're up to it? We could walk the dogs and then have a cup of coffee, or a glass of wine. Or you'd be welcome to come here. Mike's away most of the time and I'm on my own a lot."

"Maybe . . . soon."

Jessica doesn't push her further, to her relief, and she gets up hurriedly, feeling awkward and guilty.

Promising to return the favour though not meaning to, she makes her escape and walks quickly home.

* * *

When she'd first arrived at the cottage, with its squeaky front gate, its front path green with lichen and the paving cracked and uneven, she made sure not to linger at the door, not wanting to meet the neighbours. But the little house next door was always quiet and the only sign of life an occasional bark from the overgrown back garden. Once she started walking with Riley, she began to look forward to her outings with the good-natured dog. She ventured further each day, as far as the lake and its well-worn pathways. Riley seemed to love the routine, appearing at the same time every morning through a hole in the fence between the two back gardens and returning home only when she took him back at dusk. She grew to love his companionship, his soft fur, his dark eyes looking at her.

One evening, when she went next door to take Riley home, John seemed dazed and even more frail, so she offered to look after the dog for a few days until John was better. "Only if you don't mind," she said. "He does seem to love our walks and I'd be happy to have him."

He opened the door a few inches further and looked at her, frowning.

"Are you sure?" he asked. She nodded.

"That would be so kind of you. I feel bad, not being able to exercise him. Riley is my wife's dog, really — I kept him when she died but I'm too old to look after him properly. He's a good boy."

And that was it — Riley became hers. The dog came and went as he pleased through the hole in the fence, the arrangement stuck, and John seemed content that his pet had found a more capable owner.

Riley is her lifeline. She knows that. He provides comfort, companionship and a kind of rhythm. Before he arrived, she'd started to fold in on herself, living her life at her desk and on her sofa, only venturing out to the shop round the corner for the few items which were her staples. She'd begun to feel frighteningly transparent, as if she was fading away very slowly. The routine of walking seems to ground her, to give her solidity where before there had been none.

* * *

Stamping her feet at the gate and fumbling for the keys with numb fingers, she notices John at his door. He's wearing a tweed coat, several sizes too big for him, and a woollen hat. He looks shrunken, his skin deathly white.

"How are you, John?" she says when he sees her.

"It's so cold," he says, his eyes watering with the chill wind. "Can't seem to get warm."

"Do you need anything?" she says, pulling at Riley, who's struggling to get to John. "I'm going to the shop in a while." It comes out without warning.

"Come in, come in, can't leave the door open," he says, shuffling into his dim hallway and indicating the kitchen door as she wipes her feet on the thin mat. "Go on in, it's the warmest place."

"I don't want to disturb you," she says, still reluctant to go in. In the hallway it seems even colder than outside and she wonders if he's got the heating on. If he even has any heating.

"Not disturbing me — not much on, these days," he says, a flash of irony in his eyes. "Got a list somewhere. One minute."

He ushers her into the kitchen. It reminds her of her childhood home, with a Formica table, worn grey rug and wing chair in the corner, mismatched cushions pressed into a person shape and an old-fashioned antimacassar on the back. On the heavy wooden sideboard he shuffles some papers and finds a notepad. He tears off a sheet with a shaky hand and gives it to her. The writing is faint and wobbly. Tea, bread, Digestive biscuits, orange squash, fish fingers, frozen peas, washing powder.

"Is that all you need?"

"I wouldn't ask, it gives me a little trip out usually," he says. "But it is freezing out there and I'm not feeling good this week. Just get the small size of everything. Here, take this — it should be enough." He thrusts a couple of notes into her hand.

A silver-framed picture sits on the sideboard by the pile of papers — a small, white-haired woman in a patterned dress, arm-in-arm with a young, smiling man in a red t-shirt, blue sky behind them.

"My wife, Elsie," he says, seeing her glance. "We were married thirty-five years. And that's Oscar, my nephew, my only relative. Lives in Spain, lucky beggar. Wish I was there."

"Me too." She smiles weakly at him. "I'll be back soon with your shopping."

As Lisa returns home, John's groceries in hand, she realises she's getting involved. But, despite herself, she doesn't seem to want to stop.

CHAPTER TWO

Every Wednesday morning she drops Riley next door with John and walks down to the train station in the village. She travels the one-and-a-half hours to the city. She hunches by the window, staring mutely at the passing scenery, hoping no-one approaches her.

It is agony, this confrontation, every Wednesday, each week.

Post-traumatic stress disorder. She dislikes the term, feeling it reduces her to a category, so that they can file her in the right place. She doesn't want to be lumped together with other people, with other traumas. And she doesn't have a 'disorder'. Something horrible happened to her which can't be changed and it'll always be there in her past, an irrefutable fact of her life. She'd rather just leave it there.

Though, if she's honest, she is suffering and she knows it. The nights are particularly bad and often she feels numb with exhaustion in the mornings. Even when she's awake, it returns to haunt her. When she's asleep, she's unable to ward off the nightmares which plague her two or three times a week. They're horrifying, visceral. She's so freaked by them, she feels as if she's possessed by some malevolent spirit, attacking her in the night and controlling her mind.

She's almost given up trying to sleep at night, though she goes through the motions and climbs into bed every evening, late, next to Riley, his soft black muzzle quivering with canine dreams, his legs twitching. She's thankful for the TV in the bedroom, the DVD player and the stack of old movies she keeps by the bed, carefully chosen for their gentle, unreal, Hollywood-glamour stories and their U certificates. She can't watch the news — it's too sad, too bad, and most dramas and soaps too full of violence, anger and sorrow. So she wraps herself in Cary Grant and Elizabeth Taylor, Audrey Hepburn and Clark Gable, immerses herself in the black and white studio sets, the immaculate outfits and grooming. Sometimes she dozes off, only to wake at the end credits. She never, ever sleeps through the night.

Her only other distraction is a pile of books from the charity shop (not crime, not thrillers, not sad) in which she can lose herself. She avoids the internet except when she needs it for work and has given up her mobile phone, abandoned at her mum's house. Social media terrifies her.

The flashbacks have followed her too, undeterred by geographical distance.

She walks to the local supermarket to stock up. It's a small, unassuming shop, with a slope up to the door, three aisles of groceries and a fresh meat counter at the back. She takes a basket and heads for the chilled cabinet. As she moves towards the end of the shop, selecting a lump of cheese and cartons of milk on the way, there's a woman waiting at the meat counter and from the door at the back the butcher appears, a knife in his hand.

As she registers the knife, she feels the blood drain from her face. Her breath catches and her hand flies automatically to her throat. She starts to shake and the basket falls to the floor with a deafening crash. It's all there again, so real, so terrifying. She drops her bag and runs instinctively to the door. Outside on the concrete ramp she sinks to her knees, her forehead against the glass window, tears brimming, gasping for air, her heart beating out of her chest, only able to see the knife — that knife, the other knife.

She's only dimly aware of what follows. There are people around her, holding her hand and supporting her by the elbow as she struggles to her feet. The customer at the counter and the shop assistant take her into a back room and give her some warm, sugary tea while the shaking diminishes and the tears finally stop. They're kind and motherly, middle-aged women who seem to take it all in their stride, and despite her embarrassed pleadings, they walk her back the short distance to the house.

"A panic attack," says the assistant, whose name tag declares Marilyn. "My son gets them all the time, I know what it's like. Don't worry, dear, you'll be fine once we get you settled."

Back at home, she collapses onto the sofa with Riley beside her, covers herself with a blanket and hides from the world.

* * *

She doesn't say much to the psychotherapist.

In her head, she calls him The Psycho in a grim effort to amuse herself. It also helps to distance her from him, to keep him from getting too close.

She's early and wanders from the station through the streets until she feels pinched with cold. When she gets to the consulting room, the waiting area is empty. She sits and looks at the bare walls, wishing, again, that she didn't have to do this. The magazines placed neatly on the coffee table seem far removed from her life. She stares at the rug in the centre of the floor, its black and white whorls oddly mesmerising. She fiddles with the scarf around her neck, knotting and unknotting it, playing with the fringes, waiting.

He appears at the door and his smile is friendly. "Lisa, come in." He wears beige trousers and a blue jumper over a checked shirt. Informal, but neat. His hair's thick, greying slightly at the temples, touching the collar at the back.

She walks into the now-familiar room, trying to appear relaxed. She settles into an armchair, tense and uncomfortable.

"So, how have you been this week?"

What can she say? Fine? It would be a lie.

"The same." She knows it's not a good answer, but she's tired already.

She almost feels sorry for him. It isn't that she dislikes him, it's more that she hates everything about the visits and doesn't, can't, believe they'll help. The therapy draws attention to the one thing she never wants to think about again.

Yet there's no option. Sleeping pills are not a long-term solution and they don't seem to be helping much anyway.

He asks if she's using the diary. He wants her to record her nightmares, emerging memories and feelings. She hasn't forgotten to do it, she just doesn't want to. It seems wrong, somehow, to write it all down, as if in the writing it becomes more ordinary. And more real. She doesn't want it to be real.

She wonders if her case is more difficult than he's used to. Probably not, she's sure there are worse experiences out there. More terrifying than the unknown. And yet she's not making progress and it's of her own doing.

Behind him is a picture on the wall, splashes of colour on a white background, a silver frame. She tries to pick out shapes. Her eyes flick to the therapist as he speaks, and back to the picture when she answers.

On the way home the passing scenery forms a familiar backdrop for her disengaged emotions.

* * *

She hears Riley bark as she closes John's front gate. The clicking of claws on the tiled floor and soft sniffing noises precede the arrival of John's shuffling feet and his shadow behind the frosted glass. He stands back as Riley makes a rush for Lisa's legs, nearly knocking her over.

"What a fuss!" he says. "Never made that much fuss over me."

"It's self-interest. I feed him and walk him, that's all."

"He's been inspecting the gardens as usual, keeping guard on his estate." Today he looks brighter, a little less stooped.

"Come on then, Riley, off we go."

She decides to walk down to the lake to get some air after the therapy. She needs to balance the day. The light's fading as she approaches the footpath and it's that quiet, calm moment before darkness when the wind drops and everything seems to pause, waiting for the moon to rise. The lake is deep grey, its edges lapping softly against the muddy banks, and the trees, winter-bare, stand stark against a dappled, cloudy sky. There's no-one about but she feels safe here, away from the city, from the people and the past. She inhales the evening air and keeps Riley close so as not to lose him in the shadows.

That night, the rain sets in. She hears it first, drumming on the roof of the tiny kitchen, and smells it, earthy and organic, as she opens the door for Riley to go out. He takes one look at the sheets of water pounding the paving outside the back door before heading determinedly upstairs.

She shuts out the weather, turns the key twice, shoots the bolt top and bottom, and double-checks the lock on the small kitchen window. Turning out the lights, she heads for the living room, rattling the window to make sure it's secure. She locks and bolts the front door. Upstairs, she checks the windows in the spare room and then, brushing her teeth distractedly with one hand, unlocks and re-locks the catch on the bathroom window. Finally, lights out in the rest of the house, she closes her bedroom door and turns the key. Riley is already asleep on the neat grey cover of the bed. Abandoning her clothes in a pool on the floor, she climbs in.

Though she knows the house is secure and the street safe, she's glad of the extra presence of the dog. Lying next to him, her arm across his warm back, she finds solace in his uncomplicated presence. She lies there, listening to the rain, wondering if tonight, at last, she might sleep.

* * *

Marilyn, the kindly shop assistant, greets her cheerily when she walks in. After the panic attack, she would have preferred not to go back there, but there are no other shops nearby and she has to eat, so she's forced herself to leave the house.

She avoids the meat counter and tries not to look at the butcher, remembering to breathe deeply. The demons stay away. She likes Marilyn, who took the panic attack so much in her stride, and is grateful that she made so little of it. She doesn't ask too many questions; another reason why Lisa likes her.

Lisa's buying provisions for John. He calls in at the shop daily to get out of the house and to collect his newspaper, but walks with a stick to steady himself and can't manage anything too cumbersome. As she inspects the shelves, Jessica appears in front of her.

"Hi Lisa, I saw Riley outside and thought I'd pop in on my way past."

"Oh hi, I was just collecting some things for my neighbour," she replies.

"I'll help you carry it back if you like. I brought Bobby, too — he needs a walk. Do you want to wander down to the lake afterwards?"

It's late afternoon and getting dark as they drop the shopping off with John. They make straight for the footpath, the two dogs trotting ahead. A cold wind flicks their hair.

"I've got to find something to do," Jessica says. " I'm going mad on my own, with nothing to keep me occupied. My brain is dying. How can I keep it alive if I'm not doing anything with it?"

"Have you talked to your husband about it?"

"Not yet, but I suppose I'll have to. He's not the most receptive person, the last time I tried he just laughed. But I can't carry on like this."

As they leave the footpath and walk towards the road and Jessica's house, she stops and stares at a sleek BMW sitting in front of the garage. "Oh. He's back! Come and say hello."

Lisa, unprepared for this, is about to demur, but she's standing too close to the house to walk away now. The car door opens and a tall, good-looking man, his shirt collar undone and a mobile phone in his hand, climbs out. He stands leaning on the car door as they approach.

"Hello, you're back early," says Jessica, reaching up to kiss him on the cheek. "This is Lisa. We've just walked the dogs."

"So I see," he says, hand outstretched, taking hers in a firm grip. "Mike. Good to meet you." White teeth, brown tousled hair, and a slight, sweaty odour, mixed with after-shave. There's a heavy gold chain around his neck. "Please excuse me, I've had a bit of a long journey . . ." He turns back to the car to open the boot.

"I need to get back anyway. Bye, Jessica. See you soon." Lisa turns away and hurries up the narrow streets towards her house.

Back home, having fed Riley his evening meal, she makes herself a mug of tea, and sits warming her hands, wondering about the slight hesitation in Jessica that Lisa noticed when she saw Mike was home.

* * *

She dreams about the flat with its tatty kitchen and its lived-in furniture. Ali, her face pale, is standing by the window, saying something to her, trying to get her to understand, but she can't hear her, she can't grasp what she's saying. She knows it's urgent and she tries to tell her she can't hear, but there's something stopping her, something in the way.

The flat has grown into a confusing jumble of rooms and corridors, and someone's screaming but she can't find them, running from door to door, throwing them open in a panic. She runs through empty rooms into others, equally bare and echoing, and then she's horribly lost in the catacombs of an unfamiliar building, while the screaming goes on.

She wakes with a start, eyes wide, muscles rigid, her heart pumping painfully and her throat swollen with silent screams.

It's always in the middle of the night — four or five o'clock, when no-one should be awake. Wearily she turns on the light and shuffles downstairs through the cold house for a cup of tea, which she brings back to bed and sips while she watches one of the old familiar films until the cold grey morning.

It's because of the nightmares and the flashbacks that she perseveres with the therapy.

How long will it take? Will it ever get better?

She withdraws into her daily routine, wanting no past and expecting no future.

* * *

Christmas looms. In her previous life, she'd loved this time of year — the decoration, the anticipation and the parties. An excuse to be out meeting friends, drinking and celebrating. She enjoyed the traditions — the presents, the food, and the coming together of friends and family, and she insisted well into adulthood on a stocking by her bed and the full trimmings on the day.

Usually, by September, her mum, Chloe, had bought the presents, cards and wrapping paper. Some years she'd even ordered the turkey by the end of September — and started shopping for presents for the following year. For as long as she can remember, she and her mum had spent Christmas together. In the early years there were grandparents and sometimes an aunt and uncle and a couple of cousins, but the grandparents are long gone and the aunt and uncle moved abroad before Lisa had reached her teens.

When she was at school and later when she lived in the city, she and Ali would visit each other at Christmas. Lisa's mum would welcome the noisy intrusion with extra mince pies and fuss over presents and food. She would even come to Ali's house on occasion for a glass of sherry or mulled wine once the family meal was over and the girls wanted to get together.

But everything's different this year. It's November when the shops start to sparkle with decorations and even the local supermarket turns its front window into an incongruous winter scene — Rudolf grinning maniacally from a snowy forest — and Lisa's mood darkens. She dreads the familiar platitudes, the false anticipation, the requirement to be cheerful.

Chloe calls. Lisa knows what's on her mind.

"Sorry, Mum, I'm going to stay here with Riley. I'm really not up to doing Christmas. What about your friends?" She doesn't hold out much hope, but maybe her mum's neighbours will be on their own, too, and they can keep each other company. She hears the disappointment and concern in her mum's voice, but can't say what she really feels.

The truth is that she never wants to celebrate anything, ever again. As dramatic as she knows that sounds, she can't find it in her to be happy. To pretend that everything is okay. That Ali is by her side drinking eggnog and wearing a paper crown.

"You shouldn't be on your own," her mum says. "It's not good for you."

"It's what I need, Mum," she says, trying not to be too blunt. "Anyway, I've got Riley, and I like being with him." The pause at the other end of the line is a bubble of unsaid words hanging in the air between them.

"Honestly, I'm fine. I need . . . quiet. I'll come and see you soon after, I promise."

"Yes, but-"

"Mum, please."

With a sigh, her mum agrees. They say their goodbyes, leaving the bubble intact. She leans forward on the table, head in hands, wishing it could be different.

* * *

November turns into December and the weather sets in, cold and wet, with a roiling sky and a freezing wind that whips across the lake leaving angry ripples on the surface. Although the days are short and the weather foul, they walk further and longer, Lisa hunched and bundled up against the weather, the dog bedraggled, his coat soaked and dripping with mud, which he brings into the house and shakes onto the walls and the floor in the hallway. They climb a footpath beyond the lake, tramping across a field and up a hill behind the village, across farmland with grazing animals. They find that if they keep going, it stretches into a long loop, which, after a few miles, turns back around the hill behind Lisa's house. It's a good long circuit which takes a couple of hours and uses up some of the time which hangs ahead of Lisa on days when she has no deadline.

Jessica too, is dreading the festive season, though for different reasons. Her husband's family is coming to their house over the Christmas period. "I wouldn't mind," she says as they tramp along the muddy path. "Only his mum's a fantastic cook, and I'm not. Plus our house is pretty small. It's going to be really stressful. You're not going to be on your own, are you?"

"Well, yes, but I'm okay."

"Why don't you come to us? One more won't be a problem at all. It's not good to be on your own on Christmas Day."

"No, really, I'm fine. Thanks, but it's okay." Seeing Jessica's disbelieving look, she feels defensive. "I could go to my mum's, but really, just at the moment, I'm better on my own. Anyway, I've got Riley."

"True, less stressful than my in-laws, anyway! Well, you know the offer's there, and you can change your mind any time, if you like."

"Thanks." She says it, but she knows she won't.

* * *

Chloe had brought her up on her own from the age of two, when Lisa's father, a pilot, made a fatal mistake and crashed into a field. There were no survivors. The local paper made much of it and as a child Lisa had studied the newspaper cuttings in her mother's photo album. Over the years the paper faded into dark yellow against the thick black pages.

The relationship she had with her mother could, at times, be difficult. Chloe was old-fashioned in her views and believed in getting on with things, rather than examining her motivations and emotions. And she did 'get on with it', raising Lisa competently, ensuring she had a good education and a value system that she understood and adhered to, even through her teen years, when her friends were exploring the world and getting 'up to no good', as her mum would call it. Lisa had always tried to be obedient, never rebelling, not wanting to upset the one parent she had left. It wasn't until she was sixteen that she started to go out in the evenings, to enjoy her friends.

In growing close to Ali she learned that other children had proper families, with a dad, and siblings, and fun. They would laugh at the dinner table, or argue, slamming doors and stealing each other's belongings. Ali's family had opened up another world to her — and in doing so gave her more empathy with her mother. She began to understand what her mum had lost. Ali's dad, with his larger-than-life presence, deep voice and disconcerting sense of humour, was at first a frightening thing, so different and unexpected. But their family was close and laughter pervaded their home in every way. She soon began to like the maleness of it and the balance it brought to the home.

Ali had a brother — two years younger, not interested in the girls when they first began to spend time together, but nonetheless a sibling — something Lisa had longed for when she was small. At first Connor was awkward and fidgety when they were around and Ali treated him with the typical disdain of an older sister; later, though, as they grew up, he became more confident and they got on better, laughing and teasing each other as they watched films or went out.

She knew that her mum missed her dad. She spoke of him with such warmth and she never seemed interested in finding another partner. Or, Lisa came to realise, maybe she would have been, but with a child to bring up on her own, very little money and no career, it was simply too much for a woman like her to contemplate.

When Lisa had left for college she worried about leaving her mum on her own and she came back frequently at weekends. She coordinated the visits with Ali and their relationship hadn't changed in the slightest. Still so close, the two were more like sisters. So when they finished college and planned to move to the city, it seemed the obvious thing to share a flat.

Her mother, ever practical, sold the family home and moved to a terraced cottage nearby. She seemed content with her garden and her visits from the girls. She got to know a couple of neighbours who, like her, were widowed and alone. They became a close-knit social group, meeting regularly for coffee and a game of cards. Lisa was glad she was forming a new life and felt less guilty leaving her when she returned to the city after her weekend visits.

* * *

The doorbell rings. The postman, a rare visitor, hands her two envelopes, a large brown one, which needs her signature, and a smaller white one, addressed by hand. This one looks suspiciously like a Christmas card. She leaves it to one side and opens the larger envelope, which contains a printed document she needs for her latest work assignment. She settles down at her computer, forgetting the other envelope until later when she stops for a break. Opening it without thinking, she finds it is a Christmas card, and when she looks inside, she sinks down onto the sofa, staring at the spidery writing. It's from Ali's parents.

With love from Diana and Geoffrey.

Please come and see us when you're next in town, we'd love to see you.

Lisa's mum must have given them her address, despite her request not to give it to anyone. She can't blame her, though; these people more than anyone else were connected with her, through tragedy, for ever.

* * *

The police had taken her statement, such as it was, from the hospital room where she lay, a drip attached to her hand and a monitor bleeping next to her, curtains inadequately drawn around the bed, leaving gaps large enough for prying eyes. A woman police officer took the lead. She sat in the chair and leant towards Lisa's bed, brown eyes on hers. Her voice was gentle, the questions carefully worded.

"Can you tell me what time you got home?" and "Are you able to remember who was in the flat?"

Tears trickled down her left cheek onto the white cotton pillow as she tried to answer. Her mum had been there, holding her hand, and when she became overwhelmed with grief had insisted they leave.

Apart from the police, her only other visitors during that time had been Diana and Geoffrey. Her mum had stayed beside her for the short visit that seemed to last so long. They found extra chairs for them, heavy blue plastic with high backs, and they sat awkwardly at one side of the bed, away from the machinery and medical paraphernalia on the other. They'd cried together, all of them, and when Lisa's pain became unbearable, relief pumped gently into the swollen vein of her pale hand. As much as she wanted to, she could offer them very little, remembering only the early stages of that horrific night. They didn't push her, for which she was grateful. Despite their pain, Lisa knew that no-one could be more frustrated with her own patchy picture of the night than herself.

They had come back a couple of times when she seemed stronger physically, but she remembered no more than she had at first and she was so fragile emotionally that they didn't stay long, not wishing to be the cause of further distress.

Back at her mum's, frail as she was, contact with other people was out of the question, and though cards came through the post wishing her a speedy recovery, people wanting to help however they could, Lisa hardly looked at them.

* * *

She doesn't display the card. She puts it in a drawer and tries to forget it. She doesn't expect to get any others and wonders how she's going to block Christmas out completely over the next few weeks as it gets closer.

* * *

The psychotherapist, too, seems to think she shouldn't be alone. It's not that he actually says it. He has a way of asking questions, but she knows very well what he means.

She doesn't know why, but right now her instinct is to exist in a kind of personal bubble, without relationships, avoiding human contact. Maybe she's avoiding further stress; perhaps she can't trust people any more. She knows that this situation is flawed, but it's a reaction she can't deny.

He talks about group therapy — meeting others who've been through trauma. She recoils at the thought. Why would she want to hear other horrific stories, when her own has such a terrible grip on her? Maybe other people can talk about their horrors, but she can't. It's all she can do to get through each day and each night without screaming.

"Group therapy is about the last thing I'm likely to do," she says.

"You don't like the idea?"

"It's bad enough discussing what happened with you, without having other people hear it too. I don't want to listen to other people's traumas and I don't want them discussing mine. Why would I?"

"You seem angry at the idea."

"Well it's a terrible idea."

"It's quite normal to feel anger after a severe trauma," he says.

It seems to her that pretty much any emotion is acceptable after a severe trauma. She could laugh hysterically and someone would tell her it was 'normal'.

He takes her back to the event. Her voice cracks and breaks as she talks.

* * *

The day before Christmas Eve she calls in on John, to see if he needs anything. He ushers her in and she waits in the kitchen while he writes a short list of items. He's coughing — a hard, dry cough that shakes his whole fragile frame, and he asks her to collect some medicine for him from the chemist nearby.

She asks if he's got company for Christmas. "No, no," he says. "Nobody left."

"What about your nephew, doesn't he come back for Christmas?"

"Why would he? Weather's much better in Spain," he says with a wry smile. "There's only me and I'm not much cop. I expect you're with family?"

"I'm not bothered about Christmas, myself."

She thinks about him as she wanders down the narrow High Street to collect his prescription. His house is cold, he's not well and there's nobody to visit him. Does old age always look like this? She feels a sharp pang of guilt about her mum. Pausing at a garish window display, all twinkling lights and baubles, a pile of colourful fleece blankets catches her eye, and on a whim she goes in and buys one for John. At least he'll have one present, then. When she buys his food, she adds some mince pies and decides to wrap them as a present from Riley. Then she remembers she has nothing for her mum and goes back to the first shop for another blanket and some wrapping paper. She throws a packet of candles in her basket, too, for good measure.

Christmas is impossible to escape, she thinks, as she tramps back to the house with her bags. It's insistent, unavoidable. And for some, hurtful and horrible. All those trite messages, religious or otherwise, churned out year after year, make a bad situation worse for those who are unhappy, poor, lonely or just different. None of it seems genuine to her.

How far she is now, she thinks despondently, from the person she was only a few short months ago. Her life then was on a certain, normal course. She wonders if it will ever get back on track.

* * *

Chloe calls again, on Christmas Eve. She's getting together with her friends on Christmas Day and sounds quite excited about it. They're all helping with the cooking and will eat at her friend's house next door. "I've done the Christmas pudding," she says. "And Angela's doing a cake. We've got crackers. We'll all look a bit crackers, too — three old birds getting tipsy on Christmas Day!"

"Good for you, Mum," she says, "Have fun." She promises to see her later in the week and rings off, relieved that her mother will be in good company.

There's no work this week to distract her, so for the second time that day, she fetches Riley's lead and they set off into the gloom. It's not exactly raining, but there's a fine mist in the air, as if the edges of the clouds are touching the ground. Everything looks hazy and out of focus. The Christmas lights on the trees in the front gardens shine with a halo of green and blue and as dusk falls the village looks bleak, Dickensian, secretive.

It's too dark already to head for the lake, so she walks around the streets for a while, stopping here and there for Riley to sniff at fences and lamp posts. There's not much traffic and only a few people hurrying home with bags and packages. In some of the houses she can see families gathered and children playing. She feels oddly removed from them. She's not envious. She feels that Christmas doesn't apply to her any more.

That evening she wraps her three presents. She lights the stove and sits on the floor with Riley, brushing his coat until it shines in the firelight. He loves the attention and stretches his legs with pleasure while the brush gets clogged with fur and little clumps of dark softness land on the rug.

* * *

The malevolent spirit of her nightmares has no respect for Christmas.

There's the knife, shining with an eerie blue light, so close to her face, caressing her cheek, following the line of her jaw down to her neck. As it touches her skin, it's searingly hot. Someone is screaming. She sees Ali's face, ghastly in the shadows, staring in horror over her shoulder, turns to look, only she can't move, can't turn her neck. She must turn round, but however hard she tries, her muscles are frozen, her eyes are shut. The scene stops there for a long time and she can't escape, gasping for air. She wakes with a lurch to see Riley's nose right next to hers, sniffing her gently, licking her cheek.

"Oh, Riley, it's okay." His concern is reassuring and she strokes him, her heartbeat slowing gradually.

She sits up, the cold air assaulting her bare arms, and shivers as she grabs her dressing gown and slippers. She pads down to the kitchen, followed by Riley, who paws at the door to be let out. It's six o'clock. She unlocks and opens the back door and Riley bolts into the garden, tail swishing. She puts the kettle on and scuffs into the living room to check if the stove is still warm. A log is glowing slightly, so she adds a couple more and pokes at them until it looks like the fire might catch, closing the door and opening the vents while she scrunches up a few bits of paper. She chucks them in, poking them into the glowing embers until, with a satisfying crackle, an orange flame appears. She closes the door and goes back to the kitchen to let Riley in and make some tea. Outside it's just getting light, and there's a misty haze around, the paving stones by the back door glistening with moisture.

It's only then that she remembers it's Christmas Day. Cursing softly to herself, she retreats with the tea to the sofa. Worn out by the nightmare and the lack of sleep over weeks and months, she feels drained by the very thought of festivities. She puts the TV on, finds an old western and lies down on the sofa with the blanket covering her. She turns the sound so low she can barely hear it and watches the picture without registering what's happening. Eventually she dozes, the sound of the film soothing her and the warmth of the stove filling the room.

Riley wakes her, tail wagging, panting expectantly, his pink tongue hanging on one side of his toothy grin. "Okay Riley," she says, groaning. "I get the idea." She drags herself upstairs to get washed and dressed. She looks at the time. Still only eight o'clock. At least there won't be too many people around.

She throws on a coat, wraps a scarf around her neck, thrusts her feet into her boots and departs, deciding on the longer route where barely anyone walks on a normal day.

They walk for a long time. The sky brightens, a patch of blue showing through the clouds, a suggestion of a sunny day. She sees only two lone dog-walkers, who mutter 'Happy Christmas' self-consciously as they pass. By the time she returns, the patch of blue sky has disappeared and a low bank of cloud threatens on the horizon.

After breakfast she calls her mum, who's cooking, getting ready for Christmas lunch, the mumble of a radio in the background. She sounds excited and rushed.

"I'm doing angels on horseback and mince pies. I won't be able to eat for a week after this lot." There's a pause. "What are you doing for lunch, darling?"

"I'm absolutely fine," Lisa says. "I'm having something later with my dog-walking friend and her family." A lie, but it's worth it. She doesn't want to spoil her mother's day by seeming miserable.

"Oh good," Chloe says. "Glad you've organised something."

"Have a great day, and I'm looking forward to seeing you. I'll call you tomorrow."

"Happy Christmas, darling."

The one good thing about Christmas that she can see is that the TV coverage is designed for children. There's no violence, no sex, and not much to challenge the intellect. She spends the afternoon channel-hopping and avoiding the news.

At around five o'clock, when she's thinking she should deliver the presents to John before it gets too late, the doorbell rings. Riley barks and rushes to the front door, sniffing at the edges. This must be a mistake, she thinks, someone's lost, maybe. Telling herself to stay calm, holding back the fear that sets her pulse racing, she goes to the door, where she can see someone through the glass panels.

"Who is it?" Her voice quavers and she's annoyed with herself at how feeble she sounds.

"It's only me, Jessica."

Holding Riley by the collar, she unlocks the door, unhitches the chain. Bobby gallops through the hallway to the kitchen, Riley in pursuit.

"I had to get away," says Jessica. "I brought you some wine, I thought we could have a glass together . . . I hope you don't mind me popping by?" She's clutching a wine bottle and a packet of mince pies.

"Not at all," Lisa says and means it, surprising herself. She leads the way to the kitchen. "It's not very Christmassy here, I'm afraid."

"How refreshing," Jessica smiles. "I think I'm going crazy with all the Christmas cheer at our house."

As she retrieves a couple of glasses from the kitchen cupboard, Lisa remembers John. "I was just about to take something next door. Shall I ask John if he'll come for a drink? He's on his own and his house is always cold." They agree to go together.

John, too, is taken aback by the doorbell and by the sight of the two women. He's wearing an old dressing gown over his clothes, the frayed slippers on his feet and a disconcerted look on his face.

"Happy Christmas, John. Jessica's just arrived with a bottle, would you like to join us? It's nice and warm in my living room and there are mince pies . . ." Her voice fades away as she tries to think what else she could offer.

John shakes his head and starts to say no, but Jessica chimes in. "Oh please come, we'll only eat all the mince pies ourselves if you don't."

Hesitating, he looks from one to the other. "Oh go on then. Give me ten minutes."

Twenty minutes later they've opened the wine, put the mince pies on a plate, and are beginning to worry when he arrives. He has a packet of chocolate digestives in one hand, his stick in the other, and is dressed neatly, his hair combed. He eases himself into the armchair next to the stove as Lisa chivvies the dogs out of his way, and accepts a glass of wine.

They raise their glasses to Christmas and after a while they do it again. They work their way through the mince pies and start on the chocolate biscuits.

"You may think this village is a sleepy place now," he says. "But when I was growing up, it was no more than a few houses, a school and a couple of shops. The farm animals used to graze where the station is now, and the farmer drove his sheep through the main street. Most people moved away to get work, but I liked it here, so I came back after my training and married Elsie. She was my childhood sweetheart."

"It sounds lovely." Jessica says. "Do you have any photos? Was your wedding here in the village then?"

"Yes, in the local church. I do have the photos somewhere, I can find them if you like. It was quite a small affair, because we couldn't afford much."

"Only if it's easy."

It's early evening when he decides to go back. "Thank you so much, my dears, I've enjoyed myself," he says. "Nice to get to know you a bit, and to get warm! You've made it very cosy in here, Lisa."

On the way to the front door, Lisa gives him a bag with the two presents. "Here's something very small. One from me and one from Riley."

"How kind. I'll open them at home, thank you." He takes her hand and squeezes it warmly. She waits until his front door closes before she goes back in, thinking of him in that cold, empty kitchen.

When she gets back Jessica's putting on her coat and Bobby is waiting.

"They've just called," she says, waving her mobile. "Wondering when I'm coming back. Oh, well, into the fray once more."

At the door, she turns back to Lisa. "That was fun! The most fun I've had this Christmas."

Lisa realises that for a couple of hours, the first time in many months, that she, too, has had fun.

* * *

Christmas passes painfully slowly. She has no work to focus on during the day, only her long dog walks — mostly in the rain — and the odd trip to the shop. Jessica seems to be away or at least isn't walking at her normal time by the lake, and everyone seems to be busy with their families.

Sleep refuses to come.

A couple of days after Christmas Day she goes to visit her mum and sets off with Riley for the station in the village. She means to get there in the early afternoon, avoiding meal times. Her mum always cooks too much for her and she feels guilty when she can't do it justice. She carries a bag with the present and a card, along with a dog chew for Riley and a ball to throw in the garden.

Tinsel adorns the ticket office. A uniformed man waits as she fumbles for her money. "Good Christmas?" he says as he hands over her ticket.

"Yes, thanks," she says automatically. Riley sniffs at the doorway as she puts her purse away and lifts his leg distractedly. A trickle of yellow urine darkens the door jamb. A station guard yells at her from the other side of the room. "Hey, control your dog!" He comes towards her, chest thrust forward as if ready for a fight, finger pointing.

"Fucking dog, look what he's done. Why do you have a dog if you can't train him properly? Some people . . ."

The blood rushes to her face as the panic rises. "I'm sorry . . . look, I'll wipe it up." Her hands shake as she crouches down, rummaging in her bag for something to wipe up the pee, which is settling into a small pool on the floor. She finds a couple of tissues; they're woefully inadequate and shred in her hand, but it's all she has and she does her best.

She's trembling as she stands, the man still muttering behind her. She drops the wet tissues in the bin and walks away, crushed with humiliation, almost in tears. Riley is unconcerned, wagging his tail, and she crouches down to him to hide her embarrassment.

A woman approaches. Lisa tries to ignore her but she doesn't notice. "My dog pees everywhere too. It's the male of the species, can't control themselves. It was only a couple of drops. Horrible man. It's not as if the place is immaculate, is it?" She strokes Riley's back. Lisa gives her a wobbly smile and straightens up as the train approaches.

In the carriage, she sits hunched by a window, forcing her breathing to slow down. The scene in the station, a minor irritation for most people, has shaken her more than she'd like.

She can't live like this. She can't be frightened for the rest of her life. She's got to find a way.

* * *

Soon after that dreadful night in the city, lying there in hospital, she'd wondered about taking a pile of the drugs they were giving her and drifting off into oblivion. That was when she'd understood that things would never be the same. Surrounded by grief and questions she couldn't answer. Missing Ali. But somehow suicide wasn't right for her then and it still isn't, though sometimes in the dead of night when the demons visit, she wishes she had the courage.

As the train rumbles on, she imagines how it would be if one day doctors or psychiatrists were able to identify individual memories in the human brain and disable them, so that people damaged by terrible experiences could continue their lives. Perhaps one day they'll be able to. Too late for her, probably. It's with her for the rest of her life and she either has to continue this half-life, or she must find a way, somehow, to deal with it and create for herself a life worth living.

Anyway, she has a permanent reminder. The scar on her neck, easy to hide with a scarf or a high collar, is never going to fade completely. It's long — over ten centimetres — and still red and puffy, though it's a good few months since she left the hospital. Sometimes it aches, or maybe she imagines it, her mind tricking her with a memory of pain.

She can remember that she'd felt nothing at the time, or nothing except the warm tickle of blood on her throat as the adrenalin flowed. The pain had come later, when she woke in hospital with a bandage around her neck and a button in her left hand to administer the pain relief. It hurt horribly. She imagined her head loose, hanging by a thread, severed like some beheaded Tudor queen. She'd thought the scar was roughly horizontal, as the bandages seemed to indicate, but when the nurse changed them the first time, gently pulling at the dressing as it stuck to the dried blood and she winced and tensed with pain, she realised that it was at an angle, from jawline to collar bone, untidy and ragged.

"That won't be too bad," the nurse had said. "You were lucky it didn't go in further. It was within a couple of millimetres of an artery."

She thinks about that comment now, sitting on the train. A throwaway comment, of course, and not intended to be literal. But maybe true, in a way. She's luckier than Ali. That's true.

At her mum's, she drinks tea and eats biscuits while Riley gnaws away at his chew, a dried-up piece of animal skin which doesn't bear too much thinking about. Chloe's had a good Christmas with her friends and she shows Lisa the gifts they gave her — a pretty blue bowl from Angela, some scented soap from Jean. She's delighted with her fleece blanket.

Ali's parents have been in touch over Christmas, wanting to know how Lisa's getting on.

"Did you get a card from them? Why don't you drop round while you're in town?"

"Yes. I know, Mum. But I can't. Not yet. I'm not . . . I just can't. Maybe in a few months."

"You know, sweetheart . . ." her mum starts to say, and she closes her eyes, not wanting to hear. "I think they need to see you."

"I know. Can we just leave it? Please?"

"Can I tell them you'll come in a couple of months, maybe? I feel I should say something to them."

"Yes." To change the subject she gets up to put the kettle on. "More tea?"

While it boils, she goes up to the bedroom where she spent so many hours on her return from hospital. She pulls out from under the bed the bag containing her possessions from the flat, discarded without a glance when her mum brought it back. She looks at it warily, inhales and carries it downstairs, leaving it by the front door to take with her. If she's going to look, she wants to do it by herself.

* * *

Back at the village the early evening darkness has descended, bringing with it a sharpness in the air, a promise of frost. The house feels cold when she opens the front door and she shivers as she goes through to the garden to collect fuel for the stove. There's a pile of wood in the little shed close to the back door, dumped untidily there at the beginning of winter. Her bike is squeezed in next to the woodpile. It's dusty and spiders have woven threads from the saddle to the handlebars, high wires waiting for tiny acrobats. Otherwise the shed is home only to some garden tools and a broom, crammed into a corner. She puts the logs into a wicker basket and hurries back to set the fire.

Once the flames have started to lick around the edges of the logs she goes upstairs to the bathroom. The light in the mirror above the basin is harsh and unflattering as she washes her hands. She sees her face as if for the first time in years. She holds on to the illusion and examines the stranger before her. Grey-blue eyes look back at her, under a mop of unruly brown hair. Her skin is pale and there are dark smudges under her eyes. No makeup. A spot threatens to erupt on her chin and between her brows there are two vertical lines that used to go away when she wasn't frowning. Now they stay. This person looks unhappy, she thinks, and seriously unhealthy. She tries a smile and the face takes on a haunted look, as if posing for an unwanted photo, the smile fixed, not reaching the eyes.

* * *

Jessica's limping, making slow progress along the path.

"Broke my toe tripping over Bobby," she says. "I heard it break. That'll teach me to go around without shoes on. The doctor won't do anything. You just have to grin and bear it and it'll get better on its own apparently. Hurts, though."

"Do you need help walking Bobby?"

"No, thanks, really, it's fine as long as I take the painkillers. I'll just take it slowly. I'm so glad Christmas is over. It's such hard work having visitors. And Mike being home all the time. I suppose I'm too used to being on my own. Only a few more days to go. What are you doing for New Year's Eve?"

"Trying my best to ignore it. Earplugs, Riley and a duvet over my head."

“We’re going down to the Hare and Hounds — they’re doing a special party night. Why don’t you come with us?”

“Oh, no, I’m fine, thanks. I’ll be much happier at home with Riley.” Her reply was a little too quick, and she hopes Jessica doesn’t take offence. She winces at the mention of a New Year’s party.

They negotiate a narrow section of the path. The cold weather has hardened the ground and it’s less muddy than usual. The winter-grey trees look frozen, barely alive, the water in the lake black and dangerous.

“If you need company, ever, you will ask, won’t you?” Jessica glances at her sideways, the ponytail brushing her shoulder, as if she’s nervous of the reply.

“Thanks.” She feels awkward, as if she should explain. “It’s just . . . at the moment . . .”

“Sure.”

But again she asks herself, as she trudges back home, is it just at the moment? Or is this how life will be?

* * *

She sinks into the chair, her hands cold and clammy.

“How are you getting on with the diary?” He nods towards her bag, which isn’t quite doing the job of concealing the notebook. She wishes she hadn’t brought it.

“I haven’t written anything. Sorry.”

“Do you think you can start using it?”

“Yes.” Her voice sounds uncertain, even to her, though she means to be convincing.

“Don’t feel it’s like homework. Just note down what comes up — any new memories, any particular details of the memory. What triggers a flashback, or anything you think of that might be useful in these sessions. Also how you feel when it happens. It’ll help to write at a regular time each day, and date each entry, so you can keep track over time of what’s happening. Do you think you can do that?”

She looks at the picture behind him, then back at his face.

"I've got to." She draws breath, then hesitates.

"Is there something else?"

"Something happened the other day which made me realise I've got to change things."

"Things?"

"The way I'm living — how I've reacted to what happened."

"Do you want to tell me about it?"

"It was a small incident really. At the station. My dog peed in the ticket office and the station guard shouted at me. That's all. But I nearly fell apart."

"In what way?"

"I was horribly embarrassed, like anyone would be. But also I was terrified. He was quite aggressive but my reaction was out of all proportion. He wasn't going to hit me or anything, I knew that, but I couldn't help panicking."

"Why do you think you panicked?"

"Possibly because it was a man. I feel threatened by men. The confrontation, too. I felt like a child, weak and powerless. Unable to defend myself. I tried to clear the pee up, with a tissue — which was useless, I got it all over my hands. He watched me the whole time. I was so frightened, I was trembling."

"And now, how do you feel about it?"

"I feel like I can't handle the slightest thing. I've got to fix this. I've got to."

There's a pause. "It wasn't slight, though, that incident. Anyone would have been embarrassed. How do you think you should have reacted?"

"It's the disproportionate reaction. I was in pieces for hours, shaking and scared. I don't even know if I can go back there."

"Any more nightmares or flashbacks?"

"Both."

"Anything new or different about them?"

"Not really. Actually, I feel worse, if anything. More guilty."

"Let's explore that for a moment. Do you feel guilty in the moment — in the nightmares and the flashbacks — or is the guilty feeling constant?"

"Both. He was my friend. I invited him in . . ."

"He was a friend?"

She's surprised at her own willingness to voice this. It's the first time she's allowed herself to even think about the man behind the crime since the night it happened. "One of the crowd at the pub. We hadn't just met him that night."

"Had you or Ali had a relationship with him?"

"I don't think so. It's weird. I can only remember that we knew him when we saw him in the pub, and then again in the street. I felt uncomfortable sitting close to him. I remember that. I've tried, but apart from that, any other memories of him have gone. Maybe we didn't know him that well. I don't know."

"So, you feel you're to blame because you invited him in?"

The knot inside her tightens. "Not just because of that."

"Go on."

"Ali shouldn't have died! It should have been me!" It comes out as a strangled sob. "But what gets to me the most is I can't even remember what happened. She's just gone!"

His voice is calm, balanced against the anguish in hers. "Many people in your kind of situation experience this feeling. It's called Survivor Guilt. You feel guilty because Ali died and you lived, is that right?"

She nods, unable to speak, tears filling her eyes.

There's a pause as she searches in her bag and tries to compose herself. He hands her a box of tissues and she takes one without speaking.

"Should anyone else take responsibility for Ali's death?"

For a moment, she goes blank. "Well, Fergus . . ."

"So Fergus has some responsibility?"

"I believe she died because of what he did, yes. But I still feel I shouldn't have asked him in. And I should have stopped him when he started behaving aggressively."

"Could you have stopped him? Can you remember what happened?"

"I don't know. I just think — surely I could have done more?"

"Did you know what he was going to do?"

"No. I'd never have thought he'd do something like that."

"And yet you still feel guilty."

"Yes. I can't explain it."

"Is there something else that makes you feel it was your fault?"

"I . . . no, nothing."

He looks at her intently, as if he suspects there might be more, then leans back and glances at the clock. It's close to the end of the session, she notices with relief, wanting only to escape.

She walks slowly back to the station. In the waiting room on the station platform she sits with her back against the wall, her eyes on the door.

* * *

On New Year's Eve she's awake early in the morning with the light pouring through the thin curtains at the window. As she sips her first cup of tea, the cold air of her bedroom nips at her hands and she snuggles up to Riley for warmth, who looks at her with sleepy eyes, then settles back down.

"A long walk today, then, Riley." He sleeps on and she looks at her watch, hoping that the time has unexpectedly rushed by. It's still only seven o'clock, though, and she wonders how on earth she'll fill the hours that stretch ahead.

* * *

She wakes again with a start. 9.20am. It's a long time since she was in bed so late in the morning and she was sleeping deeply, undisturbed by dreams. She feels strangely groggy and stretches out to clear her head. The diary lies on the bedside table beside her and she picks it up, flicking through the empty pages thoughtfully. Perhaps I'll have a go. Or not. With a sigh she puts it back down again and struggles out of bed as Riley leaps up expectantly, knowing a walk is imminent.

As they head out into the cold, there's frost on the ground and the air has a sharpness that bites at her face. She pulls her scarf up around her neck and her hat down over her ears as they head off. She's glad of the anonymity of her warm clothes. She's going to head further out today but decides to do a circuit of the lake first. The sun's bright in her eyes as they reach the footpath and the lake reflects the blue of the sky, little ripples spreading out as the breeze catches the surface. Halfway round there's a small beach where the edge of the lake has worn away. Riley stops there for a drink. A wooden bench stands on the bank and Lisa decides to sit for a while to watch the ducks foraging for food under the surface. She feels better for the extra hours' sleep and the calm of the countryside; she resolves to start the diary when she gets back to the house. One very small step, she thinks, but she does feel slightly more positive, more determined.

When they get back to the house, they've been out for more than four hours and her cheeks are tingling. She puts some wood into the stove and goes up to the bathroom, abandoning her hat and coat on the end of the banister. Glancing into the bedroom, she notices the diary again and decides to take it downstairs as a first step towards getting started. She spots the bag from the flat, which she'd placed under the bed when it first came back, waiting for a better moment to look through it.

Suddenly curious about it, she takes it downstairs, scooping up the diary on the way. The bag sits on the kitchen table as if waiting patiently for attention while she makes herself some tea. She looks at it for a while and then, putting her mug to one side, opens it and empties the entire contents onto the table.

Well, there's her life as it was. It was only a few short months ago, but the items in the bag look like things from years before, barely remembered yet so familiar. There are three jumpers, some jeans and a few t-shirts. A couple of cotton shirts for going out in and some smarter work clothes. She doesn't expect to need those again. There's underwear, a small photo of her mum in a frame and some assorted jewellery. Her shower radio. Some books: lightweight novels, already read. A few bits and bobs from her bedside table.

Then, at the bottom of the bag, in a large brown envelope, she finds photos and notes from the noticeboard in the kitchen, and the contents of the top drawer in the sideboard, where they threw all sorts of stuff when they didn't know where else to put it.

She steels herself, clears a space on the table and empties the contents into a heap. A pink sticky note says: Mum's birthday present with an asterisk next to it, and Collect dry cleaning!! Another says: Bins — FRIDAYS. There's a torn-out ad for a local plumber — they used him when the landlord asked them to find someone to fix the immersion heater — and a card from a hairdresser in the city. There are rubber bands, sandwich bags, candles for birthday cakes and tea lights all jumbled up together.

Then there's a small pile of photographs. She picks them up and looks through them. Tears threaten from the first: Lisa and Ali, making silly faces into the camera. The two girls on holiday in Spain, tanned and long-limbed. They look young and carefree. There's one of Lisa at the flat, caught unawares with a piece of bread in her mouth, and one of Ali smiling directly into the camera.

Then she finds, under all the rest, a strip of photos from a booth. It's the two of them again, in winter scarves and woolly hats, blowing kisses. At least, it's the two of them in the first two pictures. The third shows the back of a man's head, with the girls either side, kissing his cheeks, their eyes laughing, peering into the camera. Two female hands adorned with rings and dark nail polish point down at him from above. In the fourth picture the mystery man has turned round. It's Fergus, she realises with a shock. He's grinning as Ali kisses his left cheek and Lisa kisses his right, and their two hands are still pointing at the top of his head.

Lisa's mystified. She stops rummaging through the contents of the envelope, now spread out all over the table, and sits back, trying to clear the mist from her eyes, the fog from her brain. She has no recollection whatsoever of the photo booth, the occasion, or the pictures. She turns the strip over, studies the backdrop in the booth, but there's nothing to jog her memory. Like the event itself, there seems to be no recollection of Fergus except the encounter in the pub and later in the street, and she realises that this is the first time she's even thought about how they knew him. Or how well they knew him. Perhaps her unreliable memory has erased more than just the event — it's erased almost everything else about Fergus. Perhaps she'll uncover other random things missing from her memory that will surprise and unbalance her as she attempts to recover from the trauma. Or perhaps it's because Fergus was so intimately bound with Ali's death in her mind, she's erased as much as she can of his history. With a sigh she tosses the strip of photos back into the jumble of items from the flat and retrieves the one of Ali, smiling.

She takes it with her into the sitting room and crawls onto the sofa, where she curls up into a ball, tears soaking into the cushion under her head.

She must have dozed for a while because when she rouses herself, it's already getting dark and the logs in the wood burner have settled into a red glow. She adds more fuel and goes round the house closing the curtains against the gloom. Riley wanders out into the garden and when he gets back to the door he's damp and cold with the beginnings of a new frost.

In the kitchen the contents of the bag are still strewn about on the table. She bundles it all back into the bag, except for Ali's photo, and carries it upstairs, where she puts it all away.

Back in the warmth of the living room, she retrieves the diary, sits and looks at it for a long time. Eventually she writes on the first white, empty page, in big letters: WHY? She slides the photo into the back of the diary.

After she's fed Riley and warmed some soup for herself, she selects the longest film she can find from her collection and settles down for the evening. It's only later, when she hears the crackle of fireworks at midnight, that she remembers it's New Year's Eve. Riley growls, his ears pricking. "It's okay, Riley. In fact, it's good. Good riddance to last year."

* * *

A couple of days later, the winter wind seeping round the edges of the old doors and windows in the cottage, Lisa's throat feels dry and sore. After a couple of hours she has a streaming cold. Sneezing and coughing, with heavy legs and a thumping head, she heads out for the daily walk. Jessica is nowhere to be seen but perhaps the injury has stopped her walking. She feels so ill herself that she retreats under the bedclothes with a hot water bottle. She cancels the week's session with the psychotherapist; she can barely speak, let alone travel.

Riley is happy to doze with her, though after two days of lying around he jumps up every time she moves, hoping for a walk, or at least some play. She throws a ball for him in the garden one day, but can't stay out long, despite wrapping herself in layers.

Her nose won't stop running and she's coughing badly now, neither of which is helping her sleep. Her dreams are unsettling; part-nightmare, part-fragments of her past, with school friends, boyfriends and Ali drifting in and out of empty rooms in dilapidated, unfamiliar places. One night she has the same flashback dream with the knife and the blood. She wakes often, sweating and coughing.

One morning, as she shuffles around the kitchen making breakfast, the letterbox clicks and a large envelope slaps onto the mat in the hallway. It's a work project with a tight deadline, and as she reads through the brief, sniffing and blowing her nose, she realises she won't get it done in her current state of health.

It's her first time at the doctor's surgery, which is a few minutes' walk from the cottage, down a small side street. The building is modern and practical, in contrast to the houses around it, and is surrounded by a small car park. The surgery seems clean and efficient and she signs in on a computer screen next to the reception desk. Sitting in the waiting room, she's embarrassed by her constant coughing and sniffing; her nose and mouth are now red and peeling with all the blowing and the freezing wind.

The doctor is sympathetic. "Looks like you have an infection," she says, feeling the glands at the sides of Lisa's neck.

"What happened here?" She gently touches the still-angry scar. Lisa covers it quickly with her scarf and as she hesitates, the doctor scans her notes. "Ah, I see. Let me just update myself . . ."

Lisa blows her nose to give herself time and manages to answer the practical questions about her medication (antidepressants), her therapy (ongoing) and her frame of mind (it depends on the day). Antibiotics are prescribed and the doctor recommends rest and a sensible diet. "How are you sleeping?" The inevitable question.

"Not too bad." She's reluctant to get into that discussion.

She's in a hurry to leave, not wanting to break down with a stranger, even her doctor.

As she leaves, prescription in hand, she passes the next patient going in. It's Jessica, in dark glasses, her coat collar high against her neck, scarf covering her mouth. "Oh, hi . . ." But she's gone, the door to the doctor's room closed.

The short wait at the chemist's and the walk back home are exhausting, so she feeds the fire, takes a tablet and lies down in the sitting room, coat still on, blanket tucked around her.

* * *

Twenty-four hours later she feels well enough to work for a couple of hours. She emails to rebook her therapy and calls home.

"Have you got enough food?"

"Yes, thanks Mum, I'm fine."

"Is there someone who can help? A friend or a neighbour?"

"You know there isn't." She tries hard not to sound irritated, but the words come out the wrong way.

"Well, you should get out more, it's not good for you to be on your own. You need a friend to look after you, Lisa, everybody needs friends."

There's a pause. "Oh, I'm sorry darling . . . I didn't mean . . ."

"I know you didn't." She wants to put the phone down, but feels paralysed by her mother's concern.

"I wish I could do more! Why don't you come home for a few days? At least I could cook for you, and I could walk Riley?"

"Honestly, I'm fine, Mum. I just need to rest."

"You're being too hard on yourself."

"Maybe. I've got to go now, Mum, sorry. Talk soon."

* * *

A week later, she hands him the diary, feeling slightly ridiculous. The cold has finally released its grip on her and she felt strong enough to make the journey.

He looks at the page with its single word and then up at her, his grey eyes searching. "Shall we talk about this?" he says.

She hesitates, picking at her fingers. "I just can't . . . I can't work out, why it had to happen. To me, to Ali. It feels like we must have deserved it or something."

"What makes you think that?"

"Well, I suppose we lived a pretty shallow life. We never thought about the future. Didn't think about much at all, really. Just had fun. It all sounds so stupid now. So superficial."

"And you think this means you deserved it? That your friend died, and you were badly hurt and terribly traumatised?"

"Well, no. Yes." When he says nothing, she stumbles on. "I know it's not logical, but I suppose I'm trying to make sense of it."

"That's completely understandable. But there are things in life that just aren't logical. You could have been run over by a bus; that's not logical either, and there's nothing you could do to deserve that. Did you think you were in danger?"

"No. But . . ."

"But?"

"It was my fault."

"In what way do you think it was your fault?"

"Well I've told you. I let him in. And he was . . ." she trails off, not really knowing what she's saying.

"He was a friend. Did you know what he was going to do?"

"No."

"Do you think he planned it in advance?"

"No."

"So how could you possibly have foreseen it?"

"We couldn't." But she resists the logic.

"Last time we discussed your feelings of guilt about the fact that you survived and Ali didn't. How do you feel about that now?"

"She didn't deserve it. It should have been me." Her throat, already inflamed, aches with the effort not to cry.

"Do you think you deserved to die?"

She shakes her head.

"But if you could change places, so you died and Ali lived, would you blame her for what happened?"

She stares at him with wide, tearful eyes. She can't seem to drag her eyes from his. She can't speak. She nods once, then covers her face with her hands.

He waits for what seems like an age. She knows he's trying to make eye contact, but she keeps her head down.

"I notice you won't look at me," he says, eventually.

She drags her hands from her face, bites her lip and looks at him.

"Say you were a judge looking at this case. What would you have to say about who was to blame?"

"A judge would say, did say, that Fergus was to blame."

He sits back in his chair. "It seems to me that you want to blame yourself. Perhaps you want to be a victim?"

CHAPTER THREE

The policewoman who'd come to the hospital had called one night to tell her.

Fergus had been found guilty of manslaughter and grievous bodily harm. He'd been found with Lisa's blood all over him and his fingerprints on the knife. The police had caught him as he tried to get past the shocked group of passers-by crouching over Ali's body, broken and bloody, on the steps. Some bystanders had apprehended him themselves. They had held him down until the police could make their way towards them through the crowd. With an arrest made, an ambulance was called immediately.

The police tried for a murder conviction but he claimed Ali had jumped of her own volition, and Lisa, recovering in hospital, still had no recollection of the moment. He'd admitted causing Lisa's injuries; he'd had no option when the evidence was so compelling.

Because of his guilty plea, Lisa was spared the agony of having to appear in court. She couldn't imagine how difficult that would have been.

It turned out he was known to the police, with a previous conviction for possession of drugs. He got six years.

"I'm sorry? Six years? Did you say six?" She was numb with shock, gripping the phone to her ear.

"Yes."

"But . . . he killed someone . . . is that all he gets?"

"I'm afraid so. It was manslaughter. There was no evidence that it was murder."

"But he still killed her — and he nearly killed me! Surely that's worth more than six years?"

"It's pretty certain she died as a result of his actions. But we couldn't prove murder. I'm sorry, Lisa."

"Six years just isn't long enough. He took Ali's life, my life's wrecked, her parents . . ." Disbelief gave way to anger; she had to stop herself from screaming into the phone.

"I'm so sorry."

"Wait, how much of that will he serve?"

"He'll probably be out in four. I'm really sorry."

Four years for Ali. Her mind was racing. She sank to the floor, holding her knees to her chest with her free arm.

"Where? Where will he be?"

She'd never heard of the place. She hoped it was a million miles away and hideous. She placed the phone back on the receiver.

She called her mum. "Did you hear? He got six years! It's a joke!"

"I know, darling. I've just got back from the sentencing. I'm so sorry. We were all horribly upset."

"It's wrong. It's so wrong!"

* * *

Riley has become her comfort blanket. Apart from unconditional love, he unknowingly gives her security, keeps her calm and facilitates her limited social life. He stays close when she's working and follows her when she leaves the room. Without him she'd have no physical contact, human or otherwise. She can't imagine life without him now.

Returning from the psychotherapist, she dumps the notebook with its single entry on the table and decides to go out straight away, before it gets dark. She can hear sheets of rain pounding on the roof, but she needs to get out and Riley will need a walk. She hunches into her coat, hood up, and goes to collect him.

As they make their way to the lake, she ponders the morning's discussion and whether the process of therapy, the revealing of her feelings of guilt and self-blame, is helping or hindering her recovery. Each session is painful and the emotional aftermath so debilitating it takes at least a day for her to recover.

She hadn't wanted a male therapist. Since the event she's particularly nervous around men, avoiding their presence when she can. But her GP couldn't find a woman with the right experience — of post-traumatic stress disorder, anxiety, fear, depression — and as she needed urgent help she agreed to see him, telling herself that she could stop if it didn't work for her.

Graham — the psycho — is gentle, with a quiet, thoughtful manner, and she feels less threatened than she expected. On his desk is a picture of a smiling woman and two small girls. She likes it that he's a family man. Behind the desk is a framed certificate confirming his qualifications.

He speaks quietly and seems to consider each sentence, each word, before he says it. Their sessions are punctuated by many pauses, which at first she finds disconcerting, but after a while she realises that the slow pace is helping to control her anxiety. He told her at the outset that the process would take some time, that it's important to build up a sense of safety and security.

He wants her to trust him. She's not sure she can. Not his fault, of course, but she feels resistant, angry and fragile. Those first few sessions were difficult, to say the least. She struggled to revisit her nightmares without sobbing for the whole hour and she experienced a powerful urge to get up and leave.

She had to tell him, at the beginning, the facts of the night when Ali died.

At times she thinks she's going backwards, although she's been in therapy for many weeks now. The nightmares persist and the flashbacks catch her unawares. But there's no option but to continue, at least for the moment, and the idea of changing to someone new, explaining it all over again, is unthinkable.

Despite the downpour, which is so heavy it's beginning to soak through the shoulders of her jacket, she takes the long route round the lake, grateful for the solitude. There's no-one around and she sits for a while on a bench, watching the surface of the lake, which ebbs and flows in the wind, the rain forming abstract patterns on the grey water.

She thinks about John. Will she reach old age and if so, what will she be like? Will she end up with a normal life after such a trauma? She tries to imagine herself as a wife, a mother, with a house and a garden and a husband who goes out every day to work. Perhaps her life will never be as she'd once hoped; she'll be on her own from now on and her life will be forever on a different course. With a sigh she stands up, calling Riley, who's now so wet his coat is flat and smooth.

"Come on, then, you — let's go home." And they plod, dripping, back along the muddy path, over the road and past Jessica's house towards home. She decides against calling in, though she hasn't seen Jessica for some time — they are absolutely wet through, and she wants to get home, dry off and get warm. She resolves to call in at the house one morning on her way to the lake.

* * *

She wakes with the cold. It's still early, but there's no hope of sleep and she decides to go out while there's nobody around.

There's been a sharp frost overnight and her breath is like white puffs of smoke. She walks fast until she feels warmer under her big jacket, only slowing down at the far side of the lake, where the frost is deepest in the shadow of the dense woodland and blades of grass stand upright, sparkling where the light catches them. Twigs are fringed with tiny thorns of ice, like barbed wire, as if warning off predators. When she touches them, the barbs collapse and disappear, leaving gaps in the armour.

She inhales deeply and blows out slowly, watching the steam clouds disappear before her as she walks. Last night there were no nightmares and while she didn't sleep more than a few broken hours, she feels calmer, better this morning than she has for some time.

It's just gone 8 o'clock as they leave the path and head home. She decides to call in on Jessica and finds her in dressing gown and pyjamas, a kettle in her hand. She opens the door with a smile.

"Sorry it's so early," Lisa says. "I was just passing and wondered if you were about. Haven't seen you for a while."

"No, it's fine, I'm up, just a bit slow getting my act together this morning, come on in." Jessica turns away to put the kettle on. "Calm down, dogs! Tea or coffee?"

"Tea please. How have you been?"

As Jessica turns towards her, the daylight strikes the side of her face and Lisa notices the bloom of a yellowing bruise on her left cheekbone. "Fine, apart from falling over the dog." She replies, seeing Lisa's glance at the bruise. "It's lovely, isn't it? I caught it on the edge of the table. Lucky it wasn't my eye."

"Looks painful."

"It's fine now, though it was bad for a few days. It covers up pretty well with makeup. I'm so clumsy, always banging myself. And I've had a nightmare with Bobby, he's been eating stones."

Bobby's had a number of pebbles removed from his intestine. Jessica shows her the scar, already healing well, a shaved area of pink-grey skin around it. "Cost me a fortune at the vet. I really ought to get some kind of pet insurance for him, though he won't be covered for this now, so I'll have to keep an eye on him."

A pang of guilt hits Lisa. "I haven't registered Riley at the vet. I still don't even know if he's chipped. I must check with John." The idea of Riley being hurt or unwell frightens her.

* * *

On the short walk back to the cottage she thinks about her instinct to cut herself off from people. It seems she's simply replaced the basic need for human contact with the companionship of an animal, which she loves like a person. Dogs aren't people, they don't hurt you, they don't let you down.

She calls in on John, taking Riley along with her. When he sees them at the door his face lights up and he ushers them into the kitchen while he looks for his file on Riley.

"I've had reminders from them to get his jabs done," he says, shaking his head. "I meant to pass them on to you, but I keep forgetting — memory's terrible now." He's rummaging in a drawer, where he thinks he keeps the file.

"Oh, hang on I know where it is, won't be long. Sit down, sit down."

He disappears into the hallway. The room is chilly despite the electric fire in the corner. There's frost on the inside of the kitchen window and the paint is peeling off in splinters along the edge. It probably rattles in the wind. The room has a faded, homely feel, though, as if once it was a proper old-fashioned family parlour, with its dark wood furniture and chintz curtains. But neglect has crept into its corners and damp into its wooden frames. There's a faint smell of rotting vegetables in the air.

John reappears with a brown paper folder and sits down with her at the table.

"Found it."

He puts on a pair of reading glasses, which perch precariously on the end of his nose, and starts to shuffle through the file with shaking hands.

"Oh look there's his registration paper, with his birth date. And the information on his chip. Tell you what, why don't you take the file. It's all about him, you'll find the vet's stuff there. Keep it."

"If you're sure."

The day remains bright and crisp-cold. Her own sitting room is warm, the stove refuelled, and she spends a few hours at her desk absorbed in her work. Then, stretching her stiffening shoulders, she remembers her promise to collect John's shopping and walks down to the supermarket. Comforted by the normality of the trip.

* * *

It's Jessica's birthday in a few days and Mike's away again.

"Come for a drink? I need to do something on my birthday," she says as they walk.

Lisa hesitates.

"Come on, I can't stay in on my own, that would be really sad. We'll go to the Hare and Hounds. It won't be busy on a Tuesday, especially if we get there early. We can walk there, the food's not bad. You'll like it."

"I don't know . . ."

"Come on, Lisa, it'll be fine. They're really friendly in there and you'll be with me. We can even take the dogs, if you like. What's the worst that can happen?"

She's not ready to say. Jessica has no idea.

The Hare and Hounds is probably a world away from the pub in the city. Nonetheless, she has to grit her teeth and force her reply.

"I — all right, then."

"It's a date then, good! Please don't buy me anything though. I just want to do something on the day. I'll collect you on the way there."

She doesn't feel in any way ready for this. She's going to have to steel herself, but determines that she must keep her promise and resist cancelling at the last minute, if she stands any chance of breaking the lonely cycle she's in.

* * *

That night, checking the window lock in the spare room as she does every night, she stands at the window, staring at the lights of the village in the darkness. With cruel clarity she sees not the village but the lights of the city in front of her. Ali is at her side. They're craning to see who's rung the doorbell, standing on tiptoe, laughing, then Ali heaves open the heavy sash window and sticks her head out into the night. The panic rises, then the same terrible shock of understanding, the fear, the awful weakness in her legs and the warm blood running down her neck.

Shaking with fear, her breath rasping, she feels her legs give way. She sinks to the floor beneath the window, a foetal ball of trembling limbs. Riley, close by as usual, licks her neck, his wet tongue tickling her skin. She reaches out to silken head. "It's all right," she says. "It's okay." She kisses the top of his head, wipes her eyes with the backs of her hands, takes a deep breath and stands up, wobbling slightly.

Suddenly, she's angry. Mad with herself, with her restricted life, with the demons that attack her without warning. Grabbing the diary from the bedroom on her way downstairs, she decides to record the flashback right now, while it's fresh in her mind and she can still feel the terror. Just making that small decision helps her feel stronger. She sits at the table and stares at the blank pages for a moment, then picks up her pen and starts writing.

She spends much of the time with her head in her hands, but when she's finished there are two pages covered with her scrawl. Reading it through is a step too far. She closes the notebook and puts down the pen. Small steps, she thinks, and goes to bed, exhausted.

* * *

On Jessica's birthday Lisa walks into the village to buy a card. Tying Riley to the railing outside the newsagent, she wanders in and studies the rather old-fashioned selection of birthday cards. Eventually, and with some difficulty, she finds one with a picture of a dog that vaguely resembles Bobby, decides it's the best on offer and goes to the counter to pay. A pile of local newspapers sits by the cash register and, on a whim, she buys one. It'll be the first time she's looked at any news since it happened.

"Not much going on around here," says the man behind the counter, nodding towards the newspaper as she counts out her change. "Just the usual petty thefts and school fetes. Can't think why we bother with a local paper."

She nods and passes the money into his outstretched hand. He's a big man with a paunch beneath which his trousers struggle to stay up, a brown belt tightened under the weight. His striped shirt is similarly challenged, its buttons straining over a white cotton vest beneath. His shop is quintessentially British; disordered and dusty, but with treasures to be found if you look hard enough.

Lisa's been here a few times before for office supplies, finding printer ink cartridges and copy paper alongside children's crayons and garish pencil cases. There's a notice board in the window with postcards pinned randomly to the cork, advertising items for sale and local services. As she unties Riley at the front of the shop, she casts an eye over the cards: Cleaner available, £7 per hour. Large brown leather sofa for sale. Electrician — no job too small. Rooms to let. Au pair available. Babysitter wanted. The stuff of ordinary people living ordinary lives. Before, she wouldn't have thought anything of it. Now she takes pleasure in the simple needs of the village around her, the absence of drama. She's had enough drama to last her a lifetime.

* * *

She buys some flowers for Jessica on the way back and works at her desk for the rest of the day, trying not to think about later. It will be her first evening out since Ali's death. She knows it shouldn't be a big deal — it's just a drink in a village pub, nothing to worry about — but still she feels the tension in her shoulders.

"Stop it," she says to her pale reflection in the bathroom mirror. "You can do this. You can."

She pulls on clean jeans and a warm jumper, arranging a scarf carefully around her neck. She's become expert at hiding the scar now, the scarves masquerading as a fashion statement. She feels naked without one, vulnerable to both the cold and the scrutiny.

The face in the mirror looks gravely back at her. Rummaging in the bathroom cupboard she finds a tube of mascara and some lipstick and applies them carefully, feeling out of practice. She doesn't want to look good or be noticed. That's the last thing on her mind. She's doing this for Jessica. No, she's doing it to prove she can, to break the bad spell that's destroyed her life and made her fearful, risk-averse and antisocial.

Turning away she finds Riley at her feet, looking quizzical. She's been thinking out loud, talking to her reflection, absorbed in her thoughts. "I know, I know. Must get out more. Ha."

As soon as they get downstairs the doorbell rings, making her start and prompting a volley of barks. It's Jessica with Bobby. They go through to the kitchen and Lisa hands over the flowers and the card.

"I know you said no presents, but it is your birthday."

"Lovely, thank you. Look at the card! Is it Bobby's sister?"

"Best of a pretty bad lot, actually, so you were lucky, it was nearly a cute kitten."

"That bad, huh?"

They head out with the dogs into the dark evening.

The pub is about ten minutes' walk, which they take fast to keep warm. It's quiet on the roads in the village and the only lights in the street where they're heading are those of the Hare and Hounds, a small white building set back from the road, with a few cars parked at the front. Lisa's mouth is dry and her heart starts to beat a little too fast as they approach the front door. She hangs back to let Jessica go first.

The smell of woodsmoke greets them as the door opens into a small room, where a roaring fire dominates, dwarfing the bar. There's a handful of tables with wooden benches and chairs around them. To Lisa's relief, nobody else is there, except a young girl who appears from a door behind the bar and welcomes them with a smile.

"What will you have, ladies?"

"White wine for me, please. Lisa?"

"Um, the same, please."

"How about you share a bottle?" the girl says. "It's better value if you're going to have more than one?"

"Great idea." Jessica glances at Lisa. "I'm quite capable of drinking the rest if you're not up for it. It is my birthday, and it's early yet!" She laughs, nudging Lisa gently.

The bottle comes in an ice bucket with two glasses and a bowl of peanuts, which they carry to the table by the fireplace. Lisa settles Riley by her feet and sits with her back to the wall, her eye on the door. Her chosen position once more.

Gradually the room fills up. A young couple arrives and sits in the other corner with glasses of beer, their legs touching, talking quietly. Two elderly men come in, greet the barmaid like regulars and lean on the bar. Soon there's a buzz of conversation in the room.

"Let's order food," Jessica says, indicating the blackboard. "Before they get busy."

She goes to order, leaving Lisa warming herself at the fire, which has settled into a warm glow. A black Labrador pads into the room from behind the bar and heads for the hearth, greeting the dogs with a sniff before collapsing in a heap on the warm stone floor.

"Don't mind Harvey," someone says from the huddle at the bar and a man detaches himself from the group and approaches the table. Lisa stiffens and looks around for Jessica, who's nowhere to be seen. To her relief, the man stops to stroke the dog, giving Lisa a quick smile as he straightens up to rejoin the group.

Jessica reappears, swiftly followed by the food, which is brought by the young barmaid on a tray.

"Any progress on the job front?" Lisa says, as they start to eat.

"No, not really, though I did have a look at the schools in the area. There are a couple of really good ones — I could see myself there. I've got to tackle Mike first, though, before I do anything about it."

"If it was local and you worked part-time, surely he couldn't object?"

"You would think so. But I think it's a matter of principle for him. He's quite old-fashioned in his views. Some women would love it — having money, and plenty of time to spend it. But it's not enough for me. I need more of a challenge. I can't spend my days at coffee mornings or going shopping or doing exercise classes. It's just not me. I'd be bored rigid. I am bored rigid. And anyway, I really like teaching." Jessica sighs, picking at her food.

"Talk to Mike."

"Yes, I should." Jessica looks worried, a frown darkening her face. "Needs some thought . . . and diplomacy."

They refill their glasses and Lisa begins to relax. Jessica is easy to be with and seems to respect Lisa's privacy; she doesn't pry, even though sometimes Lisa is evasive in her answers, for which she feels guilty and ungracious. And sometimes, despite a certain brittle edge to her voice when she talks about her husband, there's a twinkle in Jessica's eye and a turn of phrase that indicates a dry sense of humour. Lisa finds herself telling her about the incident at the train station.

"Oh Lord, that old grump," Jessica says. "He's horrible to everyone. How he gets a job dealing with the public, I don't know. A bloke got really upset with his petty rules the other day and there was a bit of a fight — Marilyn at the shop told me. She's a great source of information. It was all quite exciting for a place like this!"

At around ten o'clock, they're ready to leave.

"I enjoyed that," Jessica says, standing and putting on her coat. "Thanks for coming out Lisa, I know it's not really your thing."

"No, I enjoyed it too, really. I should get out more." She means it, though she's aware of the irony. She'd like to explain to Jessica why it's not her thing, but can't bring herself to. Not only would she have to feel strong enough to describe what happened, she'd have to be prepared to deal with the reaction, the questions, the sympathy. She's not ready for the sympathy.

When they get back to Lisa's house, Jessica heads on home with Bobby. Lisa goes straight to bed. The wine has made her sleepy, so once she's locked up, she settles in, relieved to have made it through the evening but glad to be back. Small steps, she thinks as she drifts off, her arm slung around Riley's sleeping form beside her. Just another small step.

* * *

The doorbell rings. Riley jumps of the bed with a loud bark. She's rigid with fear, trembling and sweating, all her senses jangling, her instincts telling her to stay put. But it rings again, urgently, and Riley, still barking, scratches at the bedroom door frantically. She turns on the bedside light and grabs her watch to check the time — still only 11.30, but too late for someone to call and anyway she knows nobody who would ring the bell at this time of the night. She tries to think logically. It can't be her mum, because she'd telephone first, and anyway what would she be doing coming here? Could it be kids messing around? Or a drunk, maybe, who's worked out she lives alone? Her mind works fast, trying to decide what to do, but then she thinks about John next door and steels herself to go down and see who's at the door, in case he's ill or in trouble and needs help.

Clutching her dressing gown around her, she unlocks the bedroom door. Riley squeezes past her and hurtles down the stairs, barking furiously, his tail wagging with excitement. Well, they know I'm in now, she thinks, hoping Riley's barking is enough to put off any malevolent stranger. She creeps down the stairs and sidles along the wall towards the front door, out of the line of sight of anyone peering through the glazed panels. Riley's gone quiet now, whining and sniffing at the bottom of the door.

"Who is it?" Her voice resonates strangely, her throat tight with fear.

"It's me, Jessica." With relief she collects the front door keys, unbolts and unlocks the door. As she opens the door, Bobby shoulders through and the dogs dash to the kitchen, almost bowling her over on the way. When she looks up at Jessica, she's shocked. The normally composed face is swollen and bleeding, one eye is so puffy it's almost closed and there's blood around her mouth.

"Oh my God, Jessica. Come in, quickly . . ."

"I'm so sorry. I didn't know where else to go. I had to get away . . ." Jessica is half-sobbing and can hardly speak through a thick top lip. She's holding a blood-soaked wad of tissues to her mouth.

"Come on, into the kitchen."

She follows Jessica in, guides her to a chair and runs upstairs to get a facecloth and cream for the cuts. When she gets back, Jessica has her face in her hands and is crying softly. Without speaking, Lisa hands her some tissues. She gathers a bowl of warm water and sits next to Jessica, lifting her face to bathe the injured areas with gentle fingers. The mouth looks bad, though the cut isn't deep, and her eye is swelling rapidly.

"Shit, that hurts," Jessica says, through swollen lips, flinching with the pain. Lisa boils the kettle and makes two big mugs of tea, adding extra sugar to Jessica's in case she's in shock. She goes into the sitting room, opens the stove and puts another log onto the dying embers, blowing gently until the glowing remains start to burn again.

They go through to the sitting room where she wraps the blanket round Jessica's shoulders. She sits on the floor beside her, her back against the sofa, facing the warmth of the fire. They sit silently for a few minutes while the flames take hold. The dogs settle down nearby.

"Are you okay?" Lisa says.

Jessica nods, though her head is down and the mug in her hands is shaking.

"What happened?"

"Mike. He came back early, to surprise me on my birthday. I was still out with you . . ." Her face puckers again and it takes a moment to compose herself before continuing. "He went mad, started accusing me of all sorts of things, pushing me, slapping me, and then he punched me, in the stomach, hard, and it hurt so much . . . I was really scared. Terrified. I only managed to get away because the front door wasn't locked. I just ran out and Bobby followed me. I'm so sorry, Lisa."

"Don't be, I'm glad you came here." They sit quietly, looking at the burning logs, the warmth surrounding them.

"What will you do?"

"I don't know. I can't go back tonight, I just can't. Could I sleep on your sofa? Would you mind? I'm so sorry . . ."

"Of course you can stay. I've got a spare room. It's pretty cold though. I'll put the heating on so it warms up a bit." She squeezes Jessica's arm gently.

She goes upstairs to flick the switch on the heating and on her way back, diverts to the kitchen and makes more tea, this time in a pot. When she goes back into the living room, Jessica is peering at her face in a little wooden-framed mirror by the window.

"Oh my God," she says. "That's hideous. He's really done it this time. How long is this going to take?"

They sit down again. "Shouldn't you tell the police?" Lisa asks.

Jessica looks stricken. "The police? But . . . he's my husband. It was my fault. I should have told him what I was doing." She stares at her hands.

"But he's really hurt you. How could it be your fault? He could've killed you . . ." Her own horrors stare her in the face.

The doorbell rings. They both look towards the sound. It rings again, as the women look back at each other in shock, while the dogs leap up with a cacophony of barking. Then everything seems to slow down, the noise is muffled and there's an ominous silence. Lisa's rooted to the spot, time suspended; the past is playing its cruel game again. Ali's there at the window, the street lights shining behind her, the bookcase, the steaming mugs of coffee on the table. It's a technicolour horror movie in razor-sharp definition. His hand in her hair, the sting of the knife at her throat, the smell of whisky.

She doubles up, hyperventilating, heart racing, knees buckling. She falls to a crouch on the floor, with Jessica kneeling beside her, hand on her back, calling her name and trying to pull her out of her state. The bell rings, insistent, the noise from the dogs is ear-splitting, but she can't move, curled into a ball, as the scene unfolds in front of her, relentless.

* * *

She opens her eyes and she's alone on the sofa. Riley is curled up beside her and the blanket covers her knees. Bobby's there on the floor, awake but calm, and she can hear someone moving around in the kitchen. She struggles into a sitting position, feeling slightly nauseous. "Jessica?" she calls out cautiously.

"Yes, it's me. Just trying to find you some brandy or something."

"There isn't any. Who was at the door?"

"It was Mike. I didn't open it. He started yelling at me and I said I was calling the police. He stopped after that. I think he's gone now."

"How did he know you were here?"

"He knows where you live, he asked me where I'd been, at Christmas. I don't know many other people." Jessica sits down beside Lisa. "Are you okay?"

"Yes. It must have been a panic attack, I'm sorry. Do you think we're safe? Has he gone home?"

"I don't think he'd break the door down, if that's what you mean."

Jessica goes back to the hallway without turning on the light and double-checks the front door. Lisa goes upstairs and peers out into the dark but she can't see anything. There are no street lights here and the clouds obstruct any light from the moon. It all seems quiet. She closes the curtains, fetches some bedding from the cupboard on the landing and piles it on to the spare bed. Jessica appears in the doorway.

"Lisa, would it be okay to have Bobby up here with me?" Jessica sounds shaky.

"Of course, it's no problem. I'll get him some water. Do you need anything else? Painkillers?"

"Yes, though I doubt I'll sleep anyway. Thanks, Lisa. We're quite the pair aren't we?"

Silently they make up the bed.

Downstairs she checks the doors and the windows, turns out all the lights, gets some water and some tablets. When she gets to her room, Riley is already curled up on her bed.

* * *

The house is completely quiet. She lies still, thinking for a long time about the events of the previous night. Mike's attack on Jessica has brought violence and drama back into her life, despite her efforts to insulate herself from the world around her.

Throwing the cover off the bed, she gathers her dressing gown around her, puts on her slippers and tiptoes downstairs to let Riley out and boil the kettle. It's still early, so she replenishes the logs on the fire, settles on the sofa in the living room and picks up the newspaper, untouched until now. Snippets about local schools, charity events and planning applications fill the pages; village life carrying on. She hopes the day will come when she's looking for excitement, rather than ordinariness.

She should be working today but with all that's happened she decides to take the day as it comes and help Jessica. Work can wait.

It's another hour before she hears movement upstairs and slow footsteps on the stairs. Bobby wanders through to the kitchen and Jessica appears at the door wrapped in a blanket, a bare shoulder and a bra strap showing. She's barely recognisable. Her face is black and purple, with dark-red stains where the skin's broken. Her mouth is bruised and puffy and her left eye swollen so much it's closed. "Hi. I look hideous, I know," she says, with a lopsided smile.

"Yes, you do, I'm afraid. How are you feeling?"

She hobbles over to the sofa and sits down gingerly. "Terrible. I feel really beaten up."

"Tea or coffee?"

"Tea, I think. If I can get it past my lips. I look like I've had the worst cosmetic surgery ever."

"Do you think you should go to the doctor? It might be worth getting checked over — particularly your stomach." Lisa's thinking she may need evidence, but decides to leave that for later, when Jessica has thought it through.

Jessica groans and lies down, the blanket wrapped around her. "God. I don't know. I'll see how I feel later. And it depends what I decide to do. Are you busy today?"

"No, I'm here all day. No need to rush, or decide anything until you feel better. You can stay as long as you like." She hasn't thought about that, but is glad she said it.

"Thank you. Sorry."

"Stop saying you're sorry. Really." She goes off to make the tea and when she comes back Jessica is sitting up.

Lisa sits down next to her. "Does he . . . has he done this before?"

"Yes, he has. A few times. He has a terrible temper. Something just snaps in him and he loses it completely. When I broke my toe, I was trying to get away from him. Usually he just pushes me around a bit. And then a few weeks ago, he hit me in the face and I was too bruised to go out for a while. You remember, I said I'd tripped over Bobby?"

Lisa nods, says nothing, haunted by her own violent shadows.

"I'm getting far too good at lying, hiding what's really going on," Jessica says.

"What else could you do?"

They sit in silence for a while, watching the flames lick the window of the stove.

"It's all over for me with Mike." A tear rolls down her bruised cheek. "I think I was always scared of him. Now I'm bloody terrified."

"How long have you been married?"

"Nearly four years. He was kind and thoughtful when I first met him, but he's changed with this job. He's always stressed and his work takes priority over everything. I want a job, and children, but he won't contemplate it. He gets really angry when I raise the subject. These things are fundamental. And my husband won't even entertain a conversation."

They sit as silent tears falls down Jessica's face.

"I mean it, Jessica, stay as long as you like."

After a while Lisa gets up and makes toast with jam and brings it all in on a tray. She gets the stove burning again and they sit for a long time, watching the flames and eating their toast, each contemplating her own personal torment.

* * *

"I'd better see the doctor, I suppose," says Jessica. "You're right, I need to get my stomach checked out, it would be stupid to leave it when it feels so tender."

"There are other good reasons to go, too."

"I know. I need another witness to corroborate my story for the police." Jessica looks deeply upset under all the bruising, her pummelled face pale and lined with anxiety.

Lisa calls the doctor's surgery and fixes an emergency appointment for later that afternoon. Then they take some close-up pictures of her battered face in the stark light by the back window. Lisa uploads them to her computer. When she sees the damage exposed, Jessica's hair pulled back from her face, she's both appalled and saddened.

Jessica needs some things for the short term — she left with nothing, not even a bag or her mobile, and she wants to call her sister. She starts to worry that Mike might take the mobile — while admitting there's no particular reason why he should — with all her addresses and contacts. To calm her, Lisa offers to walk the dogs and try, discreetly, to see if Mike is still at the house.

If he is, they have no plan — the idea of seeing him is too frightening for them both — but if he's not, at least they can go together and spend a few minutes there filling a bag for the next few days. Though Jessica left the house without keys, there's a spare set hidden in the garden, which Mike doesn't know about. Lisa wishes she were brave enough to offer to talk to him, though she's unsure what she would say even if she could find the courage. It's a pity for Jessica that the one person she knows in the village is the least able to stand up to anyone. One step at a time, she tells herself again. It's becoming an irritating mantra.

Making sure all the doors and windows in the house are closed and locked, Lisa heads for the lake with the two dogs. She imagines Mike lying in wait for her on every corner and her mind's in overdrive as she hurries on, nervous energy driving her feet into a semi-run. She decides to get the dogs exercised first before going past the house; though she's wrapped up against the weather and is barely recognisable, she knows Bobby will give her away, and wants to pass by as quickly as possible. Dogs stopping at every post won't help that plan.

She decides to ignore Mike if by some chance he sees her. Then she tells herself to stop thinking about it and just do it, or she'll go mad. She heads towards the house, eyes glued on the front, vigilant for movement. There's no car. At least not in the driveway. Trying not to look suspicious as she walks along the street on the opposite pavement, she glances towards the house and can see no obvious sign that he's there. Curtains open both upstairs and in the living room at the front. She hurries away to tell Jessica.

Back at home, she finds Jessica in a state of high anxiety at the thought of going to the house and finding him there, or of being discovered retrieving her possessions.

"Do you think I should talk to the police before I go?" she says, pacing the floor. "Maybe they'll come with me. Or at least I can say to him that he can't touch me or threaten me, because I've told them."

In the end she decides to call the police and delay going to the house until at least the next day. Knowing there's no way she'd want to go with her, Lisa urges her to make the call straight away. She leaves the room out of respect for Jessica's privacy but is waved back in to hear the one-sided conversation. Jessica raises her eyebrows and points to the handset and when Lisa nods her agreement, gives the landline number from the dial. She writes something on a scrap of paper and stands looking at it for a moment.

"They gave me a crime reference number." She looks stricken. "Oh God. It seems such a terrible betrayal. I can't go back to him, but I don't want him to go to prison."

"No. But you must report it."

Jessica nods but says nothing. She looks white with strain around the darkening blotches.

The police will be there in an hour or so. Lisa remembers the conversation at the newsagent; there's not much crime in the village to keep them busy. This will be a big incident for them.

It's late morning when they arrive. Lisa's disconcerted when she sees the chequered police car draw up outside, it's like a public declaration of the mini-drama taking place at her house. Two uniformed officers walk up the front path, a young man, probably in his early twenties, and a dark-haired woman some years older. They introduce themselves; their names wash in and out, forgotten immediately. Lisa's nervous, not only for Jessica, but on her own account. The scene's far too close to her own recent past for comfort.

She ushers them into the living room, which suddenly seems crowded, and goes to fetch some extra chairs from the kitchen, shutting the dogs away behind her. The visitors sit together on the edge of the sofa, with Jessica and Lisa in front of them on the hard kitchen chairs.

"Mrs Temple . . . can I call you Jessica?" the woman starts. She has a strong Scottish accent and a straightforward manner. Neither of them comments on Jessica's face. The young PC pulls out a notebook and pen and starts to write.

"Please tell us, in as much detail as possible, what happened."

In a low voice, Jessica starts on her story and Lisa sits quietly, looking at her hands. From time to time the policewoman interjects to clarify a point or ask a question, but otherwise the room is quiet except for the monotone voice and the occasional crackle of kindling in the stove. When Jessica falters, they ask Lisa a few questions about the previous night and what she knows about Mike.

"Right. I think we've got the picture now. Do you want to make a formal charge?" Jessica looks blankly at her and the woman explains.

"We can use police powers to intervene, arrest, caution or charge an abuser. You can choose not to bring charges, but if the injuries turn out to be particularly bad, we may bring charges anyway. If we arrest him, it might be a deterrent against him reoffending, at least for a short time. It'll also show him that we take domestic violence seriously and that his behaviour is unacceptable."

Jessica shakes her head and swallows, but says nothing.

"You don't need to decide right now. I suggest you go to the doctor, get checked out and make sure there are no serious internal injuries. You say you've taken pictures? May we see?"

Lisa brings them up on her computer and they get up to look. "Good. Can you email them to this address please?" The PC hands her a card and she nods.

"What can we do about Jessica's things?" Lisa asks. "She's too scared to go back, and I'm not . . ."

"Of course not. If you like, we can accompany you. We'll just sit outside in the car. Normally that's enough." A slight smile crosses the policewoman's face and Lisa wonders how often she's had to deal with violent men. Or women, for that matter, but in her experience, it's always the men.

"When were you thinking of going?"

"Tomorrow. I have to get to the doctor this afternoon."

"That's fine. Give us a call when you're ready to go — here's my card. You already have my colleague's. We may have some more questions, but you look as if you could do with a rest today. We can continue another time. You've been really helpful."

Jessica sinks onto the sofa and Lisa goes with them to the door.

The policewoman turns to Lisa, "If he comes here, don't let him in. Call us straight away and don't let her go near him. He's done some serious damage and she did the right thing to call us. It's good you have the dogs for protection. Are you close friends?"

"Well not really, we've only just got to know each other. But it's okay for the moment, it's fine for her to stay."

"Well perhaps she can contact someone in her family? She needs to be looked after."

"Yes. I'll check with her. Her mobile . . ."

"We'll sort that out tomorrow. But she'll probably know a number for parents, sisters, brothers? She should let someone know."

"Of course. I'll see what she wants to do."

"We'll be in touch."

* * *

Jessica lies on the sofa holding her stomach.

"How are you doing? Want something to eat?"

"That was hard. Do you mind if I go and lie down upstairs for a while?"

"No, of course, go ahead. I'll get you up for the doctor if you haven't appeared by then. I'm going to nip round next door to check on John now, I won't be two minutes, but I'll double-lock the front door behind me, just to be safe."

After just one knock at the door, John appears remarkably quickly.

"Are you all right, my dear? I saw the police car."

"Fine, I'm fine. Jessica had . . . an accident. She's going to be staying with me for a couple of days. I just wanted to make sure you were all right. Did we wake you up last night? We were a bit late."

"Oh no, I didn't hear anything. Hearing's not what it was. Is Jessica hurt?"

"She's going to the doctor later to get checked out but I'm sure she'll be fine. Do you need me to get anything for you?"

"You've got enough on your plate. Maybe later in the week, but I'm fine for now." She's relieved they haven't traumatised the old man, added insult to injury.

When she gets back, she finds herself at a loss, uncertain what to do until Jessica reappears. For once her own experience has taken a back seat, and for that, she is grateful. But the realisation of that truth makes her feel guilty all over again. She should eat, but can't make even that simple decision, so lies down and closes her eyes, glad of the temporary solitude.

An hour later, she wakes with a start. She hadn't meant to sleep, but had fallen into a deep slumber. Something's woken her. She looks around, wondering if Jessica has come downstairs, but all is as it was and Riley hasn't moved from his place in front of the stove. Suddenly frightened, she sits up slowly and slips on her shoes. Riley raises his head. "Shh, it's okay," she whispers, and creeps out into the hall.

There's no obvious shadow behind the stained glass at the door, but as she turns away, intending to look from the living room window at the road outside, she notices a small white envelope on the mat beneath the letterbox. Still treading very carefully and keeping to the side of the hall, she goes to pick it up, moving away from the front door as quickly as she can, without making any noise. She hurries to the window at the front, peers out from behind the curtain, but can't see anybody in the street.

Jessica Temple is written neatly on the envelope.

"Dammit," she whispers.

"What?" says Jessica, appearing in the doorway. Lisa hands over the envelope wordlessly.

"Oh. Actually I'm not going to open it now. I'm going to get ready to see the doctor." She leaves it on the table and goes upstairs again, but comes straight down and says, "Can I borrow a hat and a scarf? Don't want to scare the children."

Digging out hats and scarves from the coatrack in the hall, Lisa decides she'll have to go with her. If Mike is still anywhere nearby, Jessica can't risk a confrontation on her own. So, shutting the dogs away, she puts on her coat and they leave the house together — Lisa first, to have a good look up and down the road, just in case.

They arrive at the doctor's without incident and Jessica is called within minutes of arriving. There follows a long wait for Lisa. She flicks through some of the magazines without much enthusiasm, but soon gives up and contents herself with watching people coming and going.

After a full half hour Jessica reappears, papers in her hand, her face rewrapped in a woolly scarf and invisible but for her eyes. On the way home they're both anxious and vigilant, hoping to see nobody. Back safely in the warmth of the cottage, Lisa makes tea even before removing her coat. She hands Jessica a mug, handle first.

"What did she say?"

"She wants me to go for a scan for my stomach. It's probably not necessary but I suppose I should. My face will be fine in a few weeks. She's prescribed painkillers and sleeping pills. Shit. Should have got them on the way back. I'll probably need the sleeping pills."

Lisa offers to go for her and keeps her coat on, thinking she'll take Riley with her and go straight away. "Don't go near the window while I'm out. I'm going to double-lock the door again."

On the way back from the chemist she buys some ingredients for a simple supper, still feeling jumpy in case Mike is lying in wait. It's probably stupid but she's nervous enough as it is. Despite all her efforts to avoid involvement, stress, confrontation, they always seem to come to her anyway.

Back home there's no sign of Jessica. The letter, earlier discarded unopened on the table, has also disappeared. She drops her coat at the bottom of the stairs and goes up to the spare room. The door's closed.

"Jessica? Are you all right?" There's silence on the other side of the door and she's about to try the handle when it opens a crack and Jessica's damaged face appears.

"Yeah. Opened the letter. I'll come down."

"Okay. Well, come down into the kitchen. I've got your medicine, and I've bought some supper for us. We should eat. I know you probably don't feel like it, so I won't overdo it, but you need to try. It might help."

Jessica sits for a while at the kitchen table, watching Lisa prepare the food.

"He apologised. As I expected. Wants me to go and talk to him. But there's still something aggressive about the way he's talking. As if it's my fault."

"Do you want to go and talk to him?"

"No, no. No way I can do that yet. Going to stick with the plan to get the police to come with us tomorrow."

"Good. He can't just say sorry. I mean, look at you. I'm sorry, Jessica, but he can't be allowed to do this again."

"He hasn't seen me, though. Probably doesn't have any idea of the damage he's done."

"In more ways than one."

Over supper, which Jessica picks at, obviously struggling, they discuss what needs to be collected from the house and the things she has to do over the next few days. She'll call her sister once she feels strong enough and maybe arrange to stay with her for a while. She looks exhausted.

"I think you need to see how you feel once the dust has settled. No need to decide now," Lisa says.

"I suppose not. Actually, I think I need to go to bed. I feel really weird."

"You're shattered. Go on up, I'll let the dogs out and then I'm sure Bobby will come up in a minute."

It's barely eight in the evening and there's no question of Lisa going to bed, so once Jessica and Bobby have gone upstairs she potters about, tidying up the kitchen and checking her emails. She calls her mum and tells her that she's got a friend staying for a few days. Her mum sounds pleased. The fact that it's actually part of another violent drama in her life, rather than a sign she's getting back to normal, is ironic, she thinks as she puts the phone down.

Alone with Riley she sits for a while, letting the events of the past twenty-four hours wash over her. She picks up the diary and writes about what's happened, her reactions, the flashback. That'll be something to talk about at the next appointment. With a start, she remembers that it's on Friday, the day after tomorrow.

* * *

She wakes with a jolt. Did she hear something? Running through her lock-up routine, she's sure the house is secure, so what was it? Jessica or Bobby? The dogs would have reacted, surely, if there were an intruder. But still she's not reassured and, wide awake, lies listening intently for a few minutes. The abrupt awakenings are common nature for her now. She strains her ears for the slightest sound. There's nothing, as usual, but she's alert. Sliding silently out of bed she unlocks the bedroom door and creeps out onto the landing. Jessica's bedroom door is slightly ajar and she tiptoes across to check on her, pretty certain that it was closed last night when she came up. There's nobody there, no Jessica and no Bobby.

Halfway down the stairs, she sees a dim glow from the sitting room. Jessica is sitting staring into the embers in the wood burner. Bobby wags his tail gently at Lisa as she peers round the door.

"Oh, sorry," Jessica says. "I didn't want to wake you up. Still couldn't sleep."

"Don't worry, I'm not a great sleeper myself. Do you need anything?"

"No, I'm okay, thanks."

"I'm going to make a drink and go back up, doze a bit if I can. Put more wood on the burner, if you're going to stay down here, the central heating's pretty useless."

She leaves Jessica there, still staring into the fire, and trudges back upstairs. Back in the warmth of her bed, she remembers that they're going to Jessica's house today and prays they don't come across her husband. She wishes she was brave, like she used to be. Ready to take on the world. But actually, where did that get her? It didn't stop what happened or even help poor Ali. So maybe she hasn't changed that much.

Later, over breakfast, they decide to call the police and go to the house as soon as possible after Mike's normal leaving time, to get it out of the way. The sooner the better.

* * *

She doesn't go with Jessica. In the end there's no need. The police come and collect her, wait while she goes into the empty house and drop her back with the bag. There's no sign of Mike.

The detective comes in with Jessica and sits at the kitchen table handing over leaflets of organisations and writing down the names of people who might be able to help: a legal advice service, a support group for battered women, a mediator. Jessica's expression shows she's not ready for this, but she accepts the information without comment. When the policewoman has gone, she puts her mobile phone on charge, preparing to call her sister later.

"I'm a battered woman," she says flatly, but with a hint of a smile. "Sounds like a new kind of takeaway. One battered woman with chips, please."

The police have warned her to look out for Mike when he returns, concerned that he might get angry if he finds she's been to the house while he's out. But the house belongs to both of them, so she has a right to enter as much as he does. They've encouraged her to consult a family lawyer before she decides what to do.

"I've got to think about all this before I see him again. I'm going to call my sister, see if I can stay with her for a week or so. I need some distance. Once I've got more perspective and my face back, I'll try and talk to him."

Her sister, who lives in South Wales with her family, wants Jessica to leave immediately, today, but after a discussion of the pros and cons accepts that tomorrow is probably better, and Jessica borrows the laptop to book a train ticket. Lisa's relieved, as she'll be out most of the day tomorrow at the psychotherapist. She doesn't want to leave Jessica on her own, particularly when Mike might be around. Leaving Jessica to organise herself, she takes the dogs and goes out to get some supper before the shops close.

She arrives back drenched. The weather has worsened, with torrential rain and a bitter wind, and they had to run the last part. She dumps the bags on the floor and grabs a towel for the dogs, who are shaking themselves energetically, drops of muddy water showering the walls and the floor.

"Wait a minute . . . hold on, Riley!" Scrabbling madly at him with the towel, she manages to soak up the worst of it before doing the same for Bobby. There's a strong odour of wet dog. She vows to give them a proper wipe down later. She hangs her sodden coat and scarf to drip onto some newspaper by the back door. "Come here, Riley, in your bed. Come on, Bobby, lie down." Retrieving the shopping, she heads into the kitchen and drops the bags onto the worktop, then runs upstairs to dry her hair, still dripping onto her neck and shoulders.

When she comes back down, Riley has settled himself in front of the warm stove with Bobby. Jessica is in the kitchen, unpacking the shopping, two glasses of wine already poured.

"I felt we deserved it," she says, raising a glass to Lisa. A glimmer of her old self back.

Lisa nods towards the wine. "Too right."

Jessica's face looks even more colourful now, the dark bloom of the bruises deepening. It'll be a good few weeks until she's back to normal.

Jessica is chopping carrots when, after a few minutes, she glances at Lisa and stops. Under her gaze, Lisa looks up and realises, too late, that she's taken off her scarf.

"What happened, Lisa?"

Lisa's hand flies up to her neck protectively. The scar is still new and red and she can feel it standing out from her throat.

Jessica's eyes have grown large. "The panic attack . . . ?"

"It was a flashback. PTSD." She turns away.

"A flashback?"

"I was attacked. I'm sorry, Jessica, I can't talk about it."

"No, I'm sorry, I shouldn't have asked."

"Honestly, it's okay."

"But I've put you in a horrible situation if-"

"Listen, do you mind if we cook? I need to eat, otherwise the wine will go straight to my head," she replies, trying to sound cheerful, hoping the moment can be forgotten.

So they prepare the food together and when they've finished eating, Jessica turns to Lisa. "I'm so sorry to have landed on you. If I'd known about this, I would never-"

"Don't . . . really. You didn't know. Actually I'm glad you came. It's been good for me to think about someone else for a change."

* * *

The diary sits on the table in front of them, unopened. So much has happened that isn't about her. She describes to him the events of the last few days and her reaction to them. She feels weird today, as if she's floating.

"So, you say you experienced a flashback when Jessica's husband came to the door. Can you describe it?"

She stares at the picture behind him.

"No different, really. Still the screaming and the smell of whisky . . ." Steady. She frowns at the picture on the wall.

"What are you feeling right now?"

"Anxious, talking about the flashbacks. Panicky."

"What happens to you, physically?"

As she talks, it's as if she's watching herself as a different person, analysing what happens and when, as a scene unfolds in a play. She's listening to her own voice droning on and when she focuses on it, it fades away.

Sometimes she's irritated by his calm acceptance, his patient listening while she struggles with her emotions. But today she leaves his room feeling a little more positive than usual, just a fraction stronger.

* * *

That night, as if to punish her for that fleeting moment of progress, the nightmares return with a vengeance.

She's staring down at the familiar, though oddly surreal scene. The knife has turned into a sword, beautifully etched with exotic patterns that flash as the man brandishes it with exuberance, flaunting his power. The smell of whisky is overpowering. She and Ali are like hunted animals, running around the flat in terror, trying to escape, nowhere to hide, knowing that eventually they'll run towards their inevitable and bloody demise.

With a peculiar sense of detachment, still asleep, she knows this isn't reality, that it's just a nightmare, but the pain and the fear are, as always, horrifyingly present. She jolts awakes, sweating and panting hard, heart thumping. Riley, curled in the crook of her knees, looks at her intently and she almost laughs at his concern. Grateful for the relief.

With a sigh, she turns the light on, finds the remote on the bedside table and picks up where she left off the previous evening with Cary Grant and his cast of beautiful people.

* * *

When the buzzer went, they'd looked at each other, but weren't particularly concerned. People often pressed their buzzer, mistaking it for the downstairs flat — or kids pushed the button for a laugh, flitting away as soon as they looked out. If they pushed up the sitting room window, the old, rickety wooden sash, which was loose in its frame and rattled in the wind, they could lean out over the steps at the front of the house and check who was there before running down to open the door.

Ali opened the window and they peered out, leaning forward to see who it was. Fergus smiled up at them.

"How about that mug of Ovaltine?"

"Not tonight, darling." Ali was laughing. "Anyway we haven't got any."

"Let a man up for a quick piss? Please?"

Lisa leaned back so he couldn't see her, shook her head silently and mouthed 'No' to Ali, who leant out again.

"Sorry Fergus, we're going to bed."

"Go on, take pity, I'm busting. I won't stay, I promise."

Ali looked back at Lisa. "Oh, go on then," she shouted down. "But be quick, okay? We're both working tomorrow."

Lisa had gone down to let him in. He went straight to the bathroom, where he stayed for a few minutes. Ali went through to the kitchen. When he emerged Lisa noticed a sway about him, his feet not quite firm on the floor.

"On the whisky tonight, Fergus?" she said, wrinkling her nose. He gave her a sideways look and a grin. Beads of sweat stood on his forehead and there was that strange, earthy smell about him. She wondered if he'd taken something on top of the whisky.

Ali appeared from the kitchen with two steaming mugs in her hands and put them down on the coffee table in the middle of the room.

* * *

She goes to see her mum and tells her what happened with Jessica.

"How awful. Poor girl."

"I know, she's coping really well though. I can't imagine how scared she was."

They look at each other across the table, a silent recognition between them. Lisa suggests they walk Riley to the local park for some air. They stroll for an hour or so until their fingers start to feel the cold, then go back to the house before Lisa has to return to the station.

"Sorry to bring it up, love, but Ali's parents are still keen to see you."

"I know, Mum. Maybe next time. Soon."

Her mother sighs.

At the station, she sees the guard who shouted at her last time. She squares her shoulders and looks straight at him, almost inviting a confrontation, as he glances at the dog beside her. Seeing the challenge in her eyes, he turns away and she walks past with her head high, Riley trotting obediently at her heel. She's exhilarated by the moment and her small, silent victory.

* * *

She misses Jessica and the distraction from her past.

Her life has become an act of marking time, waiting. She's unsure what she's waiting for, or even what she'd like to happen. She must get over the immediate problems of lack of sleep, nightmares and flashbacks, but after that? She has no ideas, no plans and no ambitions. She's stuck in a vicious circle. The past haunts her, and she can't reach the present or the future until she's free of it.

The phone rings.

"Hi Lisa, it's Jane here — Jane Warner." It's her former boss, who gives her the work. "Listen, I've got an interesting project going on which I think might be just right for you."

She's anxious about what it might be, but reminds herself that she needs the work.

"This wouldn't involve you being in the office more than a couple of hours a month, which would be an update meeting, just with me. It's similar to what you've been doing for us, but I think more interesting — and you've done a great job so far, so I thought you might like to have a go. It would be more money, too."

"Well, I suppose I could be interested. What is the project, exactly?" She wants to turn the offer down but forces herself to consider it.

"Tell you what, could you come and see me and we can talk it through? It's easier face-to-face and I can show you what's been done on it so far. Nothing formal, just a chat. I could offer you a cup of our terrible coffee?"

Jane is a practical person, it's what Lisa has always liked about her. But she's also sensitive and seems to understand that Lisa can't take on too much.

Lisa glances at the calendar beside the phone. Its empty days stretching out for weeks, months ahead.

They arrange a meeting the following week, on the day of her therapy, to save her travelling costs.

As she puts the phone down she immediately wants to change her mind, cancel the meeting, retreat into her shell.

"No," she says to herself out loud. "No. Go to the meeting. You can do it. If you're really not up to it, you can always say no."

Sometimes she feels pulled two ways, as if there are two Lisas: the one who wants to live normally, to get on with her life, and the other sad, frightened Lisa, who will never be the person she was meant to be.

* * *

Jessica calls. Mike is out of the country for three weeks so she's coming back in a few days' time.

"How are you feeling?" Lisa says. "And how are the bruises?"

"The ones on my face have gone a lovely shade of yellow. It's delightful. I still look pretty bad, but I can cover them a bit better now. The emotional ones — I don't know yet, but

I'm not going back to him. He really scared me, and I don't believe anybody can change that much."

"I am sorry."

"Anyway, my sister and my parents wouldn't let me go back. They're furious. They want me to press charges. I'm not going to, but that doesn't mean I'm wavering."

"So, when are you coming back, then?"

"I just need to give him a couple of days, I think, to be sure he's gone. The police say I can change the locks after that, if I want to. I'll let you know when I'm back, shall I?"

"Yes, definitely, let me know if you need anything, even if it's only moral support when you get home. Plus, I'm sure Riley is missing his best friend."

* * *

He's leaning against the wall at the end of the street where she lives. With her head bent against the drizzle, her hood obscuring all but her immediate surroundings, she almost trips over him before she sees who it is. She stops in her tracks, her eyes flicking, searching for an escape.

"Hello, Lisa," he says and her heart pounds in her chest. Riley pulls towards him, tail wagging.

"It's okay," Mike says. "I just want to know how Jessica is." He looms above her. She takes a couple of steps back and breathes deeply. She pulls at Riley until he stands between them, cursing herself for not being more aware.

"I . . . she's at her sister's."

"I know. They won't take my calls. Have you spoken to her?" His voice is measured but his eyes are anxious, framed by dark shadows. A small part of her is pleased that the strain is taking its toll.

"Yes. A couple of days ago." Her voice shakes as she speaks. Her body has tensed, unbidden, the maleness of him threatening to overwhelm her. She looks around, hoping someone is there, walking by, to reassure her. There's nobody, no cars even, but she can see the end of the road ahead and she knows she can run that far. The knowledge offers a morsel of comfort.

"How is she?" He's looking intently at her, waiting for her reply. He takes a step closer. She backs away again.

"I . . . She's okay." She takes a deep breath. "She thought you were going away." She must check that, for Jessica's sake.

"I am, tomorrow. Look, could you ask her to call me? I'm not going to try to see her or anything, I just want to talk to her, make sure she's okay."

"I can ask." She nods. Doesn't want to risk more; she has to get away from him. She turns, pulling on Riley's lead, and they step into the road to cross to the opposite pavement.

"Okay, thank you," he says. "Thank you . . ." he hesitates, as if to carry on, but she can't stay, she has to get away. She waves her hand, not daring to look back.

Heart thumping, she almost runs to the end of the road, breathing hard. She resists turning round until they get to the lake. Only once they're through the gate and a good few metres onto the path does she turn to check. There's nobody behind them. She lets Riley off the lead and stands for a few moments, steadying herself on a tree trunk at the edge of the water, listening to her pulse slow, swallowing hard, gulping air.

CHAPTER FOUR

Gerrard and Blanding, business publishers, are housed in one of those tall buildings that look as if they're entirely made of glass. Behind the rather glamorous exterior, though, lies a typical publishing house: people squashed into too-little space, an air of disarray, boxes of books everywhere, computer screens back-to-back on small desks overflowing with piles of paper.

As she approaches the front door, Lisa takes a deep breath and pushes through the revolving doors into the reception area. A bright-looking twenty-something smiles at her from behind a pale wooden desk.

"I'm Lisa Mayfield," she says. "I'm here to see Jane Warner."

"Of course, take a seat. I'll let her know. Can I get you a drink? Tea, coffee?"

"Tea please, thanks." She sits waiting, feeling odd under her coat in her unfamiliar work clothes. At least they still fit, she thinks wryly. If anything, she's lost weight, judging by the trousers, which slip down her hips and have to be hitched up every so often.

The tea arrives and so does Jane, who shakes her hand and smiles. "It's so good to see you," she says, turning towards the lift. “Bring your tea — good choice, much better than the coffee.”

They sit in a small, bland meeting room, no adornment relieving the grey walls, no colour in the furniture.

“Hideous room,” says Jane, smiling as Lisa takes in her surroundings. “But functional.”

She gets down to business, describing in detail the project she wants to give Lisa. It’s more interesting and a lot more work than she’s had to date, but she’s already decided to take it on, as long as it’s within her capabilities and she can continue to work from home.

By the time she leaves they’ve agreed on her role, pay and deadlines, and there are notes and documents weighing down her bag. She’s glad of the extra load. A further weight to anchor her.

* * *

She tells him about her meeting.

“That seems a positive step,” he says. “As long as it’s not putting too much pressure on you. A lot has happened recently, hasn’t it?”

“It’s helped, in a way. It’s better if I have something else to think about, like Jessica, or work. It stops me from dwelling on . . . it . . . and feeling trapped by it.”

“You feel trapped?”

“It’s taken over my life. Everything I do is because of what happened. Where I live, how I behave, what I say, even. How I dress . . .”

“And how does that make you feel?”

God, that question. She wrestles with her irritation, forces herself to answer truthfully. “Angry, frustrated with myself. Pathetic.”

“Pathetic?”

“Not strong enough to manage my own life, to get rid of this thing that’s hanging over me. I mean, I don’t expect to be able to brush it off, but it’s overwhelmed me. I can’t seem to get away from it, even though I'm trying to make a new life." Her thoughts are tangled and she's getting confused, but she struggles on. "I don't know, really. I suppose I can't see an end to it. I feel I should be able to deal with it better."

"What do you think would help you deal with it better?"

"Moving on."

"Do you feel you're not moving on?"

"I'm trying to."

"Lisa, you are moving on. Bit by bit, you are making a life that isn't defined by what has happened to you. It may not be the same future you would have had without that experience, but nonetheless it's your future and you're controlling it."

She looks at him, trying to see the truth in his eyes, to get comfort from his words. But she's not comforted. There's a long pause.

"Is there anything else?"

She swallows. "I don't want to be a victim for the rest of my life."

* * *

Guilt. Her worst demon. A terrible, debilitating feeling. It's the thing that stops her sleeping, drives her away from people, defines her waking moments. It's all-powerful, relentless, ever-present.

But then of course it is, when Ali is dead. No matter what the situation, however threatened she'd been, however terrified, she has to live with that.

It's also the reason she's been avoiding Diana and Geoffrey. She's been avoiding everyone, but especially them. She's become an expert at the carefully crafted email; it's how she's managed to keep a line of communication open with some of the people she cares about, but hasn't the strength to see yet. She's become used to sending a polite but unequivocal email excusing herself from social events or visits.

She hasn't seen Ali's parents since the hospital and her recollection of their visit is vague. She knows they'd like to see her, but when she thinks about them, all the horror of that terrible night crowds in on her. She can't bear their pain, or their kindness.

And yet she owes them. Perhaps she's making it worse for them by staying away, selfishly denying them their personal recovery, their own way of moving on. In her heart she knows she must see them soon and in her head she's trying to prepare herself, find a way to face them and not make things worse. As the weeks have gone by, she's thought about this more and more, wracked by guilt, too cowardly to offer them the morsel of comfort only she can provide.

* * *

A few days after Lisa's trip to the city, Jessica calls. She's coming back at the weekend.

"Shall I get you some food?"

"No, don't worry, I'll go out when I get back, stock up a bit. Come over when you're walking Riley and we can catch up."

Jessica's situation has further entrenched Lisa's mistrust of men. She can't imagine ever having a normal relationship with a man. Yet she knows they're not all bad: her father, for one, was by all accounts a gentle, kind person.

This train of thought reminds her of John next door, whose age and fragility place him in the safe category. She's taken to spending time with him, stopping for a chat after picking up his shopping. He's good company, with a gentle, self-deprecating sense of humour and a natural interest in other people's lives.

He's lonely, though. He walks down to the social club in the village every so often, where he meets old friends for lunch and conversation, but sometimes, if he's unwell or when it's too cold and icy to risk the walk, he sees nobody except Lisa and the people at the shop.

She calls Riley, gathers up her keys and goes next door to see if he needs anything.

* * *

When he comes to the door, she can see that he's not his usual self. He's holding a cotton handkerchief, the edges frayed and uneven, and his eyes are watery. He asks her in to his gloomy kitchen, where he puts on the kettle, his hand shaking with the weight.

"Are you all right, John? You don't seem yourself."

"Today's a difficult day for me. The anniversary of my wife's passing. It's been five years." He picks up a small, silver-framed picture, which had been lying face down on his chair and shows it to her. A smiling, white-haired couple look out from a background of blue sky and garden, their arms around each other. His wife looks happy and he looks like a different person, bright-eyed and healthy.

"We were married for thirty-five years," he turns the picture back to him and strokes his wife's face behind the glass with his thumb. "We were best friends. Life's just not the same now."

"You certainly look happy in the photo. Was it taken in the village?"

"Yes, in our last house. It got too big for us, so we moved here about ten years ago when Elsie got poorly. We couldn't manage the garden in the other place, though we loved it when we were young. It was a proper country garden. We had roses, hollyhocks, delphiniums, it was so beautiful in summer. The lawn was a menace to look after though, I certainly couldn't do it now."

"Elsie looks lovely. Wonderful to be happy together for so long."

"Yes, couldn't have been luckier." He places the picture down and looks at it as the kettle starts to boil, its old-fashioned whistle screaming.

"I'll do it." Lisa has got used to John's kitchen and often makes the tea, saving him picking up the heavy kettle and reaching for the mugs in the cupboard overhead. He sits down, the picture back in his hand.

"When she died, I didn't know what to do with myself for a while. But her friends were wonderful. Came over all the time, especially to talk about her, remember her properly. It helped me so much. I even learned some things about her I didn't know before, if you can believe it. Things she did before we were married. I felt closer to her."

"That was nice of them. Do you still see them?"

"Some of them are still here, though only one or two. I see them at the social club sometimes. The others have died. At my age, your friends start to go. So many funerals."

Lisa changes the subject, not wanting to make things worse for him, and tells him about Jessica's plans to come back and her own changes with work. They chat for a while until he seems a bit brighter. She collects the latest shopping list, leaves him with his picture and his thoughts, and with Riley pulling on her arm, walks down to the shop.

Later, the curtains drawn and the fire warming her feet, she remembers John's words about his wife's friends and the comfort they'd given him after his wife's death, Diana and Geoffrey not far from her mind.

* * *

The familiar semi-detached house looks smaller than she remembers as she approaches from the end of the street. The front garden has been partly paved over since she was last here and a small silver hatchback sits in front of the bay window.

A few houses away she stops for a few moments to gather herself. You can do this. They're lovely people. They don't blame you. But her body is rigid, the palms of her hands slick with sweat inside her woolly gloves. She shivers, cold and anxious. For a moment she hesitates, her legs not wanting to move forward.

"Oops," says a voice from behind her and a small child runs into the back of her legs on a tiny scooter.

"Say sorry, Millie. Sorry, she's really not good at looking where she's going." The young mother smiles at her, she smiles back and the little girl scurries past, head down.

"Sorry!" A piping voice, a lisp, and she's gone, a determined little figure scooting as if her life depended on it.

The moment has passed and she walks on towards the house where Ali lived.

Once she's at the front gate, there's no turning back. The front door opens immediately and they're both there, smiling, waiting. They hug her warmly and she's in, the door closing behind her as she follows Diana into the sitting room.

The furniture is new but the welcoming warmth is still there, and she remembers the pictures on the walls and the fireplace with its china ornaments as if it were yesterday. In fact it's only a couple of years since she was last there, though it feels like a lifetime. She sits, consciously trying to relax, as Diana bustles about in the kitchen and Geoffrey hangs her coat in the hallway.

They reappear, like a double act, and start to talk to her together, though at cross-purposes — 'How is your mum?' 'Where are you living?' They're nervous too. A tray loaded with cups and saucers, a teapot and a plate of assorted biscuits has materialised and is fussed over while she stammers, trying to answer their questions while controlling her racing heart and the lump in her throat.

"My mum's fine, actually. She's got some nice friends in the street, and she likes it there. I'm living in a little village, about an hour away by train. It's nice. Quite different to life here . . ." she peters out as they look at her, waiting.

"Why there, do you have friends nearby?"

"No, not really. I needed somewhere quiet. It's peaceful, not much going on. I've got a little dog." They latch on to her story about John and Riley, wanting all the details. It's a safe subject.

She asks after Ali's brother, Connor, and Geoffrey gets up and goes to a small desk by the wall, where he picks up a picture with a dark, polished wood frame. It's Connor with Ali — larking about, making faces at the camera as they always did. Their young faces are close together, almost touching.

"They always got on so well," he says, sitting down again. "He's a sensitive lad, misses her terribly. He's living with us at the moment. He lost his job late last year. It all seemed to go wrong when she died." He shakes his head, close to tears. "Hard to make sense of it all . . ."

Lisa's caught in the fading echo of his words, unable to respond. She opens her mouth but nothing comes out. She doesn't know what to say.

Diana reaches over to pat Geoffrey's hand and he looks away, overcome with emotion. She breaks the silence. "The last time we saw you, you were all bandaged up. They seemed to be looking after you well in the hospital. How are you now?"

"Yes, they were good. It doesn't hurt anymore." She tries her best but the tears are coming, she can't hold them. "Sorry . . ."

"Oh, my dear . . ." Diana is next to her on the sofa, her arms around her. "We know how hard it's been for you." A box of tissues materialises in front of her. "We all miss Ali so much, and we miss you too."

"I feel dreadful for not coming to see you, but I've been . . . it's been . . . I can't . . ."

"Your mum's been telling us how you've been getting on. We just want you to know that we're here and we love you." Diana has tears in her eyes now and Geoffrey has risen and is standing at the window, his back turned, his shoulders hunched.

"Thank you," Lisa whispers through the tears and Diana hands her a tissue. Geoffrey sits down again. The faint smell of baking wafts into the room. She reaches for her cup and saucer, which wobbles as she draws it close. She holds the cup in both hands to steady it as she sips.

"Lisa," Geoffrey says. "Would you like to visit the grave with us?"

Guilt snakes its icy fingers around her throat. The grave. She hasn't even thought about it. The body of Ali, her best friend, Diana and Geoffrey's only daughter, is lying in a grave nearby. And she hasn't even thought about it.

"Would you like to come with us today? We go a couple of times a week. You might like to have someone with you the first time."

* * *

The church is a short drive away and Lisa sits in the back of their car, numb, as the streets of her hometown flash by.

"Shall we stop for some flowers?" Geoffrey says. "We normally buy some on the way."

"Flowers? Yes . . . of course." She shakes herself out of her trance.

They stop at a small florist where she buys a bouquet of winter blooms, white and green, their stems encased in cellophane filled with water, a makeshift vase. The woman at the counter asks if she'd like a card to go with it.

"No, no card. Thanks." She can't write to Ali. Not anymore.

The church is small and unassuming, a grey stone building nestling within a group of cottages, its graveyard at the back stretching out under ancient yew trees. Some flowers lie wilting on the grave and the black granite stone looks heartrendingly new.

In loving memory of Alison Mayfield, beloved daughter,
sister and friend
Died 20 June 2013, aged 28
Forever in our hearts

Lisa sinks to her knees, the tears falling, and places her bouquet under the words.

"Oh, Ali," she whispers. "I'm sorry, I'm so, so sorry."

She stays there for a long time, head bent, thinking of her beautiful friend, with whom she could conquer the world, gone. She wants to remember her alive. Always laughing. That mischievous look in her eye.

Diana and Geoffrey hold back, sitting on a bench nearby. Eventually, as the damp from the grass soaks into the knees of her jeans, she stands up.

* * *

Lisa's hoping to get back home, but when she starts to say goodbye at the door, they insist she goes in.

"Please come in," Diana says. "There's something we want to ask you. It'll only take a minute." Reluctantly, she follows them into the sitting room and, coat still on, sits down.

They sit opposite her and glance at each other.

Nervous, wide-eyed, she waits.

"We want to hold a memorial service for Ali on the anniversary in June," Diana says. "At St. Peter's. We'd really like you to come. That's all, just come and sit with us on the day. And your mum, too, of course. Do you think you can? Would you like to?"

They're both looking at her expectantly, but her voice has deserted her.

"It would mean a lot to us." Their eyes are on her and she can feel their need. She squirms inwardly with the weight of it.

She swallows hard. "I don't know. Can I let you know? It's just . . . I'm still not . . ."

"Of course you can let us know. You have a think and when you feel strong enough, come and see us again. There's plenty of time to decide."

She leaves them standing at the front door together, waving for a long time, as if they don't want to let her go.

* * *

At the lake the first signs of spring are showing. Fragile green shoots are pushing through the mud by the side of the path and as they walk through the trees at the edge of the water, Lisa can see new buds on the bare branches.

It's the first time this year she's noticed birdsong on her walk. The dawn chorus heralds each day now as she lies most mornings half-asleep, and though she'd rather not be awake, she likes the idea that the birds are calling to each other, making contact, declaring boundaries, welcoming the day.

Ten minutes into the walk she sees a familiar figure materialise in the distance, the pale shape of a wagging dog alongside. The figure waves and as they get closer she can see Jessica's smile.

"You look a lot better," Lisa says. Jessica's face is almost back to normal, the shadow of the bruising only noticeable if you knew. But she's pale and drawn and there are dark smudges under her eyes.

"Physically, I'm a lot better. I'm getting there." Jessica had been shocked and angry when Lisa called soon after her long and circuitous route home from the unexpected encounter with Mike. Her voice, no matter how hard she tried, had betrayed her fear. To her relief, Jessica had wasted no time. She called him and made it clear that he wasn't to talk to Lisa or anyone else about her, that she wouldn't discuss anything until he was back. He'd agreed — he'd had no choice — and had left for his trip without further contact.

The two women walk for a long time.

"I've got to sort out an agreement of some sort," Jessica says. "But I'm too scared to see him on my own now."

"I'm not going to offer to come with you." She's serious, but she smiles at Jessica's shocked glance.

"Of course not. I'm so sorry he bothered you, it won't happen again. He knows I've talked to the police."

"Have you seen a lawyer?"

"Not yet. I need to research it a bit online first, find out what needs to be done for a separation, in the short term."

"Do you think you'll divorce?"

"That's what I've decided. I can't stay with a man who's prepared to hurt me like that. There's no way we could get back together." They negotiate a narrow section of path through the trees.

"I've just got to find the courage to talk to him properly, I suppose," Jessica says.

"Do you have to talk? Why don't you email? It's probably best to have it all in writing, anyway. Then there's no argument and you can choose your words much more carefully."

It feels strange to be giving advice to someone else when her own life is so broken.

* * *

She hasn't seen John for two or three days. When she rings his doorbell, he takes an age to appear. She's about to turn away, assuming he's out, when there's a sound at the door and she hears the key turning.

"Oh, I'm so sorry, did I get you out of bed?" He's in a worn dressing gown, his ankles poking out from beneath flapping pyjama trousers. His bony white hand clutches a blanket around his narrow shoulders. "Are you not feeling well?"

His voice is dry and croaky. "Touch of bronchitis, been in bed for the last two days. Come in, come in."

She steps into the gloomy hallway and waits while he closes the door.

"Have you seen the doctor? You really don't look well." He looks even whiter, more transparent than usual, and she asks how he's been managing, if he's eaten at all.

"No, I can't get out." He coughs and the whole of his frail body shakes. He grimaces as if in pain and wipes his mouth with a crumpled tissue.

"The doctor will come to you. Shall I call him?"

"Oh, I don't know. I'm not too bad. What can he do?"

"He can give you antibiotics. Let me ring, John, please."

"Oh, well, okay then, if you think it's worth it. Come in, I'll find the number."

He shuffles towards the kitchen, his slippered feet making little swishing noises as he moves. She follows him in and puts the kettle on, noticing the dirty dishes by the sink. As usual it's cold in the kitchen and the electric heater is off. Handing her a slip of paper with the doctor's name and number, he sinks into his armchair, coughing. She extracts the blanket from behind him and covers his legs.

She makes the call and arranges a visit. It'll be a couple of hours or more, but the doctor will come.

"Shall I wait with you?" She takes her coat off and starts the washing up without asking.

"Thank you, but no, you don't need to wait. Could you come back and let him in? I'll go back to bed in a minute." He seems exhausted, rests his head on the back of the chair, his eyes closed, while she moves about, tidying the crockery and making tea.

"Of course. There you go." She sets the mug down on the table by his chair. "Might be a bit hot, so leave it a couple of minutes, maybe. I'm going to the shop, shall I get you some bits?"

"Yes, please. Thank you, thank you. Usual things . . ." His voice trails off. She opens a couple of cupboards. They're almost empty and the bread bin on the side contains only a stale crust in a bag and a pile of crumbs.

"I'm going to get you a good stock of things you can eat easily. And some soups that you just need to heat up. Shall I collect your newspaper?"

"Don't worry, dear, can't read in bed, anyway. Wait until I'm better . . ." That cough again, hard and painful.

"I'm going to go now. Drink your tea and I'll be back with your shopping before the doctor gets here. Can I take a key, so I don't disturb you?"

He points to the sideboard where she finds a key with a blue plastic tag. "That's the one," he says, and sits back in his chair. "Thank you, dear. I'm just going to finish my tea and go back to bed. Just call me when he comes."

She turns on the electric fire and leaves him sitting there, his eyes closed.

* * *

Doctor Morris is with John for a long time. Lisa waits downstairs, cleaning and tidying the kitchen to occupy herself.

He reappears suddenly at the kitchen door as she's scrubbing at the hob, which is covered in bits of blackened food.

"I'm done."

She jumps, not having heard him coming downstairs, and drops the knife she was using to scrape at the surface. "Oh, sorry," he says. He's young, perhaps in his thirties; a big, black coat swirls around his legs when he walks.

"It's fine," she says, flustered.

"Are you a relative?"

"No, I live next door. I do his shopping sometimes and look after his dog."

"He has a dog?" He looks around the kitchen.

"Well, he's really my dog now. John couldn't keep him, so he came to live with me. John looks after him when I'm out." She doesn't know why, but she feels the need to explain.

"Would you be able to get his prescription? He needs a couple of different medicines for the next few days."

She nods. "No problem."

"Does he have anyone looking in on him? A relative, son, daughter? I asked but he seemed confused."

"I don't think there is anyone. He has a nephew, but he lives in Spain. Otherwise nobody, only friends at the social club and me."

"Right. I'm going to get a nurse to pop in for the next few days to check on him, help him bath and eat and so on. I'll come back on Wednesday. I'll go back up and explain it all to him now. Apparently you have the key?"

They agree that she'll have another key cut and that the nurse will call in at Lisa's to collect it the following day. He asks for her telephone number, just in case, and she gives it reluctantly.

Only a handful of people in the entire world have her number. Right now, she'd prefer it to stay that way.

* * *

John's recovery is slow. The nurse calls by and updates Lisa on his progress. He's still confined to bed, only managing to walk to the bathroom and back, but is feeling slightly better and has managed some soup for lunch. The nurse is leaving him a cold supper tray each day. She seems satisfied with his progress.

"Slowly but surely," she says. "It takes a long time to recover from things at his age. You did the right thing to get the doctor in, though. It could have developed into something a lot worse without treatment."

After she's gone, Lisa gets her coat, puts Riley on the lead and locks up behind her. They head for Jessica's house, where she leaves him wandering round the garden with Bobby. She makes her way to the station and checks the time of the next train to the city.

* * *

She picks at the stitching on the arm of her chair, avoiding his eyes.

"You said you thought I might want to blame myself. That I might be choosing to be the victim."

"Have you thought about that?"

"At first I didn't understand what you were getting at, but then I thought that maybe there's some reason for me wanting to take the blame, that maybe I'm getting something out of it."

"Are you?"

"I've gone over and over it in my mind. I can't work it out. What benefit would I get out of taking the blame for something I didn't do? Maybe I did do something that caused Ali to die, and I'm frightened of what I might remember. Or maybe I'm just being the victim, looking for attention. But I don't think so. That's the last thing I want at the moment. So why would I want to be a victim? I'm not getting anywhere with any of it."

"Have you put this all in the diary?" There's a hopeful tone to his voice.

"No, I haven't."

"Is there a reason for that?"

"It's too confused. I feel like I'm going round in circles."

"And the flashbacks, and the nightmares?"

"I can't seem to find the words. It makes it sound too simple, too banal. I can't describe it. It's just all too horrible."

"Tell me what it is you can't describe — your feelings, the nightmares, the flashbacks?"

"All of it. My feelings, because when I write it down, it doesn't go anywhere near describing what I'm feeling. And the other things — what happened. I don't want it to be a story, I suppose."

"A story?"

"Yes. If I don't write it down, it's not so real. At the moment, it's only what I remember and what he — Fergus — remembers. Nobody else knows what really happened. So if I don't write it down, nobody ever will know. So it won't really exist." She pauses, trying to catch something that flits through her mind. But she can't quite grasp it, it keeps floating out of reach.

"I don't know what I'm trying to say, really."

"I think I understand." There's a pause. He seems to be considering what to say next. She braces herself.

"For next time, do you think you can try again to write it down?" he says. "It can be really helpful, particularly if you're confused. And it can trigger your memory."

She nods, wondering if she'll be able to force herself.

"You know that this room is a completely safe environment?" he says. "Nothing you say here will go any further than these four walls. And the same goes for anything you write down. It's completely confidential."

"Yes, I know. It's not that."

"Are you concerned that you haven't told the police everything?"

"Not really, though I haven't told them anything I've remembered since hospital. He's already been sentenced and that's not going to change, whatever I remember now."

* * *

When she arrives to pick Riley up, it's already late afternoon. Jessica invites her to supper. She's worn out after the session this afternoon and would prefer not to go, but there's a pleading note in Jessica's voice.

They eat early, sitting at the kitchen table. Lisa picks at her food.

"Sorry, Jessica, I'm not great company when I've just been to the psycho."

"That's okay," Jessica offers a small smile. "It must be hard."

They sit in companionable silence for much of the meal, each with their own thoughts.

The trill of the phone in the hallway interrupts the silence and Jessica leaves to take the call. Lisa clears the table and prepares to go home; she's so tired she can barely stand.

"That was the police," says Jessica when she reappears in the kitchen. "They said that now would be a good time to change the locks and put window locks everywhere. It feels like an act of aggression to me, though. It could really piss him off if he gets back and realises he can't get in to his own house."

"It could. They're probably right. You said yourself you're scared of him. Have you emailed him yet?"

"No — I started but I haven't sent it yet."

"Why don't you email him about the locks? Tell him the police advised you to change them. Then at least he'll have a chance to get used to the idea, rather than it being a shock when he gets back."

"You're right, I should do it. I'll have another go tonight, otherwise I won't sleep. And I'll get on to a locksmith tomorrow."

"It's good to have a plan in place sometimes. Just taking each day as it comes and setting out small tasks that you know you can complete. It's what I do with my work sometimes, or even something as small as walking Riley. Sorry, but I'm whacked. I need to get home and get some sleep, if I can. Walk in the morning?"

They fix a time for the next day and Lisa leaves, battling against a strong wind which races through the trees and rattles the gates along the street.

But sleep is a long time coming that night. This time, she can't get Fergus's leering face out of her head.

* * *

She thinks a lot about Ali's memorial. Though it's still nearly three months away, the anniversary looms large in her mind. She can't imagine how she will get through it. The first anniversary is the worst; you start to move on from your grief after the first year. That's what they say. But Ali's death is omnipresent, in her dreams and in her waking hours and there's been no let up. If anything, as she pieces together her memory of what happened, the jigsaw gradually reaching completion, it's become more difficult than it was at first. Perhaps she won't be able to grieve until the demons leave her and she can sleep — and live — without the fear.

The idea of attending a service to mark the occasion, possibly the start of a new phase of recovery, brings her no comfort. Because of the flashbacks, which happen without consideration for where she is or what she's doing, she can't trust herself to get through even a single hour safely. The thought of it happening in front of all the people who are also mourning her friend, fills her with dread.

She calls her mum, who wants an update on Jessica. They talk for a while about what's happening with her before Lisa has the courage to tell her about the memorial.

"Mum. Geoffrey and Diana want to hold a memorial for Ali on the anniversary. They want me to go with them — and you."

"I think that's a good idea. I'll put it in the diary."

"Yes, but Mum . . ." She swallows, unable to express herself in the face of her mum's simple practicality.

"Lisa? Don't you want to go?"

"I do. I do — and they said I wouldn't have to do anything. But I don't know if I can."

"Oh, sweetheart. It's a good while yet, so you might be feeling better by then. And I'll be there. I'm sure it means a lot to Diana and Geoffrey, and Connor, for you to go."

"I know. I know all that. And I missed the funeral, so I should go to say goodbye. But it'll be really hard. I still miss her so much."

She hears the sadness in her mum's voice. "I know. Perhaps it will help you, though?"

"Perhaps. Anyway, they're going to want an answer, and I don't want to say yes and then let them all down. I hate being like this. It's pathetic I know. I just feel like I'm not ready to say goodbye yet."

"Do you want me to talk to them? I can say I'll be coming and we're hoping that you'll be up to it. At least then they've got an answer, of sorts. Then, if you're not up to it on the day, they'll be disappointed, but they'll understand."

"You're right. Would you talk to them, then?"

"I will. I'll call you when I've done it, let you know what they say."

"Okay, thanks Mum. Look after yourself. Love you."

"You too."

* * *

There's another date that plagues her in the small hours of the morning, when she can't escape. Four years for Ali.

Three years after the first anniversary, he'll be out.

She can hardly bear to think about it, but she finds it plaguing her every thought. Four years is far too short, not only for taking Ali's life but for the people left behind to recover. It hurts to imagine him going back to a normal life, working and socialising and taking up where he left off. The fallout from what he did is so much greater than his punishment. That will be finished, over with; a criminal record might inhibit him, but not that much. He's young, with the rest of his life in front of him. What about Ali? What about her life?

She doesn't know where he'll go afterwards, though she knows where he is now — banged up in the north of England somewhere. But what if he comes back to the city? It would be far too close for comfort. The idea of him being nearby, that she might come across him by chance, is too awful to contemplate. And what if he tries to find her? What if . . . ?

The questions spin around her head on a loop. She has to get better. She has so little time.

* * *

The phone is ringing as she opens the door. She throws down her keys and unhooks Riley from his lead, still kicking off her boots as she reaches for the phone.

"Hello?" she says, breathy from the struggle with her boots.

"Hello, Lisa, it's Mike."

For a moment, she can't work out who he is. There's a pause while her brain ticks, like a timer, towards understanding. As soon as she realises, the panic bubbles up inside.

"How did you get my number?" Her voice is harsh, the anger rising. He'd promised Jessica he'd leave her out of it.

"It doesn't matter. I just wanted to-"

"It does matter! How did you get my number? Why are you calling me? Where are you?" Now she's shaking with fury. The thought occurs to her that if he could find her number, then anyone could. She's not safe.

"Steady Lisa. You don't want to upset yourself, do you? Not after what you've been through."

"What? What did you say?" Her voice comes out as a whisper, the anger giving way to fear.

"I've been wondering about you. After all, you know all about me from my wife. I know what happened to you. And to your friend."

A cold shiver creeps down her spine as his words trickle through the phone. "My friend? What — what are you talking about?"

"You're the best of friends now, with Jessica, just like you were with the other girl. And what happened to her? She died, didn't she? I don't want Jessica seeing you. I'm frightened for my wife."

She squeezes the handset as if to shatter it with her bare hand. "You're what? You're frightened for Jessica? After you nearly put her in hospital? You could have killed her! You have no idea what you're talking about."

"You turned her against me, you manipulative bitch. It's your fault. You want to control everyone, don't you?"

For a split second, she's dumbfounded. Calming her voice with difficulty, she says, very slowly and clearly: "I'm calling the police. Now. And I'm going to get a restraining order against you. Jessica should do the same." She slams the phone down so hard it clatters to the floor and Riley slinks off into the kitchen, tail between his legs.

* * *

Graham opens his door and smiles at her.

"Come in, Lisa. I was just running through my notes from last time." He moves to sit in one of the armchairs as she puts her bag down and settles into the other. As he sits, his trousers ride up over red socks, incongruous against the grey of his trousers. She notices for the first time that his eyebrows, heavy and black, almost meet in the centre of his forehead.

"What's come up for you this week?" he asks.

"Jessica's husband called me."

"I see, and what happened?"

"I was shocked. He shouldn't have my number. I suppose, thinking about it, there are lots of ways he could have got hold of it. But it frightened me."

"What did he want?"

"I don't know really. He said he didn't want Jessica to see me. He'd found out what happened to me and seemed to think I'm a threat. He pretended he was concerned for her. But he wasn't, obviously, he was just threatening me. He accused me of turning her against him."

"How did that make you feel?"

"At first, really frightened. But then I got angry. He beat her and he's telling me he's worried about her? And he's obviously been digging into my background."

"So what did you do?"

"I told him I was going to call the police, get a restraining order and tell Jessica to get one too. Then I cut him off — I just didn't want to hear any more. He seems to have gone off the rails, with her wanting a divorce."

"Some people need to be in control. They find it hard when things change. Are you still frightened?"

"I couldn't get the restraining order because he hasn't actually done anything, but I did talk to the police about it and they said they'd keep an eye on him. It's made me even more anxious about security, though. I don't know where he was when he called, he could be anywhere. And he seems to blame me for everything that's happened. I just hope Jessica gets it sorted out soon."

"You got angry, you said."

"I got very angry — I broke the phone. After all I've done to protect myself, he gets my number, tries to threaten me."

"How did that make you feel — the anger?"

She pauses, wonders what he's getting at. "Powerful. For a moment. More like the old me."

"Good. Has anything else happened this week?"

"Well . . . it's the anniversary. Of the day Ali . . . died, in June. Her parents are holding a memorial service and they want me to go."

She tells him about her visit to Diana and Geoffrey. The journey together to the grave and their plans for the anniversary in June.

"Would that be difficult for you?" he says.

"Yes. I mean — I wouldn't have to do anything and my mum will come with me. But there'll be so many people there I haven't seen since it happened."

"Go on."

"I know they'll be sympathetic. Feel sorry for me. I don't think I could bear that. And, just focusing on Ali, even for just an hour . . . I can't trust myself not to panic, and that would be terrible."

"In what way would it be terrible?"

"Because I wouldn't be able to hide it. There would be a scene . . ."

"Those people have lost Ali too. They're also grieving. I think it's more likely they'd be extremely sensitive to how you're feeling, don't you think?"

"Maybe."

"Do you think they might not be?"

"I don't know. I suppose I still feel it was my fault somehow, and so I don't deserve their sympathy, even to be there at the memorial, really." She picks at the skin on her finger, next to the nail. A small, perfectly round drop of blood forms. She wipes it absent-mindedly on her jeans.

"Perhaps we can make some progress with the flashbacks before then. You know, the first anniversary of a tragic event can help enormously in coming to terms with things. It seems to me a good thing that it's being marked in a positive way, and it may help you." He's looking hard at her now, trying to keep eye contact.

"Maybe. I need more progress." It sounds lame, but overwhelmingly, urgently, she wants to get out of this terrible cycle of nightmares and flashbacks, weakening her and controlling her.

"Okay, let's think about that. I sense that there's something else on your mind though. A lot has happened this week for you."

"I keep thinking about when he gets out of prison."

"And that frightens you?"

"Yes. A lot. If it was now, I think I'd react badly. I'd be scared."

"How do you feel about him now?"

"I hate him. I hope he rots in Hell."

She spits the words out, surprising herself.

He pauses for a moment, a frown creasing his forehead. He uncrosses his legs and leans back in his chair.

"We want to get you to a place that whatever happens, whether he stays in prison or not, you don't feel threatened. Do you feel you're not making progress, or that it's not happening quickly enough?"

"I don't know, really. I don't know what to expect. But the lack of sleep, and being so afraid all the time, it's difficult to live normally. I feel like I'm just marking time. But now, more than ever, I feel as though I want to break this cycle that I'm living in."

"I understand. I wonder — are you able to come more often? We could increase to twice a week and really focus."

"I've got this big work project going on, but yes, I've got to. I'd like to."

He reaches over to his desk and opens a large diary, appointments written in neat biro blocks. "This week is busy, but I can do two next week, and also the following one."

She reaches for the notebook, the bulk of it still pristine, and writes down the days and the times he reads out to her.

He nods towards the diary in her hands. "In the meantime, I'd like you to concentrate on writing things down. Your fears, your thoughts, any flashbacks, the nightmares. As much detail as you can. I know you find it hard, but ultimately I believe it will help us to work this through. It might surprise you, you know."

She nods. If that's what she needs to do, then she'll force herself.

"We'll look at the anniversary first, then the longer-term issues. How does that sound?"

* * *

Two sessions each week will stretch her, both emotionally and practically. As for Riley, she doesn't want to bother John while he's still recovering from his spell of bronchitis. Twice a week seems a lot to ask while he's so frail.

Jessica already has the perfect solution. Her garden is secure, with stone walls and a lock on the side gate — and there's a small shed she uses as a summerhouse when it's warm. When they're both out, they'll leave the dogs together in the garden, with the summerhouse door propped open so that they can shelter from the weather. Lisa will keep the spare key for the side gate, so that she can get into the garden if Jessica is out. They try the system one day while Lisa visits her mum and Jessica has an appointment nearby. It works perfectly.

Mike won't be coming near, at least for the moment. When she heard about the phone call, Jessica was furious. Within a few days she'd managed to get a temporary restraining order against him.

"Thank you so much for looking after Riley," says Lisa as they collect the dogs from the garden and start down towards the lake. "And it's reassuring to know Mike can't come near."

"As long as he obeys the order," Jessica says. Then, seeing the alarm in Lisa's eyes, hurries on: "Oh, I think he will. I'm sure he's not keen to be in trouble with the police."

"Good. For both of us."

Down at the lake, clumps of daffodils are flowering beside the fence and the mud along the path is beginning to dry out. The temperature has risen in the past few days and there are schoolchildren playing on the grassy areas, a watchful parent nearby. The water laps onto a tiny shore where the dogs drink noisily. It's the first time Lisa has seen anyone other than dog-walkers enjoying the lake. Something tells her the quiet times by the lake will change once the summer comes.

* * *

Three flashbacks in a single weekend. Two in one day. A man coming towards her in the street as she walks back home from the lake triggers an image of Fergus in the city street that night. The two places couldn't be more different. But as he passes she hunches down into her collar. She doesn't look at him, pretends to be waiting for Riley, who in turn is waiting for her.

As she draws the curtains in the sitting room, the window rattles. Ali is standing beside the window. The scene appears to her, imposing itself, insisting. The image won't go away. She's in the flat, where the window is open, the yellow street light behind it bright on Ali's hair. Ali's shouting to her, but she can't hear what she's saying. She's trying to lipread but can't work it out. The feeling of frustration, of being unable to move or cry out, assails her, her breath becoming sharp and shallow, sweat breaking out on her forehead and in the palms of her hands.

When it's over — a few brief moments feeling like hours — she gets a glass of water from the kitchen, puts on the TV and watches a talent show, the sound turned up, Riley at her side.

On Sunday, she decides to work. With more trips to the psychotherapist, she needs to work whenever she can. And it occupies her mind. Yet still, in a moment of distraction, she finds herself watching the steam from the mug she's just placed beside her. Ali is before her once more, carrying two steaming mugs from the kitchen. She hears his footsteps, feels his hand in her hair, smells the rank odour of whisky.

* * *

A warm breeze ruffles her hair as she leaves the house and heads for the station for the second time in a week.

She's been writing in her diary. It's not helping. When she reads over her scribbling, the words don't do the horror justice. But she's willing to do whatever it takes to help move forward.

* * *

She stares at the painting, trying to find the pictures she's seen before, but the shapes seem to swirl about before her eyes.

"Many flashbacks?"

"More, if anything."

"Any different?"

"Intense. Terrifying."

"Are you remembering more?"

"It comes back in bits. Sometimes it's just a feeling, or a smell. Sometimes there are new things, like what he was wearing and what he said."

"Take me through the events of that evening again. What you do know. It's some time since we first looked at it and we may trigger something that didn't come up before."

Her stomach performs a nauseating flip.

"Keep your feet on the floor and try to locate the feeling. Can you tell it as if it's happening now? Remember, you're completely safe here. You can stop at any time."

She closes her eyes and the scene appears in sharp definition before her. "We're back from the pub. It's not late, about 10.30. We're in the sitting room when the doorbell rings. Ali opens the window to see who it is and calls down. It's Fergus, he wants to come up to use the bathroom. I go down to let him in."

"What is he wearing?"

"Blue t-shirt, jeans. Brown leather loafers."

"Go on . . ."

* * *

He wandered around the sitting room, touching the furniture.

"How about a cuppa for me, then?" He inspected the pile of CDs on the bookcase. "And some music — something nice and slow so we can get up close and personal."

"Er, I don't think so, Fergus, we're pretty tired." Lisa was immediately regretting their decision to let him in.

He swung round and looked from one to the other, still swaying slightly. "Do you two always get tired together then? Shack up together?" His words were slurred, an unpleasant leer on his face. "I like that idea. I'll join you."

They both reacted immediately, jumping to their feet.

"Right, Fergus, time to go," Lisa said and went to open the door, trying to steer him in the right direction.

"Come on, Lisa, you know you want to," he said, lurching towards her.

"Out, Fergus," she said, side-stepping him.

"Okay, okay! Just a quick glass of water, then, before I go. I'll get it." He was already moving towards the kitchen, so they let him go, saying nothing. They didn't sit down.

They heard him crashing around, cupboard doors banging, a tap running. After a brief pause they heard the sound of a glass slam down on the kitchen work surface. He reappeared and made for the front door, where Lisa stood. She held the door open and tried to wave him through. He came towards her but instead of going past, he grabbed her by the arm, forcing her back into the room and kicking the door shut. The speed of his move took her by surprise and she went without a struggle.

CHAPTER FIVE

Mike's back. Jessica has arranged to meet him in a local café.

"Are you sure that's a good idea?" Lisa says, thinking of the phone call.

"He wanted to come to the house. I couldn't agree to that. He was okay with the idea of the café." They sit together in Lisa's kitchen, the door to the garden open for the dogs. It's been a few weeks since Mike left and though Jessica has contacted him, nothing has been decided.

"I feel like I'm in limbo," she says. "I'm beginning to worry about money. I don't have an income except for the housekeeping. He controls everything — bills, mortgage, credit cards, bank account, the lot." Her forehead creases into tiny lines of worry.

"You haven't got any savings?"

"No. It's just the way it's always been for us. He's always been in control. Stupid of me to allow it, I know. If he stops paying now, I'm in trouble."

"The money side will be okay. We'll sort something out, together. But I'm worried about you meeting him alone. Surely you shouldn't? What if he gets angry? Even if you're in a public place, he could do you some serious harm. Do the police know?"

"You're right. But what should I do? I've got to sort it out. The police have done all they can for now."

"Did you find a mediator? I'd say that would be the best way to meet up with him, and you might be able to get something agreed quickly. It would be much safer."

"I've got a name, but I haven't fixed anything. I need to get on to it. In fact, I'm going to go and do that now." She gets up and goes to the door, Bobby following.

* * *

There's a headache looming above her eyes. Opening the back door of the house for Riley, she notices that the overgrown garden has been cut back, its patch of lawn mown and the beds around it tidied up. The landlord must have been in, though she'd had no warning.

The idea that someone was in her home when she wasn't around unnerves her. The niggling thought is sitting there, waiting for her to dwell on. Waiting for the panic she knows it could induce. She doesn't allow it. She forces herself to remember that it's not actually her home anyway. And the landlord is more than welcome to do what he likes with his own property.

Wandering outside for some fresh air, she stretches in the sunshine and looks around. Despite the neglect, some plants have pushed through and one or two shrubs have been revealed, their new leaves unfolding in the unfamiliar warmth. A small apple tree at the end of the garden is in leaf.

The hole in the fence is still there and she looks through the broken slats into John's garden. Nothing has changed — the grass is knee-high and ivy grows out of control in clumps along the back fence. Bindweed and thistles cover the shrubs along the fence opposite. Remembering his comments about the garden in his previous house, she wonders if the mess bothers him. She goes next door.

John greets her with a smile, fusses over Riley and insists she stays for a cup of tea. He seems better, with a little more colour in his face, and he's walking more freely, no blanket around his shoulders today. The kitchen still feels chilly despite the warm sun outside and it has the stale smell of a place unused to fresh air.

"It's a lovely day. Shall I let some air in?" She fills the kettle, flicks the switch and moves towards the window.

"Oh no dear. That window hasn't opened for years. Completely stuck, though it still lets in the draughts. Open the back door if it's warm enough."

From the kitchen the garden looks even more overgrown. Riley shoots out and disappears into the tangle of weeds and grass.

"My garden's been tidied up," Lisa says. "It looks much better now. Do you want yours done? I could see if the man will come back?"

"I've lost track of the garden. Can't do anything like that now." He looks out of the window at the unkempt area, a note of sadness in his voice.

"Would you sit outside sometimes if I get it sorted out? It might be quite pretty in the summer."

"Yes, if it's sunny, I probably would. We used to, when Elsie was alive. But no need to go to any trouble."

* * *

"Miss Fulbrook, what can I do for you?" The voice on the other end is business-like.

"Lisa, please. I just wondered who did my garden."

"Yes, apologies, we should have warned you. We like to get it done a couple of times a year. Our normal gardener, Matt, did it."

"Does he have a key?"

"No, I went with him and locked up when he'd finished. Was everything okay?"

"Yes fine, thank you. It looks lovely. But . . . could you let me know next time, please? Just in case . . . ?" Her voice tails off. She's not quite sure what reason she'd give if he asks.

"Of course. I'll make a note. Is everything else all right with the house?"

"Yes, it's all good, thank you. I wanted to ask, do you think Matt might be able to do my next-door neighbour's garden? His name is John, do you know him?"

"Yes, I've met him a few times, nice old chap. I'm sure Matt could do it. He will charge, of course."

"Do you know how much it might be? It's quite overgrown and a bit of a mess."

"Tell you what, I'll give you Matt's number and you can get him round to have a look. Then he can give John a proper quote. How does that sound?"

She calls Matt, not wanting to trouble John again. Matt sounds cheery and friendly and already knows John, though he hasn't seen him for a while. They agree on a day for him to come and look at the garden.

She puts the phone down and can't help feeling an unfamiliar twinge of pride, as though a flame inside is slowly catching on.

As she stands there, the phone rings again. It's her mum.

"I spoke to Diana about the memorial. She was really pleased you're going to try to go."

"I can't guarantee it, Mum." The flame inside is flickering, its warmth fading as the cold harsh reality of the here and now sweeps in.

"I know and I explained. She's very understanding. She'd like to talk to you, though, beforehand, if you're up to it."

"What about?"

"Oh I think about the arrangements for the day. Will you call her?"

"I'll try, Mum."

Lisa glances at the calendar beside the phone. The memorial is less than a month away.

* * *

She wakes from another restless sleep soon after dawn. She lies motionless and tries to dispel the remnants of unpleasant dreams. Very rarely does she succeed and drift off. More often, she can't stave off the recurring images and, heavy with weariness, she gets up, goes downstairs to put the kettle on and starts her day. Sometimes she works at that early hour, her eyelids drooping, and other times she just throws a coat and boots over her pyjamas and sets off with Riley for the lake.

There's no-one around. There's debris around the benches where there was none in the winter months; the light evenings have attracted more people. Today the lake is completely calm. No wind disturbs the glassy surface. Mayflies dance their peculiar jig at the water's edge. She inhales the aroma of wild flowers and savours the silence.

Last night, unable to put it off any longer, she'd called Ali's parents.

"Hi Diana, Mum said you wanted me to call about the memorial?"

"Lisa! Hi, yes, we don't want to put any pressure on you. We just wanted you to know what's happening."

"Right, okay. I understand that. I'm sorry I can't commit entirely."

"If you do come, will you sit with us in the church? And your mum, of course."

"Will you be at the front? I don't know . . . I might be better near the door. Just in case." Right at the back, one foot holding the door open, ready to run . . .

"We will be at the front, but it's entirely up to you. If you feel more comfortable at the back, we'll understand. Please don't worry about it. You know the offer is there and we'd very much like you to join us."

"Thank you."

"The other thing is, we're having a few people back to our house afterwards and we'd like you and your mum to come too, if you can. Just a few close friends and relatives. If you're not up to it, we'll completely understand, but the invitation is there. We don't want you to feel you're not welcome."

"I . . . thank you."

The handset shook in her fingers as she said goodbye.

* * *

The therapy gets harder each time and the diary's filling up with her nervous scrawl. Today she must record her reaction to last night's phone call and her conflicted feelings about the ever-approaching memorial service.

In her heart, she wants to go, to pay tribute. She owes it to Ali, to acknowledge her life, her friendship and the bond between them. And she owes it to Ali's family. But her soul, the very essence of her, screams and cowers and shrinks in horror. The guilt at not remembering Ali's final moments weighs heavily on her.

* * *

The memorial is a week today. She sits, picking at her fingers. The skin around her index fingers is red and raw now; she's had to put plasters around her thumbs to stop them bleeding. Her head aches and the muscles in her neck are taut.

"He went to the bathroom. There was something odd about him. He smelled of whisky, but it was more than that — I wondered if he'd taken drugs or something. He was sweating and could barely even walk straight."

"Go on."

"He didn't want to leave, he sort of hung around, wandering around the sitting room. He said something about a threesome and we asked him to go."

"Were you frightened?"

"Not then, no. He wasn't aggressive or angry then. He said he wanted a drink of water, so we thought that was okay. He went to the kitchen and when he came out, he went towards the front door as if to go. I was standing there, holding the door open for him. But he didn't. Instead he grabbed me."

She swallows hard. This is the part where she usually stops. She hasn't been able to get any further since the policewoman was sitting next to her in the hospital room.

"You must have felt threatened, at that point?"

"Yes, but I was angry, too. He was holding my arm so tight it hurt and he wouldn't let go. I didn't struggle — not straight away, anyway. It was all so sudden. He pulled me into the room and kicked the door closed."

"And then?"

She feels the blood drain from her face. She squeezes her eyes shut, trying to block the vivid images crowding in on her. The bookshelves, the ceiling, the street lamp through the window. His voice in her ear, Ali screaming.

* * *

"Let's do it differently then, eh? Your call. What's it to be?" His face close to hers, too close.

"What are you doing? Fergus!" she said. "Let go!"

"Think you're too good for me now, do you?" He spat the words out. He was forcing her arm behind her, her shoulder at a painful angle, while she twisted and pulled with the rest of her body, trying to get away. Ali was there, yelling, pulling at him, trying to release Lisa from his grip. "What are you doing? Stop this, Fergus!"

Her arm was free — but there was a hand in her hair, her head yanked back painfully, something cold and hard at her throat. She resisted the urge to flinch. From the corner of her eye she saw Ali recoil in horror.

"Fergus — Jesus Christ! For God's sake, what are you doing? Let her go!"

Lisa froze. She tried to speak but nothing came out. His breath was warm on her neck, the smell choked her. She knew that there was a knife. It was scraping at the tight skin of her throat, and she couldn't help but flinch at its touch. Ali came towards them again, words tumbling out of her mouth, her voice rising to a scream.

"Don't, Fergus. Just let her go . . . don't do this, we're friends . . . please . . . let her go! Stop it! Stop!"

"Shut the fuck up, you. Well, Lisa?"

She felt the grip on her hair tighten as he tensed and she stumbled slightly, her legs giving way. There was an odd, tickling sensation at her neck as the blood trickled down.

* * *

A dark curtain threatens to drop and she falls forwards over her knees, gasping for air.

* * *

A couple of weeks later, John's garden is transformed. Matt has even found a small bench, which he puts just outside the back door. There's a patch of lawn and some mature shrubs, previously hidden amongst the tangle of weeds and bramble. A path of cracked paving stones leads from the kitchen door across the grass, spotted with patterns of yellow and grey lichen and hemmed with soft patches of moss.

John sits outside when it's sunny and Riley settles at his feet when Lisa is working at her desk. John is grateful and seems a little more cheerful. There are moments of melancholy, when Lisa knows that John must be thinking of Elsie, the time they would spend together in the garden, but when he looks at her with tears in his eyes, there's also a smile there.

As well as the more frequent trips to the city, she has a deadline for the first half of the project and she spends most of the next two weekends finishing it off. When she's not with Graham, she avoids thinking about the memorial service. She's barely seen Jessica and feels guilty, mentally pencilling in a visit when she next takes Riley for a walk.

When her mother calls, she knows it's time to make a decision. It's only a week away.

"I know, Mum. I don't want to let them down."

"Why don't you come and stay the night before? You can bring Riley to mine. Then we can go together."

"Maybe."

"They've offered us a lift. I wasn't sure you'd want to though."

"No. I don't. We'll take a taxi. Then if I can't face it, it won't matter so much."

"Okay, darling. I'll be right next to you the whole time."

After the call she sits with her head in her hands for a long time.

* * *

The memorial falls on a Friday.

Inevitably, all that week, her mind is full of Ali. They'd been friends since school. They'd gone to parties together, knew the same boys, and hung out at the same places in town. Ali was tall and blonde, with the kind of brain that was always three steps ahead of you — annoying, but also quick, surprising and insightful. She had a wonderfully dry sense of humour. She took no nonsense from anyone. Ali was popular, the leader of the two, and Lisa admired the intelligence and confidence which emanated from her friend. It was never a jealousy thing. They were close, comfortable with each other, never bored or irritated. They talked about everything and everyone and knew each other's intimate secrets, anxieties and insecurities, to the point where they barely seemed to need anyone else.

When they moved to the city, it was full of possibility for them both. They had no responsibilities and not much more on their minds than having fun. Ali had a job in a small advertising agency and Lisa became an administrative assistant in a publishing house. Neither job demanded too much from them. Sometimes they got together with each other's workmates — Ali, in particular, had made some good friends and always included Lisa when they went out after work — more often, though, they went out locally, to the pub, where they soon got to know a good crowd of people. There were parties almost every weekend and plenty of interested men, though neither Lisa nor Ali was looking for anything serious.

With no responsibilities except to pay the bills and get to work on time, they lived like students and barely thought of the future beyond the next weekend. Lisa had loved her life, then, before.

* * *

She's barely eaten or slept. In her dreams, she's lost something or someone and she's searching everywhere, asking everyone, but no-one knows.

When she looks in the mirror, a ghost looks back at her.

On Thursday she packs carefully for the next day. Black trousers and jacket, grey t-shirt, smart shoes. Black scarf to wrap around her neck. Makeup to cover the dark smudges under her eyes. Overnight kit. A bag for tissues, keys, money. Another bag for Riley with food and a ball. She finds the picture of Ali and tucks it into the pocket of her jacket.

She'll arrive at her mum's house for supper. She needs to be on her own for as long as possible. She's too anxious to be any kind of company. When she's finished packing, there are still many hours before she needs to leave. She calls to Riley and locks up.

She can't face anyone, even Jessica, today, and feels guilty that while she is going through her own personal turmoil, others around her are suffering too. When this is all over, she tells herself, I'll sort my life out once and for all. When this is all over.

She walks a different way, up the hill behind the house and through an overgrown footpath to the other side. The path winds through farmland towards another small village and then back past the top of the lake, in a full circle. Oblivious to her surroundings, she walks the uphill part as fast as she can, wanting to be tired, to concentrate on something other than tomorrow, and her breath comes in sharp stabs as she reaches the top. But the fresh air and the exertion do nothing for her state of mind and the brick in her stomach refuses to budge.

She arrives back at the house hot and sweaty and stands for a long time under the shower, her head bowed forward as the water pours down.

* * *

She leaves early for the train. Walks fast to the station, then round the block because she doesn't want to wait half an hour on the platform. But her bag gets heavy and she's tired already, so she settles for a fifteen-minute wait. She keeps her eye on Riley.

On the platform there's a young lad, his hair carefully trimmed and styled, a tattoo snaking up his arm. She watches him as he walks up and down, talking on his mobile, oblivious. His trainers look new. She's careful not to make eye contact. A woman in heels and a tight skirt sits next to her on the platform seat and starts to text. Riley sits quietly. Nobody pays her any attention. She's dressed all in black, sunglasses hiding her eyes, scarf over her chin, her normal disguise.

In the carriage she finds herself an empty area and squashes herself into the window seat. Riley lies beside her, his head on her upper leg. He's caught her mood and is subdued and watchful. She stares out of the window, unseeing. A trolley comes down the aisle, pushed by a bored-looking girl with dyed black hair and piercings.

She thinks about the next day and her shoulders tense. She shrugs to release them but it doesn't help. Her body refuses to do what it's told, these days.

There'll be so many people, people that are interested in her too. A ghoulish desire to know the details. Murder, manslaughter. They hold a strange fascination for people, even ordinary, thoughtful people.

They won't ask, she knows that, but they will wonder — and afterwards they'll talk about it, each with their own theory of how it happened. Perhaps they can fill Lisa in on what they think happened that night.

She fidgets in her seat, unable to relax, and Riley lifts his soft black head and looks at her. "I know, I'm a wreck," she mouths to him.

The train is slow, ambling from stop to stop. She begins to feel as if every stop is taking her further away from safety. She strokes the soft black fur on Riley's head and he closes his eyes.

* * *

It's six o'clock when she arrives at the house and supper is already cooking. It's fish pie and apple crumble and she can smell the food from the front door.

Her mum bustles about, clicking the kettle on, fussing over Lisa's bag, wanting to hang up her clothes for tomorrow.

"I'll do that in a minute," Lisa says.

She lets the dog out into the back garden and follows him onto the lawn. There are pots of geraniums by the back door and one on a small round table on the patio. She sits, elbows on the table, watching Riley get familiar with the garden smells.

"There was a hedgehog on the grass the other day," her mum says, putting a tray on the table and sitting next to her. "I expect Riley's got the scent." She pours the tea and Lisa sits back.

"Do you think you'll be all right tomorrow?" It's the question she expected. She wishes she knew the answer.

"I don't know, Mum. Maybe." They sit quietly for a few minutes, sipping their tea.

"You look thin."

"I know. Just in the last few days. I'm not interested in food." Then she catches the look on her mum's face. "It's okay. After tomorrow . . ."

"Yes. You'll feel better once it's over."

Lisa sighs and goes inside to find a bowl for Riley's supper. She puts some food and water down and goes back out.

"Mum. Do you mind if we don't talk about it tonight? I've been thinking about it for days. And weeks, now. I really just need to get my mind off it and be ready for the memorial."

"Of course," her mum replies. "It's good to have you home." She kisses Lisa gently on the cheek and pats her shoulder as she walks into the kitchen.

* * *

Sleep is not her friend. She stays up late to avoid it, long after her mum has gone to bed, watching a chat show on TV, flicking past the news. Riley, for whom sleep is not a problem, curls up beside her.

It's past one o'clock when she finally decides to go up, her step on the stair soft, followed by a rumble of paws. She lies down, Riley next to her. For a long time she stays in the same position, eyes open, not expecting sleep to come. A nightly ritual. But it does and her dreams are full of strange images, colours and sounds. Faces float in and out, childhood friends appear and disappear. She's in the flat in London, alone, wondering where Ali is. And then she's in a strange town, lost among derelict houses, the streets full of rubble, a tension in the air. Bizarre shouts and loud noises assail her as she runs from place to place, looking for somewhere safe, but she can't find what she's looking for.

She wakes around dawn. This is it. Today's the memorial. An entire year ago to this day, her best friend was killed. Murdered.

Hours pass quickly and before long, she can hear the soft noises of her mum surfacing. The bedside clock reads eight o'clock. At about this time on the same day last year, she was getting ready for work and Ali was alive — probably brewing coffee in the kitchen. She can see her face, singing to the radio that she always had on at breakfast, eating toast on the run, no time to waste. She would always leave before Lisa, who only had a short journey to work. After she left there'd be a brief moment of peace while Lisa got ready.

She tries to keep Ali's smile alive in her mind as she readies herself, far too early. She pulls the photo from her jacket pocket and props it on the table in the bedroom while she dresses, then lies down and cradles it in her hand.

"Lisa?" Her mum's face appears round the bedroom door. "Are you all right?"

"Just trying to prepare myself."

"You should have something to eat before we go, love. How about some toast?"

"No, honestly, I'm fine. I can't eat anything at the moment. Maybe later." Her mum nods and goes off to get ready. Lisa returns to her silent vigil.

The clanging sound of the doorbell makes her whole body tense. "Mum?"

She's already at the door, asking the driver to wait. The panic starts to rise.

"Lisa? Are you coming?" Footsteps are climbing the stairs.

"Just give me a minute . . ." She goes through to the bathroom, shuts the door and leans over the basin, staring at her reflection in the mirror. She's done her best to hide the dark smudges under her eyes, but still a pale, frightened face looks back at her. She runs her hands under the cold water and notices that they're shaking. She takes a few sips of water from her hands and wipes her mouth, smudging the lipstick on the towel as she wipes the drops. She takes a deep breath. You can do this, she says to her pale reflection. Just go.

And so she does. Her mum holds her hand all the way in the taxi. She puts her dark glasses on and fingers the picture of Ali in her pocket. You can do this.

* * *

They're early. They ask the driver to park in the street that runs alongside the church while they wait. Lisa feels helpless, as if pulled along by events, drawn in by some unseen power.

She looks at the church, but the sunlight is too bright, the colour of the flowers on the graves too garish. It all looks false, like a film set waiting for the stars to arrive.

She watches the path leading to the church doors. A few people arrive, in ones and twos, and go through.

They wait until they see the Mayfields appear and walk up the path, Diana dressed in green, leaning on Geoffrey's arm. Connor is walking slightly behind, tall and ungainly. They get out of the taxi and follow them in, her mum holding her arm. She keeps her dark glasses on and her head down as they enter the dimly-lit church; touches her scarf that covers her neck and her jawline.

The organ plays quietly and a few people are dotted here and there in the pews. She can't look at them. Her mother leads her to the front where the Mayfields are sitting, encouraging her when she hesitates. As she sits, Diana squeezes her arm, there are tears in her eyes. Geoffrey nods. Connor stares at his hands. She feels sick and shaky. She's vaguely aware of people shuffling into their seats behind her, but she stares forward, her neck and shoulders rigid, trying to control her emotions.

The service begins with a brief acknowledgement from the vicar. How sad is the reason for their gathering today, how young was the victim, how terrible the tragic events of that day a year ago.

The rest goes by in a haze, her mum prompting her to stand, sit and pray. She doesn't pray. She clutches the photo of Ali in both hands, as if she'll never let it go. The urge to wail and scream clutches at her. When Geoffrey stands to give a tribute to his daughter, she barely hears the words. There's a buzzing in her ears, her eyes brim with tears and her whole body shakes, despite her mum's arm around her and Diana's warm presence beside her.

"Full of life . . . beautiful . . . everything to look forward to . . ." the words wash over her. A dark curtain starts to fall.

"Go . . . I've got to go . . ." The bile is rising and she stumbles head down past her mum to the end of the pew, past all the people, to the doors.

She follows the gravel path to the back of the church and clutches at the cool stone wall, gulping air into heavy lungs. She bends forwards and retches, over and over. There's nothing to bring up and her body strains with the effort, her throat sore and dry.

After a while, it stops and she looks up. She's shocked to see that the sun is shining, cars are still going past in the street, people are going about their business as if nothing has happened. She walks slowly through the churchyard, searching for Ali. She's still there and there are new flowers everywhere. It's beautiful.

"I'm so sorry, Ali. I'm so sorry." She says it out loud, and carries on saying it to herself, kneeling by the grave, head bowed. Oh, Ali, I'm so sorry. Why was it you? It should have been me.

She's still there when her mum finds her, but she's calm now, a numbness taking over.

"It's okay, my darling girl." Her mother folds her in her arms, kneeling on the soft grass beside her.

"Has it finished?"

"Nearly. Last hymn, I think."

"Can we go? I don't want to be here when everyone comes out."

"We can go."

They stand together, looking down at Ali's resting place. They leave the churchyard. Lisa looks back, Ali will still be there tomorrow.

* * *

They sit in the garden with Riley. Lisa feels drained and can hardly speak. The phone rings and her mum gets up. She's gone a few minutes, then reappears. "It's Diana. Will you talk to her?"

"What will I say, Mum?"

"Don't worry, she understands. She wanted to check you're all right and to ask you something."

They want her to call in tomorrow, before she goes back. Feeling she's let them down today, she agrees, though reluctantly. She was hoping to leave early, get back to her home as soon as possible, to shut herself away. But she owes them that much, so arranges to go mid-morning.

* * *

The memorial is over but the day is not. Though she's sick with fatigue and emotion, she's enervated, her body's in overdrive and she can't keep still.

She takes Riley and though her mum protests — concerned that she's not eaten or slept — they go out for a long walk, leaving the town after a couple of miles for the footpaths and farm tracks of the countryside. Soon they're lost in unfamiliar territory but she carries on, not caring, forcing her body to climb steep paths and rugged fields where the paths run alongside unfamiliar crops and dense hedges. She keeps the dog close. He seems to understand her need to drive on and keeps in step, trotting by her side and looking up at her for reassurance when they climb a stile or change direction.

After a couple of hours, she's hot and irritated by the long sleeves of her t-shirt, which won't stay rolled up. Riley's panting, his pink tongue lolling as he walks, bubbles of saliva at the corners of his mouth. When eventually they find a small stream he takes great gulps, the water spilling from his mouth, his long ears trailing in the flow.

Now that they've stopped, she looks around for the first time. The landscape is unfamiliar and they've seen nobody for a few miles now. The air is still. There's a silence that's different to the calm back home. The thought makes her uncomfortable and so she leaves the stream, beckoning Riley to come along with her, and heads up a rising track so that she can get her bearings. At the top of the track is a small farmhouse, with outbuildings full of machinery in various states of disrepair and horses in the adjacent field. A woman in riding boots and jodhpurs busies herself with one of them as Lisa approaches.

"Hello, sorry to bother you but I've lost my way," Lisa says as the woman straightens. "I need to get back to the town."

"You've come a long way," the woman says, the horse's reins in her spare hand. "Follow me, I'll show you."

They follow to the top end of the field where it's high enough to see the track they've just left. They can just make out a town in the distance, shimmering with the reflected light of many windows.

"There's the town. You need to go back down the track, follow it round to the right and take the left turn at the junction. That road will take you right there — it's not too busy, so you should be okay."

"Okay, thanks."

"It's a good couple of hours, though. Do you need some water?"

"Yes please, that would be great. My dog's had a drink, but I didn't bring anything."

"I'm going back to the house, come with me, I'll get you a bottle." They follow her down to the house, where a black and white collie runs up to greet Riley with a bark. They wait by the gate until she reappears with a large bottle of water.

"There, that should keep you both going until you get back," the woman says.

* * *

It's early evening when they return to the house.

"I was beginning to worry," her mum says. "You went out without any money and no phone, of course."

"Sorry, I just needed to get out and walk off some of the stress. I need a bath." She clumps up the stairs as her mum calls after her: "I'm getting supper ready — come down as soon as you're finished."

In the bath, her stomach rumbles ominously, though she doesn't feel hungry. Her legs look thin and pale in the water, her skin grey and unhealthy.

* * *

That night she lies in bed with the light on, Riley sleeping beside her. She holds the picture of Ali and weeps, soaking the pillow beneath her ear.

How could it be that one moment, a year ago almost to the minute, Ali is alive and vibrant, the next, broken and gone? How the hell did that happen? How did she, Lisa, whose life was at the very same moment hanging by a thread, end up alive, while Ali was dead?

And why? For what? What did Fergus want that night? What was he looking for? Did he really mean to harm them? To kill? What on earth was it all about? There's no sense in any of it.

She lies there through the night, tortured with questions which multiply the more she wrestles with them. They beat at her mind, pounding at the door, insisting on a resolution.

But there are only questions. She finds no answers. None at all.

* * *

Diana opens the door with a smile. She looks smaller, somehow, and her body feels bony and fragile when she hugs Lisa.

"Come in, dear. Are you feeling better?"

"Yes, I'm fine. I'm so sorry to rush off like that."

"Oh, really — we were just concerned for you. It took a lot of courage for you to come, and we're very glad you did."

"It was a lovely thing to do and I'm glad I came, really. I know it doesn't seem it."

They go through into the sitting room and sit down.

"We were surprised and very touched, at the number of people who came. So many faces we hadn't seen for a long time, and so many flowers! It was a wonderful tribute to Ali."

"Yes." She looks down at her hands. "She was very popular."

"Yes."

In the pause that follows, Geoffrey appears and they exchange kisses on the cheek. He disappears into the kitchen to make coffee.

"We've been sorting out her room." Diana's eyes glisten. "Not to clear it — we're not ready to do that — just to get a bit more organised. We found some things of hers you might like."

"Oh, you did? I . . . but . . ." The guilt twists in her gut. She wants to blurt out that it was all her fault, she doesn't deserve their kindness, but Diana has already turned and is leading the way upstairs to Ali's bedroom.

It's exactly as it was. The bed is made up, with the same linen that Lisa remembers from her teenage years. They would sit for hours on that bed, messing it up, curling up under the covers, listening to music and doing their nails. The books on the shelf are the same familiar titles, novels from English classes: Persuasion and To Kill a Mocking Bird rubbing shoulders with childhood paperbacks from Jackie Wilson and J.K. Rowling. The same small decorative boxes are on the windowsill and on the bed sits Ali's old cuddly toy, a soft brown teddy bear called Sid.

For a moment she's transported back, as if she's never been away and Ali is still there, about to appear at the door. She examines the bookshelf, touches the bed and stares at the posters on the wall. She can almost smell the nail polish, hear them giggling.

"We haven't changed much at all in here," Diana says. "I suppose we won't for a while. Some of her old clothes went to the charity shop though, it seemed wrong to keep them all here. But the rest, her trinkets and so on, we couldn't just throw them out."

Lisa stands by the window, looking at the little boxes that Ali liked to collect from junk shops and car boot sales. None was more than about three inches across; the smallest were the ones Ali loved best. Some were enamel with garlands and ribbons painted on the lids, some delicate bone china or pottery, one or two made of silver, tarnished now through neglect. She remembers those because every now and then, when she was there with Ali, there would be the distinctive smell of silver polish in the room and the little boxes would shine brightly. Ali would play with them as she stood at the window, rearranging them from time to time, polishing them as she went, and putting them in groups according to size or colour. She can almost see Ali standing there, laughing as she polished.

Lisa picks up the smallest. It looks old and delicate, the engravings on the lid faint. She rubs it gently with her finger to remove the tarnish.

"Would you like to have one of those?" Diana's voice interrupts her reverie. "I'm sure she would want you to, and we can't keep them all."

"Oh, that's . . . really? I don't . . . I can't." She's paralysed with guilt. She can't look at Diana, hopes she doesn't notice.

"Really. They'll only be gathering dust here. Look, there must be at least twenty. Please have one — something to remember her by. You two were like sisters. I know you're hurting too."

Lisa's eyes fill and she wipes them with the backs of her hands.

"Go on. How about this one? Well, anyway, you choose."

Because she can't speak, she holds up the little silver box in her hand and Diana nods and smiles. She scrabbles in her pocket for a tissue, wipes her eyes and nose.

She doesn't deserve this. She feels like a fraud.

"Come on, let's get that coffee." Diana guides her back down the stairs to the living room, where a tray of cups and a plate of biscuits awaits. She puts the silver box down on the table and accepts a cup gratefully, glad of the distraction. She doesn't usually drink coffee, but the bitter liquid helps soothe her throat.

"Geoffrey, Lisa's having one of Ali's little boxes."

Geoffrey smiles. "Good. She would have wanted you to have it."

Behind them the front door opens and shuts with a loud bang and Lisa's cup wobbles dangerously as she starts at the noise.

"We're in here, Connor," Diana calls. "Come and say hello to Lisa."

He comes into the room, tall and lanky, hair falling over his eyes. A pale blue t-shirt, faded and worn at the hem, covers his thin body. Jeans and trainers, the young man's uniform, cover his lower half. He doesn't smile.

"Hello Lisa." He sticks his hand out formally. His hand squashes her soft fingers in a vice-like grip. He steps back towards the door again.

"Hi Connor, how are you?" It's not the right thing to say, but in the moment she doesn't know what else to say.

"Fine." He's still not smiling and there's something unspoken, aggressive even, about his stance.

"Come and join us, have a drink." Diana indicates an empty chair at the other end of the sofa.

"No thanks, I've got to go out again."

"Lisa's going to have one of Ali's little boxes as a keepsake," Diana says, looking at Connor for a reaction.

"Right. I've got to go. Bye Lisa." And with that, he's gone, his feet pounding upstairs two at a time. Diana and Geoffrey look taken aback, staring at the still open door.

"Don't worry about him," Diana says, turning back to Lisa. "He's not a good conversationalist at the best of times."

"Took it all very hard," Geoffrey says. "He idolised his sister, as you know."

"Yes." But even if she's over-sensitive, she recognised that look of anger in his eyes as he took her hand.

* * *

A few minutes before she leaves, she hears Connor's footsteps on the stairs again and the front door slams.

She says goodbye in the hallway. Diana hugs her, insisting that she comes back very soon to see them. She's wrapped the silver box in tissue paper and Lisa puts it in her bag. Geoffrey kisses her on the cheek again and nods. His daughter's death seems to have diminished him, taken the old ebullience away, leaving a quiet awkwardness in its place.

As she leaves the house, Connor is in the driveway, leaning on the open door of a red hatchback, talking on his mobile. He looks at her, cuts the call and drops the phone onto the driver's seat. He steps towards her, towering over her.

"Bitch."

It hits her like a hammer and she recoils with shock. She looks up at his angry face and starts to shake, steps back and stumbles, almost falling to the ground. His eyes are wide and staring, his chin juts forward, tension hardens his neck and shoulders.

"I . . . Connor, what . . ."

"You always wanted her life. I know your game. I know what you're up to. Wheedling your way into my family, taking her things. You bitch. How come you lived and she died? Tell me that!"

She flinches at the venom in his words, her mind racing, wanting to reason with him, find the right things to say. But the question is the very question she's been asking herself. The knowledge renders her speechless and the words won't form on her lips.

He's looking at her with wide eyes, his hands clenched, waiting for her response.

She wants to shout: NO! I'm not like that! I loved Ali, she was my best friend.

But nothing comes out.

"How come you lived? You could have saved her, but you saved yourself. It's true, isn't it?" He's not shouting, but the threat in his voice is clear.

He steps forward. Her body reacts with pure instinct: RUN. She takes off at full pelt, bag flying, feet scrabbling, adrenalin coursing. She hurtles down the street, rounds a corner, hits her shoulder with a painful jolt on the brick wall on her left.

As she runs, she listens intently for the sound of running feet at her back.

CHAPTER SIX

Ali is okay. She fell onto the steps, but she got up again and she's fine.

"It's just a bruise," she says, looking up at Lisa at the window.

She smiles and walks back up to the flat. But as she reaches the open door to the sitting room, she starts to fade and fold, and Lisa rushes towards her. Her body is disappearing, becoming translucent, then just a shining light with the contours of Ali's body. She continues to smile and her hair lifts as if there's a breeze, and then she's gone. Lisa lies on the floor and she can't move. Her eyes are nailed shut, her mouth is full of sand. Her head has been severed from her body, but she feels no pain, only terror, because she's stuck to the floor and she can't get away. She moans and struggles, but nothing happens. A black curtain descends.

She opens her eyes slowly and her first thought is of Connor. She grabs a pillow and puts it over her head, hoping to smother the memory of his words. But she can't block them out. After a few minutes she replaces the pillow and stares up into the darkness.

When she'd left Connor and run away she'd kept running for a long time, only stopping to ease the pain in her chest. A stitch stabbed at her side. She leaned against a brick wall fronting one of the terraced houses behind her.

His words were repeating in her head. How come you lived and she died? How come you lived? You could have saved her, but you saved yourself.

* * *

The next few days are spent cocooned at home in a deep, dark fog. She emerges only to walk Riley and to pick up groceries.

As if to punish herself, she thinks for hours about Connor and his words. What makes him think she wanted to hurt Ali?

She examines his accusations, individually and in detail.

You always wanted her life.

Maybe she had envied Ali's 'normal' family life, the happy family unit — but surely that was understandable, given her own situation? And anyway, it wasn't actual envy, it was more admiration, recognition of what a family could be like. No, she won't accept that she'd been jealous of her friend, or wanted her things. It just isn't true.

The other accusation is far more difficult to face.

How come you lived, and she died?

I don't know!

Or do I? She tries to separate her guilt from what actually happened that night, but the scene is blurred and she turns it over and over again, desperately trying to tie it down, half-remembered details swirling.

How could he think she had any say in what happened? She was nearly killed herself, after all. And she loved Ali, why would she ever have wanted to hurt her?

You could have saved her, but you saved yourself.

But she'd been hurt, bleeding, unable to fight back. The only reason she'd survived had nothing to do with her own actions; it was only through luck, or fate, that he hadn't actually severed an artery. But could she have saved Ali? What makes Connor think she could have done? What had really happened?

The more she thinks about it, the more she thinks that Connor knows something that she doesn't.

* * *

Graham puts down his notes and looks up. It's about to start.

The last few days have been particularly low. She's exhausted by the nagging monologue in her head. Getting weaker by the day, she feels flat and empty, ready to give someone else the job of running her life.

"Tell me about the memorial."

There's a pause as Lisa collects her thoughts. "We sat with Ali's family. I didn't get through it all. I panicked and left halfway through. I felt sick."

"Did you feel it was good to have been there?"

"I'm glad I went, for her parents."

"And for you?"

"Yes, I suppose so. It did bring it all back, the attack. But when I remembered her as she was before it was . . . comforting."

"You say you panicked."

"I was so anxious, scared of seeing people I'd recognise, people I hadn't seen since Ali . . . died. And I hadn't eaten for days. It wasn't really a panic attack. I felt sick and I had to rush out. I went to the grave and said I was sorry to Ali — for leaving her, for her dying and me not, for not saving her. It seemed to help, saying sorry. Even though she wasn't actually there, I felt close to her, beside her grave."

He leans forward, hands on his knees, and looks intently at her. She notices how clean his fingernails are.

"Do you believe you could have saved her?"

"Yes . . . no . . . I don't know really. Her brother thinks I could have." She describes the incident with Connor.

"Do you think what he said is true? That you always wanted her life?"

"No, definitely not. I didn't want her life. She was my best friend, but I wasn't jealous, ever. We were really close, but I didn't want to be her."

"So you don't accept that part. What about the other part? What makes him think you could have saved her?"

"I don't know . . ." She stops to think and something dawns on her — a flash of understanding, a hazy memory, floating. She's shocked into silence.

"Lisa?"

"No, it's . . . I really don't know." Her mind is racing, chasing after it, but it slips away.

Graham lets it go, though he knows she's thought of something, she can tell. She's familiar with his ways, now. It'll come up again. By then, maybe she can be sure.

"Has it occurred to you that he may be looking for a reason, like you?" he says.

"A reason why she died? Yes, probably. I was the only other person there, so he blames me. His sister's dead and he's grieving, trying to make some sense of it. Perhaps he's just lashing out. He doesn't know what he's saying. I know all of this."

"It's possible. What do you think?"

"When he said it, it was a real shock. I thought that perhaps he knows. Perhaps he picked something up from the court hearing or the sentencing or something. Did something else happen that night that I can't remember, that makes him think it was my fault?"

He makes a little steeple with his fingers and touches his mouth to his thumb-knuckles.

"You could ask him," he says.

* * *

She doesn't want to see anyone. She leaves the house only to take Riley round the block. She can't face Jessica. Or John. Everything is too much for her and she hates the feeling of helplessness.

She's in mourning for Ali. It occurs to her that a year after Ali's death, this is the first time she's really faced her grief. It's been triggered by the memorial. She's knows this. She just misses Ali.

She wants only the sanctuary of her home and the companionship of her dog. She ignores both the TV and the computer, surviving on tinned soup and buttered toast, boiled eggs and tea.

* * *

A knock at the door pulls her from her reverie. A walk with Jessica is her first time out properly since the memorial service. Jessica is wearing bright colours, a pink t-shirt and white jeans, and she looks different, younger, more relaxed.

Once they're away from the road, they let the dogs off the lead and follow them down the path towards the lake. It feels so long since they've seen each other.

"I'm sorry I've been so off the radar. I promise this isn't going to be how things are. I know you've got your own situation and I should be there for you. It's all just so much right now. The memorial was harder than I ever imagined."

Jessica stops walking and hugs Lisa. She holds tight as the tears start to fall. "It's okay, Lisa, I'm here."

They break apart and Lisa wipes at her eyes with the sleeve of her jumper. She tells Jessica about the confrontation with Connor.

"I thought the memorial was going to be hard enough," Jessica says. "But that was cruel, on top of it all. What was he doing?"

"People behave differently when they're grieving, I suppose. His mother warned me he wasn't coping well."

"Well it hasn't been a walk in the park for you," Jessica says.

"It's been terrible for all of us."

They negotiate a gate into the field at the back of the lake and take the footpath to the hill behind Lisa's house. The dogs race ahead.

"Tell me what's happening with Mike."

It's hard to believe it's already five months since Jessica arrived unexpectedly at Lisa's front door, her face battered and bleeding. "Quite a lot. We've seen the mediator twice. Mike refused to engage with the process. He sat there not making eye contact, shuffling through his papers. I think he only comes along because he thinks I might take him to the cleaners. Not that I could, even if I wanted to."

"Have you managed to make any progress?"

"He wants to sell the house. My parents, bless them, have offered to help me buy him out. I'm not sure though, there's still quite a big mortgage on it and I don't know if I can take it on. I need a job first."

"So you're going for a divorce?"

"Definitely, that's why we need to get all this agreed. I think I've got grounds." She gives Lisa a wry smile.

"Will you leave the area? He was brought up round here, wasn't he?"

"I want to stay here. I suppose he might decide to settle here again, but I doubt it. It's much better for his work to be in the city, near the airport."

"I hope he stays away — and I'm glad you want to stay."

"I'm kind of fond of the place," Jessica says. "I'll apply for a teaching job in the area, anything part-time. It's late in the academic year, but you never know."

"You've been so brave," Lisa replies. "I'm proud of you."

"I just want my life back. It should never have got so bad, but now I can finally be myself. It's hard. Of course a part of me would take him back in a second. But I have to remember why I'm doing this. What happened. I deserve better," she says. "We both do." She squeezes Lisa's hand.

A family passes them on the path, two children on brightly coloured bikes, their helmet-clad heads huge on small bodies, their legs pumping. They stop to let them by.

"By the way," Jessica says when they're out of earshot. "I don't think he'll bother you again. He seemed pretty embarrassed about it when the mediator mentioned you. I think he's over that stage now; he just wants to get it sorted."

"Good. How do you feel about him now?"

"I'm relieved he's gone. All I feel for him now is contempt. I hate his flashy jewellery, his designer clothes and his fast car. I hate the way he licks his lips when he's nervous. His tongue looks like a pink slug. Isn't that awful?" She flashes a look at Lisa like a guilty child.

Lisa laughs and it feels strange, as though there's a crack in the mask she's been wearing all this time.

* * *

As a distraction she forces herself back to her desk in an effort to catch up on the time missed — she's been 'off sick' for far too long and she can't afford to lose the income. They'll stop giving her the work if she becomes unreliable. She sits for hours at her desk. It's July now, and warm, so she leaves the kitchen door to the garden open and a gentle breeze drifts through.

In the early evenings she walks, sometimes with Jessica and Bobby, but more often on her own with Riley. The walking calms her. Gradually she begins to feel just a little more objective about Connor's accusations, a little more accepting of her grief.

Down by the lake families sit and picnic on the green spaces, their laughter echoing across the water. In the winter she'd been grateful for the lack of people and when the weather changed, she'd felt her sanctuary had been invaded by these strangers. But now she's accustomed to the presence of others, the gentle hum of background noise.

Nature has woken up. Ducks gather together and bobbing lines of their offspring paddle after their mothers, dipping and calling. Lisa's rewarded on occasion by the flash of a kingfisher dipping across the edge of the water and dragonflies playing in the reeds, iridescent colours flashing in the bright sunlight.

As much as she can understand Connor's grief, his questions are still there. In the back of her mind emerging often to be turned over yet again, to be pulled apart and examined and put back together. There are still no answers.

* * *

The shopping's heavy and she feels a twinge in her side as she puts the bags down and gets out her key to open John's front door.

"Only me," she calls.

"Come on through."

She goes into the kitchen, where the back door is propped open, the light falling in a lopsided square on the floor. Seeing John sitting outside, she puts the kettle on and gets to work putting the shopping away. These days he has help with the housework, so the kitchen is generally clean and tidy and his washing and ironing is done for him. Lisa still helps with the shopping, though. She likes the excuse to keep an eye on him.

With the warm weather, he's been out more, going to the social club and meeting with friends. But today his cough has returned and he seems tired, so she makes him a cup of tea and offers to cook him some soup for supper while she's there.

"Would you, dear? That would be so kind. I'm really tired today." His eyes look paler than ever and the hand holding the mug shakes slightly.

"How long have you had that cough?" she says. "That's what's wearing you out. Perhaps you need some antibiotics again."

"Couple of days, not too bad. I don't want to bother the doctor again, he's far too busy to bother with a cough."

"Let me know if you need me to call him, or to get you something from the chemist though. Tomato soup?"

She warms the soup and makes buttered toast and sits with him at the kitchen table while he eats. She knows he likes the company and she's finished work for the day.

"It's my birthday next week," he says, wiping an orange streak of soup from his chin with a paper towel. It leaves a faint glow on his pale skin. "I'm really getting ancient. Eighty-nine! Can you believe it?"

"Do you have any plans?"

He shakes his head. "Well, I'm not going dancing, that's for sure."

"I'll get a cake, and Jessica and I will come and eat it with you. And Riley, of course."

"Cake! Well that would be rather nice, thank you. Don't get eighty-nine candles though, will you?" He chuckles at his joke.

While she clears up he sits in his armchair and dozes, and when she's done she signals to Riley, closes the back door and leaves quietly.

* * *

"Mum?" She tries to mask the anxiety in her voice. "I've been meaning to ask you something."

"Go on then."

"You went to the hearing, didn't you?"

Lisa's mum has come to visit for the first time. When she moved to the cottage, Lisa had needed her new home to be hers alone, a safe haven to live, work and rebuild her life. She wanted the space to recover, a quiet place to reflect.

Somehow though, the summer warmth has opened up her defences and she's tidied the spare room, placed fresh flowers on the chest of drawers and cleaned the house from top to bottom. Her mum is impressed. She's been given a full tour of the house, admiring the cosy sitting room, the tidy garden and the views.

They're sitting at the kitchen table, cups of tea already poured.

"Yes, I did," her mum said. "I sat in the gallery with the Mayfields. It was . . . difficult for all of us."

"I've never asked you about it, but I've been wondering. What was it like? What happened?"

"Are you sure you want to know? It might upset you all over again. And I don't know, but there's something different about you. You seem lighter."

"Yes, I'm sure. I think I'm ready to know now. Can you tell me about it? I think it might clear up a couple of things for me."

* * *

A month after the event, Lisa was still in hospital recovering and the court hearing was due. Her mum had called Ali's parents and they'd travelled together.

"Did Connor go too?" Lisa says.

"Yes, all three of them. We sat together in the public gallery, in the front, so we could see everything."

"Could you see Fergus?"

"Yes. When he came in, I couldn't take my eyes off him. He seemed so young — just a boy, really — and he was nervous, fidgeting all the time, looking at the floor mostly. Not at all how I'd imagined him. His mum was there too. I felt sorry for her."

"Did they question him?"

"No, he didn't get to say anything really, throughout the whole thing. They asked him for his plea at the beginning, and he said guilty to both crimes — grievous bodily harm for you and manslaughter for Ali. Then it was all the prosecutor. He talked about the night it happened, starting with you and Ali at the pub. He went through the evening in detail."

"Can you tell me? It might help me remember."

"Well, he described you arriving, what you were drinking and where you were sitting. It was very factual, matter-of-fact. You both left shortly after ten o'clock, stopping at the shop near the flat to buy milk. Fergus caught up with you outside the shop."

"Yes, I remember that far. Did they say if he followed us on purpose?"

"No, nothing like that."

"So what happened after that?"

"He came to the flat, rang on the bell, you both saw him from the window and you went down to let him in — to use the toilet. When he came out of the bathroom, he wanted to stay and talk. He went to the kitchen for some water and while he was in there, he picked up a kitchen knife." Her mum pauses, takes a deep breath. Lisa takes her hand across the kitchen table.

"But he couldn't remember anything after he came out of the kitchen. There was no explanation of what happened from then on. We waited — we were hoping for more, but they said he had no memory. Poor Diana, it must have been agonising for her."

"But he did remember taking the knife? And grabbing me?"

"He remembered picking up the knife. I don't know if he remembered grabbing you. That wasn't mentioned. They started talking about forensic evidence after that."

"It seems so weird that he didn't get questioned," Lisa said. "I suppose that was all behind the scenes. But what if he was lying about not remembering?"

"That would have been up to the police to find out, I imagine. All we had to go on was what the prosecutor said. There was nothing about the police questioning. Because he was willing to plead guilty, they only needed to present the facts, so the judge could make her decision."

"So what forensic evidence was there?"

"Apparently there was evidence that Ali was standing by the window, I don't know what it was. When they caught him, Fergus said she'd jumped."

"He said she jumped? But why would she jump? He must have pushed her. He was lying! Ali wouldn't have done that, Mum, you know that, right?"

"Well I suppose she could have been so frightened, she panicked — but anyway, he changed his story. There was evidence he touched her and she fell backwards out of the window onto the steps. It certainly didn't seem like she jumped.

It's more likely she was pushed, or just fell by accident, trying to get away. She died from a head injury."

"Oh God, Mum." The tears fill her eyes, threaten to fall.

Her mum's tearful too, dabbing at her eyes with a tissue. "I know. Poor Ali. And terrible for her family, having to hear it described like that."

Lisa squeezes her mum's fragile hand in front of her. "I'm so sorry you had to go through that."

"I had to, you couldn't possibly have gone."

Lisa sits and thinks for a moment, digesting the information. She can see the scene at the flat, feel his breath on her neck, his hand in her hair. And Ali — Ali is there, close to them, screaming, pleading for Lisa's life. But after that, nothing. Why won't it come back to her?

"How did they know he'd touched her?"

"Your blood was on her t-shirt, and his DNA. Transfer, they called it."

"And where was I while this was happening?"

"They found you on the floor by the coffee table, unconscious and bleeding. That's all they said."

"And this was all from the prosecution? Fergus didn't say anything?"

"He didn't have to. He'd already admitted both crimes."

"But they believed he couldn't remember? Didn't they question that?" Though her own memory is buried, a side effect of the trauma she's suffered, she can't believe that the same has happened to the man who caused it all. He must be lying to protect himself — to avoid being tried for murder.

"Not in court. Whatever happened, it seems that because he admitted both crimes, there was no need for him to say anything at the hearing."

"So," she says, trying to sort out the confusion in her mind. "Even though neither of us could remember what really happened to Ali, he pleaded guilty to manslaughter? Why would he, if he could get away with saying he didn't know?"

"Because he'd been in contact with her, and because of what he'd done to you. It was obvious he'd behaved in an extremely violent way, threatening your lives. They reckon his behaviour caused Ali to fall and die as a result, which is manslaughter."

"And he admitted grievous bodily harm for attacking me?"

"Straight away, apparently. Thank goodness he did, or you'd have had to appear in court and testify against him."

"That would have been unbearable. I'm not sure I could have got through it."

"It was pretty awful even without you having to testify."

"Was there any defence?"

"A lawyer read out a statement from Fergus. He apologised. He said he was drugged up and very drunk, he'd broken up with a girlfriend and was upset. That was his excuse, anyway. He said he didn't mean to hurt anybody, and he was very sorry."

"He was told to say all that! Why did he do it then, Mum? Why did he try to kill us?" The fury that's been smouldering inside her suddenly erupts and she jumps up and goes to the kitchen sink, holding on to the sides with shaking hands. The cool porcelain, rock-solid and real, steadies her. Everything else in her life seems unstable, impossible to grasp, and she leans forward, unsure if she feels sick or faint. Her mum follows and lays a gentle hand on her back.

"I know. None of it makes sense. I knew this would upset you."

"It all seems so pointless. Ali died for no reason and my life's wrecked. And we still don't know why he did it — or even what happened. We've got no idea." She runs the cold tap and splashes her face with water. The cold is like a penance; she sips from her hands and the water runs off her chin and onto her neck, calming her with its cool touch. As she dries it her fingers skim over the still-red scar, the everlasting reminder.

* * *

Her head aches with the strain of trying to remember. She searches for clues in what her mum has said — anything that might trigger a fragment of memory, but there's nothing. She sighs and comes back to the present, puts the kettle on and sits down.

"What happened then?"

"There was some legal stuff that didn't mean much to me, then they fixed a date for the sentencing," her mum says. "Do you remember any more of it now?"

"I don't know. I'm not sure." She's beginning to wonder what's real and what's nightmare. "How was everybody after the hearing?"

"We were all pretty shellshocked. I can't remember what we talked about, even."

She gives her mum's hand a squeeze. "Thank you for going — I know it wasn't easy."

"Does it help to know what happened?"

"Yes, though it's all still jumbled up in my head."

She needs more time. She's not sure what she'll do with the information she's just heard, whether it'll lead her anywhere at all, let alone somewhere useful. So far, it's given her no new clues, no direction or further understanding of what happened.

"Mum, did anyone talk about how we'd met Fergus? How well we knew him?"

"No, I don't think so. Can't you remember?"

"No, that memory's gone as well. It's probably not important."

But it might be, she thinks. And it might reveal a reason why it all happened.

Glancing out of the kitchen window, she notices Riley disappearing through the fence into John's garden. She remembers John's birthday coming up and reminds herself to sort out a cake and a card.

"Did anything more come out at the sentencing?" she says, turning back to her mum.

"Not really. It was all over very quickly. There was a bit of legal talk and the charges were read out again. Then the judge passed sentence. It caused a bit of a furore in court. We were so upset — and the papers made a meal of it. They tried to get pictures of us on the way out. Geoffrey was furious."

Lisa has avoided the media coverage, not wanting to see the story dissected, those terrible, life-changing moments reported in cold detail. This is as much information as she needs for now.

* * *

Lisa and her mum walk by the lake in the warm sunshine. They stroll, reminiscing about Lisa's childhood, her father and the holidays they enjoyed together. They watch the ducklings and laugh as the tiny creatures dive and bob back up, experts at feeding already. Lisa enjoys the freedom of light summer clothing — though she still covers her throat with a scarf — and has taken to wearing jeans and t-shirts on warm days, her pale arms soaking up the rays.

In the evenings, they eat outside until the light fades and they talk or sit watching films when it gets dark. In the mornings, Lisa gets up early to work at her desk, so she's got time to spare for her mother later in the day.

The day before John's birthday, they buy the ingredients for a cake and make it together, as they used to do when Lisa was small. They buy candles, a card, and a balloon that says.

On the day they've arranged to arrive around tea-time. Jessica comes to call for them on her way, and after the exchange of pleasantries and introductions, they gather up the birthday things and troop next door. They find him in the kitchen, his hair combed and proper shoes on his feet, the kettle already boiling.

"Hello, hello! Come in," he says, easing himself out of his chair.

"Happy Birthday, John," they chorus.

A smile lights up his face when he sees the cake and the balloon.

"Look at that! I haven't been so spoilt for years."

Lisa helps him open the cards and they squeeze together round the kitchen table. There's a single candle for him to blow out and although this prompts a coughing fit, he soon recovers and tucks into the piece of cake Jessica has cut for him.

"Lovely," he says, winking at Lisa. "You must get your mum to stay more often." Crumbs stick to his chin, giving him a comical look.

"Oh she doesn't want me around too much," her mum says, smiling. "She has her own life to lead."

And to sort out, Lisa thinks.

John starts coughing again, his thin body shaking with the effort. Lisa helps him to his armchair while Jessica gets a glass of water. He's only eaten a small piece of cake, but shakes his head when Lisa offers to leave it next to him.

"Thank you, it's delicious, but not now. I'll have some more later. There's a cake tin in that cupboard, if you'd be so kind." He leans back in his chair and closes his eyes. "I'm sorry, I get worn out quite easily these days."

"Don't you worry at all," Lisa replies, leaving him to rest.

They wash up and tidy and by the time they've finished he's asleep. They creep out, closing the front door carefully behind them.

"I'm not sure about that cough," Lisa's mum says as they walk back. "I think he should see a doctor, especially if it's been a few days."

"I'll check on him tomorrow," Lisa says. "Last time I asked, he brushed it off, but I'll ask again."

"It's good you're keeping an eye on him. What happens if he gets too ill to look after himself?"

"He gets some help already, after the last time he was ill, but I don't know. He's only got his nephew, and he lives abroad. I suppose his doctor would have to take the decision if he needs full-time care."

"Yes. It can't be easy being that age, and alone," her mum says.

* * *

She sits quietly at the far end of the café, her back against the wall. She's early and has already finished her drink. The dregs congeal into a syrup in the bottom of the mug. She wonders if he'll come. When she called him, he was taken aback, hesitant. He had agreed to meet — but maybe he just wanted to get her off the phone.

She'd agonised over contacting him, going over and over what he'd said, torturing herself. In the end there was no choice but to talk to him, find out what brought him to make those accusations, to be so sure.

Diana had answered the call.

"He's not here, I'm afraid. Is there something I can help with?"

"No — I just wanted to catch up with him." It was lame, but it had to do.

"I should tell you, Lisa, he's been behaving strangely. It's all got to him. He's seeing a therapist. I don't know if he can be any help."

"It's okay, I just want to keep in touch. Do you have his mobile number?"

It took a few days to summon up the courage to call him and now she's there, she asks herself for the hundredth time if this is wise. But she's practised what to say many times and she's determined to get the answers she needs.

Then he's there in front of her, unsmiling, a tall, dark presence. She jumps and the table shakes.

"Connor. Thanks for coming. Are you going to get a drink?"

It takes a few moments for him to be served and she has time to compose herself, determined not to panic. He comes back with a coffee and sits opposite her, dwarfing the table in front of him. His face is pale and a dark stubble shades his cheeks. His clothes are worn and hang off his slender frame, as if he's lost weight. He looks too long for his chair.

She waits for him to settle and begins.

"I wanted to talk about what you said the last time we met, outside your house. You seem to hold me responsible in some way for . . . for what happened." She forces the words out. They hang in the air between them.

He leans back in the chair, knees apart, head on one side. He says nothing. But she has steeled herself for this encounter.

"Connor?" She tries to get eye contact. He looks at his coffee mug, plays with the handle. "Why do you blame me?"

He looks at her then and his eyes flash. "You lived. Ali died." His voice is low, but he spits the words out and she shrinks back from his anger.

Don't be intimidated. "But, just because I lived, doesn't mean I wanted her to die. Or had any hand in her dying . . ." She swallows hard. Pushes her mug to one side on the table, then pulls it back in front of her again, like a shield.

You have to do this.

Connor is silent, his coffee untouched. She tries another tack.

"Listen, I wasn't at the hearing, or the sentencing, as you know. I don't know what Fergus said and my mum has only just told me what she remembers. Did he say something to give the impression . . . to make you think . . ." You must say it. " . . . it was my fault she died?" She falters and the tears threaten.

He looks at her then, the pain in his eyes taking over from anger. "I don't know what to think. You were there. You could have done something!"

"Honestly, Connor, I don't think I could have done. I can't really remember but it looks like I collapsed, I'd lost a lot of blood. You don't really think I wouldn't have tried to stop him if I could?"

"But why did he let you live? Why did he release you and attack her instead? There was no evidence, apparently, and he couldn't remember, he was so fucked up on drugs and booze."

She drops her head into her hands. "God, I don't know, Connor. He was off his head. Perhaps he thought he'd killed me . . . I would have done anything, anything, to save her. I need you to know that."

Stop. Don't say any more. The tears have won the battle and she scrabbles in her bag for a tissue. She looks up again and he's wiping his eyes with the backs of his hands. When he's done, he picks up the coffee mug and drinks. Then looks at her again.

"I never envied her, not for a moment," she says. "I loved her, she was my best friend, and I thought she would always be."

He shakes his head, starts to speak, then shakes his head again. "I'm sorry I said that."

There's a long pause. He seems to be struggling to say something, so she waits, miserably. "I don't know, Lisa. I suppose I'm looking for someone to blame."

"Oh Connor — you can blame me. I already blame myself, for letting him into the flat, for not shoving him out when he started behaving strangely, for surviving, for living . . . If I deserve to be punished, then I'm carrying out my own sentence, every minute of every day. But I didn't want her life and I didn't cause her death."

For a moment they stare at each other, their souls bare. "I believe you," he says eventually. "I'm sorry if I made it worse."

She closes her eyes in relief. Small steps.

* * *

When he's gone, she sits there for a very long time, watching people come and go, drink coffee, talk, laugh. She takes comfort in the familiar noises.

Despite her relief at Connor's words, it still taunts her — a memory that sits just out of reach, beyond her powers of recollection. She almost grasped it in that last session with Graham, but it came and went so fast, she just couldn't be sure.

There's something — something she hasn't yet remembered, which will explain it all. It just won't be forced.

With a sigh she stands up and leaves the café.

CHAPTER SEVEN

She shakes her dripping umbrella outside the door before stepping inside. Her feet are wet in their canvas shoes and the legs of her trousers are still damp when he invites her into his room a few minutes later.

She writes regularly in the diary now, but she's still unsure of her memories. Connor has fuelled the powerful desire to know the detail, to confront the event and her own actions, however painful. She knows it could be the path to recovery, but that's not the reason she's embarked on this quest. She's unable to stop herself. She has to know.

She notices that today, uncharacteristically, he's wearing odd socks — one black, one blue, and he looks dishevelled, with dark circles under his eyes. That's ironic, she thinks. He can't sleep, either.

She wonders about his other clients. Are they all damaged, like her? Have their lives been interrupted by some dreadful event beyond their control, or do some people just develop differently? Perhaps there's some connection incomplete, some gap in the physiology, within some people from the beginning. Or perhaps some of them have such terrible stories to tell, he loses sleep over them, like she does over hers.

"Last time, we discussed what Connor said after the memorial," he says. "Did you think any further about that?"

"I met up with him." If she'd been expecting surprise, she got none.

"Was that helpful?"

"I don't know about helpful. He's looking for someone to blame and that someone is me." It hurts to say it, but it's true.

He nods. "Do you think you deserve that?"

"Well, I told him I didn't envy Ali and I didn't want her life. I think he knows now it's unfair to accuse me of that."

"And?"

"He blames me because he thinks I could have saved her, but saved myself instead. I've been going round in circles thinking about it. I don't know if it's true or not."

"Last time, you seemed to think of something — or maybe you remembered something — which made you stop. We were talking about what Connor said to you outside the house."

"Yes. I had a flash of memory, but I couldn't quite grasp it and it hasn't happened again."

"Do you think it's important to remember everything?"

"I do, yes. I've talked to my mum about the hearing and she told me what she remembers. I thought it might trigger something, but it didn't really help."

"So you want to know it all?"

"Maybe then, once it's all clear, I can stop feeling guilty."

"Have you considered the idea that, in the details, there might be something that makes you feel worse, perhaps even more guilty?"

* * *

She has remembered something. Perversely, her mind has released a memory that doesn't seem significant, though it does explain the photo of the three of them.

It's triggered by the smell of fresh paint at the post office, and the man up the ladder, his workman's boots at eye level as she stands in the queue. The flashback is quick and clear, but it doesn't floor her in the same way as the others. It's more benign, and though she's disconcerted and shaken, she manages to resist the impulse to run.

He'd come to the flat to decorate, on the landlord's instructions. He'd been there when they arrived, having slipped his schedule and run over time, so when they moved in they were greeted by newly-painted bedrooms, a bathroom covered in paint-spattered sheets, and a kitchen still drying. He hadn't even started on the living room. The smell of paint pervaded the flat, and they threw all the windows open to avoid being overwhelmed by fumes.

But Fergus, white spots of paint in his hair, was friendly and apologetic — it wasn't his fault, after all, if the landlord had let the place before it was ready. He introduced himself and promised not to get in their way; anyway, they were out at work during the week and he could get on with it without bothering them. They liked him immediately, with his ready smile and his blue eyes.

One day he was still working when Lisa got back, and when Ali appeared he downed tools and suggested he buy them a drink at the pub. "For the inconvenience, you know," he said. They had no problem agreeing to that.

That had been the start of their trips to the pub round the corner and the beginning of the regular group of friends — some already familiar with Fergus, some who seemed to join them by chance. He would talk to anyone and if he arrived on his own he didn't stay alone for long. They would get there early, down a few drinks, eat chips or nachos and head off mid-evening. Thursday nights became a habit. Once or twice they went together to the cinema close by, to the early showing. Fergus sat between them and they passed popcorn to and fro, slurping Coke and giggling like teenagers. She remembers they were affectionate with each other, tactile. They linked arms, kissed him on the cheek, wrestled with him as if her were their brother. The girls liked his easy humour, his sociability.

They seemed to stay later and later at the pub and sometimes they had too much to drink. But it didn't matter, they could get home easily, and if one of them wanted to leave and the other didn't, they felt safe enough walking home alone. Sometimes Fergus would walk them back and stay for a coffee to sober up. Sometimes, when they were early, they'd watch a bad TV show together before he went home. In the early days of their friendship, he even slept overnight on the sofa on occasion when he was working on the flat the next day.

Once or twice Lisa came home to find Fergus there and wondered if there was something developing between him and Ali. Their banter had become flirtation. Admittedly it was no different with Lisa — but there was a closeness between the two, a hint in the body language.

She mentioned it in passing, not wanting to sound possessive, made a joke of it. Ali laughed it off. Though she liked Fergus, he wasn't her type. She was far more interested in the new man at work.

Beyond this Lisa's mind goes blank. Though she now knows how they knew Fergus, she's no closer to understanding the nature of their relationship when Ali died. She has a sinking feeling that there's something important waiting to emerge. And a new emotion accompanies it. Shame.

* * *

Riley bounds around her legs as they leave the cottage and head next door. "Go on, away!" she laughs.

"John? Are you there?" There's no sound from the kitchen. But then she hears coughing from upstairs, so she climbs the first few steps of the staircase to call to him. Riley waits obediently at the bottom.

"Are you all right? John?"

The coughing comes closer and he appears at the top of the stairs, his hand trembling as he steadies himself on the banister. His frail body shakes with each cough and he bends over, his other hand holding a handkerchief to his mouth.

"I'll get you some water. Don't try to talk." She runs to the kitchen, grabs a mug, half-fills it with water and hurries back up the stairs. "Sit on the top step and take a sip or two." He does as he's told. Gradually the coughing subsides and he's able to take a normal breath or two.

"Oh, dear. Oh dear. I'll be okay in a minute." His voice comes out as a hoarse whisper.

"Take your time. I'll help you down when you're ready."

After a few minutes he hands the mug back and they take it slowly down the stairs to the kitchen, where she helps him to his chair. She sits in front of him. His eyes are closed, his eyelids patterned with tiny trails of blue.

"John? I think I should call the doctor now."

He nods without opening his eyes. She scrabbles through his scraps of paper and finds the number, dials and waits for a reply, listening to his laboured breathing, thick and rasping. Within minutes she's organised the doctor to visit. She sits down next to his chair.

"Oh my dear, I'm sorry to be such trouble."

"You're not, John. I just want to make sure you're okay. It's what neighbours are for!" She tries to make her voice sound cheerful, masking the concern that's creeping through. "The doctor's coming, and I'll wait with you until he's here. You should have told me it was getting bad . . ."

"It got worse today. Had a bad night."

"I'm always in, you know — you just have to ask. You could call me if you don't want to go out. You have my number."

"Thank you . . ." He starts to cough again and she gets more water to put beside him. He takes a few sips and rests his head on the back of the chair, exhausted.

She sits for a full forty minutes, beginning to nod off herself, before the doorbell rings. Riley jumps up. "Stay," she says firmly and he sits back down next to John.

It's the same doctor as before, Doctor Morris, the man with the flappy coat — only this time he's not wearing it, looking younger in an open-necked shirt, the sleeves partly rolled up.

"Oh hello," he says. "Weren't you here last time?"

"Yes, hi, come on in." She indicates the kitchen and he strides through. The room is dwarfed by his presence, his energy absorbing the space around him.

He moves straight towards John, pulling the stethoscope from his bag.

"John, I think we need to admit you for a few days, sort out your lungs." He speaks loudly, as if John is hard of hearing.

John looks at him blankly.

"Your lungs are congested and I think you need to be in hospital where we can keep an eye on you. I'm going to get an ambulance to come and get you."

"Oh dear. Hospital." He looks up at Lisa, fear in his eyes. She feels a rush of sympathy for this elderly, lonely man.

"It'll be all right," she says. "You need to be looked after. I can keep an eye on the house for you. And I'll visit, too. You'll be back before you know it." She cringes inwardly at the cliché but doesn't know how else to comfort him. He beckons her to him and she leans down to hear his whisper.

"Don't let them keep me in. Can't stand hospitals." Perhaps he's scared he might never come out.

She takes his hand and squeezes it gently. "I won't let them. Please don't worry. Do you want me to call anyone?"

"There isn't anyone."

She waits with him for the ambulance and packs a small bag, feeling like an intruder. The bedroom is gloomy, layers of dust lying undisturbed on the surfaces, and there's a faint whiff of urine.

The paramedics are cheery and matter-of-fact. They help him into a wheelchair and into the waiting ambulance. And with that, the house is left empty.

* * *

She calls in to update Jessica and finds her reorganising her living room.

"Spring clean," Jessica says, smiling.

She tells her about John. It's shaken her. It seems that wanting a peaceful life is no guarantee of getting one; things happen anyway.

"I don't think we're here for a quiet life," Jessica says. "I think we just have to take what life throws at us and we can't expect to control it in any way. Whatever you do, stuff happens and there's nothing you can do about it. You just have to adapt and move on."

She's impressed with Jessica's certainty, her apparent ability to weather the storm.

"You sound like my mum," she says.

"That's not so bad — I like your mum."

Despite her confidence, Jessica has her own worries. Mike has gone, together with some of his belongings, and the house seems strangely empty. Despite the fact that he travelled so much when they were together, she feels very alone. She's longing to get a job so that she can focus on something new. In the meantime, she's creating an office for herself in the spare room upstairs and changing things around to stamp her new status on her surroundings.

"I don't want to do too much though, in case we decide to sell," she says. "Then I'll have to do it all again somewhere else."

"What does it depend on?"

"Just me, really, and whether I want my parents to support me. If I buy him out, I would be back to being financially beholden to them. I'm not sure I want that right now."

"If you sell, could you buy a place on your own with your share?"

"Possibly. That would be great, though it might be a strain on the finances at first. I need to do a bit of research — get the house valued and look at the cost of a smaller place. "

"Perhaps you could rent for a while, until you find the right place."

"Or I could keep this and let out a room. I don't know, I really need to do my sums. Changing the subject, will you come to the country show with me next weekend? It's here, by the lake, and we can take the dogs . . ."

* * *

Lines of booths selling everything from bread to jewellery to local crafts rub shoulders with old-fashioned village activities, including a coconut shy, the stocks, fishing for plastic ducks in big blue dustbins, and traditional quoits. In the centre is an enclosure with a sign announcing a dog show, ferret racing and a tug of war.

Marilyn, the kindly woman from the local shop, is running the tombola and persuades the girls to buy tickets. Lisa comes away with a bottle of wine and some vinegar.

The dog show attracts dogs of all sizes and breeds. Jessica enters Bobby for the most beautiful dog category and he behaves immaculately, his eyes fixed on Jessica, the feathers on his tail waving constantly. Lisa watches from the boundary fence, laughing. She can't remember the last time she felt so relaxed. Bobby wins second prize, to Jessica's obvious disgust. She pins the yellow ribbon to his collar.

"It was definitely rigged. He's way prettier than that Labrador . . ."

They stand for a while, watching the ferret racing, when a voice startles them both. "Hello, we meet again." It's Doctor Morris, casual in shorts and a t-shirt, holding a large paper coffee cup.

"Oh, hi," she replies after a slight delay. "Sorry, I didn't recognise you!" The blood rushes to her face.

"No problem, I'm not in work mode today."

"Jessica, this is Doctor Morris. He's John's doctor."

"Andy," he says, shaking Jessica's hand.

"How's John, have you heard?" Lisa says.

"He's not under my care while he's there, so I haven't seen him, but I believe he's getting better. It's a good hospital. I'm sure he's well looked after."

"He hates hospitals. I hope he gets out soon."

"Well, he's eighty-nine, it takes much longer to recover when you're that age. But he has all his marbles and he seems pretty fit apart from the bronchitis. Anyway, it was lovely to see you, enjoy the fair!" And with that, he smiles and makes his way to the tombola.

When they move on, Jessica nudges Lisa. "He's nice."

"Stop it. He's John's doctor."

"Yes. But he's still nice. He's probably happily married, with four kids."

"Probably. No sign of them, though. Are you looking, then?"

"Not really. But everybody needs somebody." She flicks her hair from her face. "I'm pretty sure Mike has a new paramour."

"Really? Do you mind?"

"Good luck to her — she's welcome. Actually I'm glad. He's someone else's problem now. I just hope she knows what she's letting herself in for."

They walk towards the brightly coloured tents and booths lining the edge of the field.

"Well, I've got a long way to go yet, before I start looking for more complications in my life," Lisa says.

Some of the booths are run by local groups — dog training, a running club, the local Round Table, looking for new members. Jessica stops at a small table next to a rack displaying a variety of bicycles. Cycling for Softies proclaims the sign. Come and join us every week for a gentle cycle ride around the area — everyone welcome, all abilities, sizes and ages.

"Every Sunday morning, eleven o'clock," says the woman looking after the stand. "We're all new to it, so everyone's in the same boat. We thought it would be good to see the countryside and get some gentle exercise at the same time. My husband's leading it — he's worked out some nice routes for us to start off with."

"Sounds great." Jessica takes Lisa's arm and draws her further in to the stand. "What do you think? Have you got a bike?"

"I have. Haven't used it for ages, though. I'm really quite unfit."

"All the more reason to give it a go. If you don't like it, you don't have to carry on."

She wavers, not wanting to say no to Jessica, but that familiar sense of anxiety seeping in. "I don't know . . . I'd have to brush the cobwebs off and get it serviced . . ."

"Great — we're on, then." Before she knows it, she's signed up to the new cycling group. Reeling a little, she tries not to show how uncomfortable she feels. Uncomfortable, and ever so slightly excited.

As they walk on from the cycling table, Jessica gives her shoulder a squeeze. "It'll be good for you — I know it."

She nods, says nothing. She's grateful to Jessica for understanding, and for her encouragement.

It's a small step for most people, but a huge one for Lisa.

* * *

Lisa calls the hospital.

"He's coming along quite well now," the nurse says. "He's not coughing so much and he's eating a bit more. The pressure in his chest has certainly eased."

"Okay, do you know when he be able to come out?"

"I think we probably need to keep him for a couple more days — give him a chance to get some strength back — but we'll know more when the doctor comes round."

"Is he up to having a visitor?"

"Oh yes, I'm sure he'd like that."

The hospital isn't far, just on the other side of the village from Lisa's street. It's surprisingly modern, with many-paned windows and a long, tarmac driveway.

John is sitting up, looking brighter, wearing old-fashioned striped pyjamas that are faded and soft. He smiles when he sees Lisa and waves to the chair next to his bed. It's hard, plastic and uncomfortable.

"Lovely to see you, dear — thank you for coming. Sit down, sit down."

She hands over the day's newspaper, a book and some biscuits she's picked up on the way. He offers her one and then struggles to open the packet, his hands trembling. She takes it back from him and tears it open, exposing the first two biscuits. He takes one and crumbs shower down on the sheet that covers his chest.

"How have you been?" Lisa says. "I'm told you're improving."

"Am I? Nobody tells me." There's a twinkle in his eye. "Perhaps they'll let me out of here then."

"A couple of days, they said."

"Good. Need to get back." Lisa wonders what he's keen to get back to, but doesn't ask. "Can't sleep in here. Old chap over there snores — sounds like a steam train."

The bed opposite has a small lump in it, which Lisa hadn't recognised as a person, but when she looks again there is a slight dent in the pillow. The 'old chap' must be very thin; he's practically invisible under the bedcovers. A TV hangs from the ceiling at the end of John's bed. A quiz show slightly flashing. Seeing her glance at it, John asks her to turn it so that he can see it better and to turn up the sound for him; he can't work out the buttons on the remote control. She shows him what programmes are on and turns the sound up until he seems comfortable with it. They sit in comfortable silence. The only noise comes from John when he mutters the inevitably correct answer to one of the questions.

An orderly arrives with some tea for them both and eases John into a sitting position, plumping up the pillows behind him and brushing away the crumbs. Lisa pours from the tin teapot and they watch the news together.

When she leaves, his eyelids are already drooping. Looking at his fragile hand on the sheet, she feels a pang of deep sadness.

* * *

Her bike is sitting there, neglected, with rust sprinkled along the spokes and on the rims of the wheels. She can't remember why she even brought it to the cottage when she moved. Some small optimistic thought behind it.

"Hm," the man in the bike shop says, giving Lisa a dubious look and sucking his teeth. "Not a keen cyclist, then."

She's not in the mood. "No. Can you service it?"

He wheels it into the workshop at the back and lifts it onto the heavy wooden table. Bikes of all sizes and in all states of repair seem to hang from every possible point and tools in plastic boxes line the shelves on one entire wall. He tests the brakes and spins the wheels.

"What kind of cycling are you wanting to do?"

"Just to get some exercise and go from A to B. Nothing too serious."

He looks from her to the bicycle, a wry smile on his face.

"To tell you the truth, I'm not sure you want to spend any money on this bike. It's had it, really — too much rust. We've got some great second hand ones in, hardly used. I can find you a super one, which will last a long time if you treat it right. I'll give you a good price."

When she leaves the shop, she's pushing a sleek blue bike — 'nearly new ladies' bicycle, suitable for gentle exercise' — with new tyres and a soft saddle. So, she seems to be joining the cyclists.

* * *

One woman dead, one badly injured in horrific knife attack.

Bloodied man grabbed by passers-by.

Her fingers tremble as she scrolls down to the rest of the article. It was written the day after it happened. There's a picture taken from across the road, striped police tape cordoning off the house and a group of uniformed officers gathered in front. She swallows, wipes her hands on her jeans and reads on. She's come this far, she has to go on.

A young woman died when she fell from the window of a first-floor flat in Newcombe Road yesterday evening; another woman was found seriously injured inside. A man in his thirties was apprehended by passers-by as he left the building and was later arrested.

'I heard a terrible scream,' said neighbour Max Jacob, who went out to see what was happening. 'When I got outside there was a body lying on the steps with some people crowded around it. Then a man ran out of the building — it was pretty obvious he was trying to escape and he was covered in blood. A couple of people grabbed him and wrestled him to the ground. The police and the ambulance were there within minutes.'

The police found a badly injured woman in the upstairs flat. She was taken to St. John's hospital, where she is recovering.

There's an even shorter report in a national newspaper without the picture. And then she finds a much longer item and she's immediately struck by the photo. Ali smiles directly into the camera. She remembers it being taken. It's a holiday snap from a trip to Greece. She's tanned and wearing a white dress, a silver necklace round her neck. Her arm is around Lisa's waist and Lisa's looking up at her and grinning, her dark curls contrasting with Ali's blonde, blow-dried locks.

The article describes the scene outside the flat — the scream, the knot of people around Ali's body and the struggle between Fergus and the men who stopped him. It quotes a police officer. We received a call at 23.15 on the night of Thursday, 20 June, and attended the scene in Newcombe Road, where we found the body of a woman, later identified as Alison Mayfield, on the steps outside number 21. The window above was open. A man, later identified as Fergus Collins, was apprehended at the scene and taken into custody. Collins remains on remand until the court hearing.

"In the first-floor flat we found another victim, Lisa Fulbrook. She was badly injured and there was evidence of a struggle. She was taken to hospital where she is recovering. We are waiting to interview her about the incident."

Lisa feels sick.

Nothing. She's learned nothing that she didn't already know. She's not sure what she was expecting, but she was hoping for more. More detail, more insight — just more.

Not a single mention of the relationship between Fergus, Ali and Lisa — not even that they knew Fergus prior to the event. Is that significant? Maybe they didn't need to find out, because he admitted the crime. But surely, if they wanted to understand why Fergus had gone to the flat, they would have asked? Even for the sake of completeness, to get the facts straight, it would be relevant. Maybe not. Perhaps they had enough to get a conviction, end of story. Well, there was something she could try to find out. Somebody must know.

She goes back to the search page on her screen and types in a date, the name of the Crown Court where the hearing was held and then Fergus Collins sentence. A page of results flicks immediately onto the screen. She steels herself and selects one of the results.

Both the tabloids and the local papers focus on the length of the sentence — all 'shocked' at the lenience — and the families' emotional reaction at the result. There are dramatic headlines:

The Price of a Woman's Life

Her Life Cut Short — His Barely Pauses

She ignores them, determined not to be sidetracked. She skims over the pictures of the Mayfields — Diana weeping, comforted by Geoffrey, Connor looking tense and grim — and focuses on the facts. The other papers give her a little more fact and less drama. She reads everything she can find, trawling through the coverage from top to bottom.

But after two hours of searching, she's no further forward. The press reports are not going to give her anything. She stretches her stiffening back and sits back in the chair with a sigh. What next? Perhaps she should try to get a transcript of the court hearing, although she's pretty sure it won't give her more than she already knows. Returning to the screen to find out how to go about it, she's distracted by a headline alongside the story of the attack.

Police to be trained in helping crime victims seek 'restorative justice'

She clicks on the link and reads on: Police officers across England are to be instructed in how to support victims using 'restorative justice' under a new training scheme funded by the Police Commissioner.

Restorative justice brings together victims harmed by crime or conflict with those responsible. It holds perpetrators to account for what they have done and helps them take responsibility and make amends.

Specialist accredited trainers will help officers gain a deeper understanding of how restorative justice works and the likely outcomes and benefits for victims.

A representative for the Police Commissioner said: 'For victims, meeting the person who has harmed them can be a huge step in moving forward and recovering from that crime.'

* * *

John's home. The first she knows about it is the ambulance sitting outside when she gets back after an early morning walk with Riley. There's nobody in the vehicle and John's front door is closed, so she decides not to call in.

Last night she was awake for hours. Bad dreams invaded her sleep and she's left with a feeling of dread. She's weak with fatigue. Normally a walk helps raise her mood, but today the skies are dark and black clouds loom over the lake, their sinister billows reflected in the gloomy water. Even Riley seems cowed and stays close to her heels as if for protection. She forces her heavy legs back through the village streets towards her home.

Some days are like this. Though there are moments when she feels more positive, there are also moments, hours, days of flatness in between, when she doubts she'll ever feel strong, confident and ready to face the world again. Her life is stagnant, leading nowhere. No joy lifts her spirits. On days like today she wants to lie down with a blanket over her head and shut out all her thoughts. On days like today, her dog is her only friend. She's trying though. Even reading through the news reports is a sign that she's starting to move forward.

But John's home and the ambulance has gone. There's no food in his house, not even a pint of milk, and there may be nobody else to help him out today. At about four o'clock she forces herself off the sofa where she's been lying, gazing at nothing.

The computer stares at her from the desk like an accusation. She ignores it, collects John's key and her bag and goes next door.

She opens the door quietly and calls out. There's no answer, so she goes through to the kitchen. Finding his chair empty, she returns to the hallway and climbs the first few steps of the staircase.

"John? Are you there? It's Lisa . . ."

"I'm here, Lisa — in bed." His voice is muffled, as if he's just woken up.

"I'm just going to the shop — shall I pick up some things for you?"

"Yes, thank you. I'm tired out. Be up when you get back."

"No — don't get up, no need. Just wanted to check, to make sure you had something to eat. I'll just grab a few bits."

"Thank you, dear."

She checks in the kitchen cupboards, writes a short list and sets off for the shop. It's started to rain, the kind that soaks and chills, and she speeds up, wishing she'd worn more than the thin black top she'd thrown on this morning.

When she gets back to John's, miserably wet, she finds a nurse waiting on the doorstep.

"Oh, good," the nurse says when she sees the key in Lisa's hand. "I rang the bell but I don't think he heard me. I'm here to check on him. Did you do his shopping for him?

That's kind. I'm Jenny, and I'm going to be looking after John, probably two or three times a day, though there might be another nurse who comes as well . . ." She continues to talk on the way into the house, and keeps up a constant monologue while they unpack the bags of food. Lisa begins to feel exhausted by the barrage of chatter. The nurse finally goes upstairs. With a sigh of relief she escapes to her sanctuary next door.

A couple of days later there's a different nurse leaving the house when Lisa reaches her front door.

"How's John doing?" she asks.

"Not too bad — getting better slowly. He's up and about now. We come in to get him up in the mornings and come back to get him to bed."

"That's good. It must be taking the strain from him somewhat."

"Are you the neighbour who helps with the shopping? He's getting a hot meal delivered every day, so you don't need to worry too much about food. Just the basics, if you're happy to do it."

"Of course. I'm glad he's on the mend."

"Yes — seems like a nice man."

* * *

The doorbell rings, three times. Riley barks and sits wagging his tail. It's Jessica, and it's half past ten on Sunday. No wriggling out of this one, then. Lisa sighs and opens the door.

"A vision in Lycra," she says, waving Jessica through.

"I wish. I had to dig deep in my wardrobe for something halfway appropriate."

Lisa has made no changes to her clothing; it's still pretty much always black, always a scarf, always unassuming. She's not relishing the thought of the cycling group. She feels like locking herself in and closing the curtains. But Jessica is having none of that. She seems to sense Lisa's reluctance and starts to organise her, not giving her the choice.

"You'll need a water bottle and sunglasses. Stick them in your backpack. Let's go."

The bikes are propped outside in the front garden. She follows Jessica through the gate and down the road, trying the bike out, fiddling with the gears and wrestling with the urge to turn round and go home. She pedals on towards the meeting point on the south side of the village, her hands gripping the handlebars as if to stop them running away with her.

A group of around eight people has gathered, the youngest in her teens, the oldest perhaps in his seventies. The bikes are a mixture too, with a couple of proper mountain bikes rubbing shoulders with sit-up-and-beg styles complete with shopping baskets.

"Good to see you all. It's a lovely morning for a gentle bike ride!" A man wearing a hi-vis jacket announces as they all gather round. "We're doing a circuit today around the outskirts of the village. Takes about two hours at a slow-to-steady pace. If it's too much for anyone, we'll slow down, or take a break — and we'll have regular stops anyway to look around us. We're not in a race, we just want everyone to enjoy themselves and appreciate the scenery. Obviously, stick together as far as possible, but don't hold up the traffic or we'll get into trouble. Jan will stay at the back to make sure we don't lose anyone. Okay? Let's go!"

They set off. Lisa holds back, pedalling apart from the others and concentrating on the new sensation, her leg muscles gradually waking from a long period of inactivity.

They're soon out of the village, on an unfamiliar, quiet road, which turns through fields of ripening crops. Cows watch with huge curious eyes as they pass and dogs bark, unseen, from cottages and barns. After a slight incline of a few hundred yards, the leaders stop at a viewing point. Miles of countryside stretch out into the distance, chequered with fields of yellow, green and brown. Tiny white houses and barn buildings are dotted about and far away into the distance is a line of grey buildings, marking the outskirts of the next town.

Lisa stares and lets the calm wash over her like a gentle shower.

* * *

"Cycling? You haven't done that for years," her mum says.

The excursion on Sunday had opened Lisa's eyes to her surroundings. And she'd soon got over her anxiety; the other cyclists had seemed as happy to leave her to her own devices as she was to leave them.

She feels as though she's had a glimpse of how things could be. Her spirits had lifted and for the first time in over a year she'd felt a glimmer of something — happiness? No, not happiness, not quite. Perhaps peace, of a kind.

"I'm glad I went." She watches as her mum folds clothing into neat piles on the kitchen table — a routine she's watched since she was tiny.

"Will you go again?"

"I expect so. I don't think I'll ever be a keen cyclist, but a gentle tour around the area is fine for me. The countryside is lovely round there."

Her mum gives her a sideways glance, an eyebrow lifted very slightly. She sees hope in that look. She turns away, not ready for optimism. It's not resolved. Not yet.

* * *

A couple of days later her legs ache so much she can barely move and she's saddle-sore in places she didn't know she'd used.

"I'm so unfit," she says to Jessica as they walk around the lake. "I didn't realise how bad it had got."

"It's only that you did something very different — you're fit for walking, but not for cycling. We'd better go more often."

"Yes — but my muscles would disagree. I feel like I've run a marathon. I wonder if Riley would come with me if I tried cycling with him on the lead . . ."

"I wouldn't. It might be a bit dangerous until you're more stable."

"You could be right. Anyway, I enjoyed it. Thanks for encouraging me. I would definitely have pulled out without you."

"Said it would be good for you. So I don't need to feel guilty for railroading you? It's great for our fitness, in a number of ways."

"I know, I know. Still not sure I can handle the social side, though."

They walk in comfortable silence for a few moments along a narrow part of the path, where nettles grow high on each side and the lake is obscured by the late summer foliage.

"So, generally, is it getting easier, do you think?" Jessica says, when the path widens and they can walk side by side again.

"I don't think 'easier' is how I'd put it. I'm a bit stronger, maybe, in some ways. I can't get it out of my head, though, and I still don't sleep well. There's something there but I just can't reach it."

"What does the psycho say?"

"He doesn't really say anything. It's more prompting me to work on it myself. It's up to me, really, in the end."

* * *

The light fades from the garden and Riley's asleep on the sofa. She reaches for the diary, sits down next to him and starts to write her own account of the night that Ali died.

It's hard going, but no worse than she expected. She starts with the pub — the people they saw, who they sat with, their conversations, their drinks. She focuses on the details, hoping that they will trigger what's missing. She takes her time, eyes closed in concentration, brow furrowed. She's never done this — not even for the police, not in this minute detail. They'd stopped asking once they had the admission of guilt from Fergus.

The pages fill up. A pulse in her forehead starts to throb as she concentrates, but she keeps going. Her scrawl gets more unruly as she works and she chooses every word carefully, crossing it out with a heavy line if it's not what she means.

She reaches the moment outside the shop when they left Fergus to go home. She takes special care over what she writes from that point on. She chronicles her story from the flashbacks she's endured over recent months and from her dim recollections, as if they're two separate strands meshing together to reveal the full, horrible truth.

She remembers climbing the stairs when they got home, Ali going ahead of her and dropping her keys when she reached the door to the flat. She describes their home in detail — the tatty furniture, books on the shelves, the mugs on the coffee table. The open window and Ali leaning out to call to Fergus when he rang the doorbell. She recalls running down to let him in and his sickly, whisky smell. Her stomach churns. She puts down the pen and goes to the kitchen, pours a glass of water, her mind still held by the scene. She returns to her task, forcing herself to keep going.

When she reaches the part with the knife, her hand starts to shake and she stops writing as an image flashes.

It was one of our kitchen knives. Which one? The knife wasn't used as evidence at the hearing, so her mum hadn't seen it — and hadn't mentioned a description of it either.

A wave of nausea rises from deep within her, the rancid taste of bile flooding her mouth. She drops everything and runs upstairs to the bathroom, where she empties the meagre contents, retching and retching on emptiness.

* * *

She stops there, exhausted from the effort and the sickness. Over the next few days she can't bring herself to return to it, bile rising in her throat each time.

As a distraction, she asks Jessica to the cinema. Jessica picks her up and they drive to the nearest multi-screen, eight miles away. The film is mediocre, the characters clichéd, Lisa's requirement for non-violent, non-weepy films having narrowed their choice significantly. It serves its purpose, though, and for an hour or more she's swept into another world, following a different story.

* * *

When she eventually gets back to the diary, on a night when she can resist it no longer, a question raises its head.

Only two people know the truth. The other one is Fergus.

Should she go to him for the answer?

Even the thought of it is terrifying. She's read that restorative justice is supposed to help resolve the victim's fears and to empower him or her. She can see how that might work in certain cases, but would it help her tie down the truth? Would she go through all that fear, the stress of seeing him again, only to come out none the wiser? Does he remember more than she does? If he does, will he admit to it? Maybe he remembers less — what then?

She examines her need to know, picks at it, worries at it, not sure where the urge will take her.

All this questioning, this need to remember, has been triggered by Connor and his accusations. There's no evidence that she's culpable in any way; nobody is questioning her role in the tragedy. She's the victim of an unpredictable, violent offence, just as Ali was.

But actually, she knows what's driving her on.

It's the half-memory that came to her when she was with Graham.

Fergus might be the key to unlock that memory. By meeting him, it might just help her well and truly move on. To grieve for Ali and be the person she thought she could be.

* * *

"You want to visit Fergus?" Graham says.

"No, I don't want to visit him at all. I don't want to see him, ever again. But I really need to know what happened. The details. The truth."

"The truth?"

"I know that I haven't remembered something crucial. I've searched the media, asked my mum about the hearing. But there's something else." She looks down at her hands.

"I'm wondering what's making you feel that there's more to know," he says. "Is it possible you might be punishing yourself, looking for something to validate your feelings of guilt?"

"Maybe."

There's a pause while he waits for her to raise her eyes to his. She does so reluctantly and waits.

"I think it might be useful to re-examine those feelings. Are you comfortable doing that now?"

"Okay."

He waits.

"We talked about survivor guilt and me feeling guilty because I survived and Ali died. I know it could have been either of us who died. Or both, even. We couldn't possibly have known he would turn violent. He'd given us no reason to suspect it in any way. I was the one who physically let him in that night, but that was just chance — Ali could easily have gone down to let him in. So I don't think that's why I'm blaming myself."

"Go on."

"I could easily have died that night. Another inch or so and the knife would have cut an artery and I'd have bled to death. Or he could have grabbed Ali and I could have ended up falling out of the window."

She's listening to herself trying to give all the logical reasons not to feel guilty. The words sound credible. But her feelings aren't logical. "Whichever way I look at it, it still feels like my fault. To me."

"Let's take a slightly different tack. What do you think his intentions were towards you both?"

"I don't know. As far as I remember he mentioned having a threesome. That's what he said, so we thought it was about sex. But when we said we wanted him to leave, it changed. He got aggressive. That's when he seemed to focus on me."

"On you?"

"Maybe because I was trying to manoeuvre him out of the door — I was nearer to him than Ali. I can't think of any other reason that makes sense."

"Do you think he intended to hurt you when he arrived at the flat?"

"No. I don't think so."

"Why did he suddenly change, do you think?"

"I've got no idea. He didn't know either — or at least, that's what he said to the police. Unless he was lying, or has remembered something new, he still doesn't know why he flipped, or what he was going to do. As far as I know."

There's a pause while he reflects. She picks at her fingers, then at the arm of the chair, waiting.

"If you were able to talk to him, now, if he was in this room, what would you say?"

"I'd want to ask why."

"Be more specific."

"Why attack us — why us, and what happened that night to make him turn so violent?"

"Anything else?"

"I'd want to know exactly what he remembers, find out what exactly happened to Ali."

* * *

"What shall we do with this?" Lisa holds up a cricket bat, with signatures scrawled on its side.

"Oh God. His prized possession. That'll have to be wrapped up properly and go on the keep pile."

Jessica is clearing out Mike's belongings and Lisa's helping to separate their two lives. They've already cleared the attic and his things are piled up on the landing to be sorted into those he'll want to keep and those he won't. Jessica had offered to do the unpleasant work herself, not wanting him to spend hours at the house.

"I'll wrap it in a t-shirt for the moment," Lisa says. "We're going to need some boxes, the keep pile is huge."

Jessica stares at the collection of pewter beer mugs and the old vinyls. "Yes, this is the worst bit, I think. The bedroom should be much easier as it'll mainly be clothes. We'll stick it all in the garage for him to collect."

Jessica gets on with it without sentimentality, which is a relief for Lisa. She's still too fragile to provide emotional support to someone else. Only yesterday, out walking through the village with Riley, the strong smell of whisky from a broken bottle in a waste bin triggered a vivid flashback, leaving her shaking and hyperventilating; she'd had to lean on a wall for a few minutes until it had passed. Her recovery is achingly slow, and though she has moments of positivity, she still dreads the next confrontation, the loud noise, the trigger that sends her back to that dreadful night.

Jessica appears at the bedroom door, her hair dishevelled, her face flushed from the effort of dragging a large suitcase full of clothes onto the landing.

"I never realised how many suits he had," she says, puffing with the effort. "And shirts, and shoes, and belts, and . . . just . . . kit." She sits down on the top step and pushes her hair from her face. "I'm all dusty and sweaty. How about a break?"

"Good idea."

They sit down in the living room with a cup of tea. "It's therapeutic, even if it's hard work." Jessica says. "I feel I'm doing something positive about my life, at last, not just sitting here in limbo. It's a second chance to do what I really want to do, not just wait for it to happen to me."

Lisa thinks about what she's just said. Yes, that's what I need. A second chance.

* * *

Something's different. It's the air in the hall, the light from the kitchen door falling on the terracotta tiles, the dust drifting down like tiny snowflakes on a winter's night. She closes the front door quietly, opens her mouth to call, then shuts it again, reluctant to disturb the heavy silence. Riley, usually the first to push through to the kitchen, stops and whines gently.

"Shh, Riley," she says, and gathering her courage she walks towards the kitchen door. As she pushes, it creaks and she eases herself through the small opening, trying not to make more noise. Her eyes take a moment to adjust to the light from the kitchen window after the gloom of the hallway.

John is there in his chair as usual, his hands in his lap, the blanket she gave him for Christmas over his knees, his eyes half-open. A ray of sunlight falls across his silver hair, combed thinly over translucent skin, and lands in a warm glow on his pale cheek as his head rests gently against the wing of his chair.

He's dead.

He looks so calm sitting there. She pulls off her jacket and draws up a chair in front of him. "Oh, John." She reaches across and touches his bony hand, feels for a pulse, just in case. There's nothing and the skin is cold. She bows her head and the tears fill her eyes.

She feels no need to rush. She sits for a while with Riley on her lap, keeping John company. She will miss his gentle presence, his modest conversation and the relationship they've built over the year since she first saw him in the garden. She'll remember him every day as she wakes to see that soft muzzle lying beside her. She owes him a huge debt of gratitude, for she knows Riley has saved her. Without him, she would have faded into obscurity.

Finally, having said her silent goodbyes, she stands, goes to the telephone and calls the doctor.

* * *

Half an hour later she opens the door to Doctor Morris and leads him down the corridor to the kitchen. She puts Riley in the garden to keep him out of the way and watches while the doctor examines the frail figure propped in the chair. It only takes a moment, then he closes John's eyes and straightens up.

"You're right, he's gone. I'll take over from here. Any idea about next-of-kin?"

"There's a nephew in Spain. Oscar, I think John said his name was. But I don't know his number, or where exactly he is."

"Nobody nearer?"

"I don't think so. He has a few friends here, but no relatives that I know of. I'll have a look for a phone number now."

It feels wrong to be looking through John's things, but the doctor is occupied with paperwork, so she starts to look through the pile of papers on top of the cabinet, where bills and statements, handwritten notes and photographs lie in an unruly pile. Luckily, there's also a small address book and as she flicks through it she finds a well-thumbed page with Oscar Grey's address and a phone number.

"I think I've found it."

"Would you be able to make the call?"

Her heart skips a beat. This is entirely different, she reminds herself firmly. "I think so." She dials the number quickly, so that she can't think about it too much, and when the phone is answered almost immediately by a woman's voice speaking in Spanish, she's dumbfounded for a moment.

"Er — sorry, do you speak English?"

"A little."

"Is Oscar Grey there please?"

"Oscar is working. You want I give him a message?"

"Oh. Yes — can you ask him to call urgently, please, it's about his uncle, John Grey. It's very important." She gives John's number, slowly, and her own, not sure what else to do.

"Important — yes, I tell him."

She replaces the receiver and exhales.

She hovers by the phone, feeling out of place, desperate to retreat to her own environment, but embarrassed to leave too soon. Doctor Morris glances at her. "Don't worry, I'll be here for a while, no need for you to stay if you'd rather go home."

"Oh thank you — are you sure?"

He nods and smiles, so she calls Riley in from the garden. Before she leaves, she leans over John and kisses his cold forehead. "Goodbye from both of us, and thank you," she whispers, tears threatening. She feels the doctor's eyes on her as she goes.

* * *

At home, she lies down on the sofa and falls into a fitful sleep, drifting in and out of disturbing dreams, an ache of anxiety constant in the shifting scenes flitting through her mind. A flurry of activity in the street drags her back to consciousness and, forcing her legs to move, she goes to the window.

A funeral car sits outside John's house, its back door open, a malevolent creature waiting to swallow its prey. As she watches, sombre-suited men carry a stretcher out, their burden tactfully swathed in dark fabric. She watches them leave, standing back so she can't be seen. Then, not knowing what else to do, she gathers her jacket, the house keys and the dog and sets off to see Jessica. As she closes the front door behind her, Doctor Morris is at John's front gate, about to leave.

"Are you all right?" he says.

"I'm fine, thanks. Did his nephew call?"

"Yes, it's all sorted. He's coming on the next flight out of Barcelona — he'll be here later tonight. I've had John taken to the mortuary. His nephew will take over from there."

"Will he be able to get into the house?"

"Don't worry, I've left John's keys in a safe place, so he'll let himself in. It may be late, so don't be alarmed if you hear him arrive."

"Right, okay, thanks."

He's looking at her intently. "Are you sure you're all right? It's not the easiest thing to have to deal with."

“I think so.” But when she clips the dog lead onto Riley’s collar, her hands are shaking. She puts them in her pockets, feigning nonchalance.

“Look, get in touch if you need anything. I’m on call anyway.” He hands her a card. “Sometimes these things come back to visit you.”

If only he knew.

* * *

Oscar rings on Lisa’s doorbell and introduces himself. He’s tall, with a mop of brown hair and a light tan.

“I’m sorry you had to find him; the doctor told me. Are you all right?” he says.

“Yes, I’m fine, thank you.” She’s not fine, though. She feels like she’s swimming through jelly; her mind has gone fuzzy.

“He wrote to me every so often. He said you’d become friends and given Riley a home.”

“Yes. He was a lovely man. We’ll miss him very much.”

When he’s gone, she calls to cancel the week’s therapy — she can’t face it. In the back of her mind she knows she’s avoiding something, but she misses John’s steady presence, more than she thought.

She gets on with her work over the next few days, but her mind isn’t engaged and she doesn’t trust herself to do anything that requires any intellectual effort. She’s too tired to walk, though she trundles round the lake for Riley’s sake, and too tired to sleep, her legs twitching and her shoulders tight. She worries vaguely that she might be heading for some kind of a breakdown. Another death, albeit very different from the first, is still another death, at a time when the fall-out from the first is still very much affecting her life. It’s all crowding in on her.

Jessica’s upset at John’s death, but not surprised. Lisa admires her practicality, her way of getting on with her life despite the setbacks. She’s realised what a pragmatic person

Jessica really is now that she has the strength, not given to dwelling on things. She's got two interviews in the diary for part-time teaching jobs and is full of optimism about her life's new direction. Talking to her, Lisa can't help but feel detached.

* * *

For Lisa, funeral attire is everyday. Her reflection in the mirror is the same as usual: a pale, serious face, unsmiling eyes with dark smudges below, a grey scarf wrapped around her neck, her body hidden under a black top and trousers. The vertical lines above her nose make her look slightly cross. She lifts her eyebrows and they disappear, then frowns again and leaves to meet Jessica on the way to the service.

Only a handful of people come to John's funeral. Two elderly men arrive together, one with a stick, walking painfully and slowly into the village church. Both men in suits, handkerchiefs neatly folded in the top pocket, shoes polished, hair neatly parted and slicked down. Even without the occasion, Lisa would have guessed they were friends of John's.

Oscar and his wife greet them at the church gate. They walk together into the church and take their seats towards the front, where the coffin waits. Lisa imagines John's frail body within, gently decaying. It's cold in the church, its stone floors and draughty stained-glass windows chilled by the October wind. She shivers, only partly from the temperature. At the last moment, as the vicar prepares to speak, Doctor Morris arrives and joins the small group of mourners in a pew towards the back.

Lisa's mind is still foggy — which, given the potential for this to be a stressful day, might or might not be a good thing. She recalls the funeral she didn't get to as the vicar drones on. She stands, sings, sits and prays automatically, without absorbing anything much, and she has to force herself back to John, to acknowledge him, even at his own funeral. This occasion is quite different from Ali's memorial service, though, and to her it seems sad but appropriate, as opposed to utterly, hopelessly tragic, and tinged with horror.

After the service the small group, including the vicar, reconvenes at John's house for tea and sandwiches. Lisa brings Riley to his old master's house, perhaps, she thinks, for the last time. Jessica, across the small living room, soon gets into a deep conversation with Oscar and his wife, but Lisa is awkward and tongue-tied among so many strangers. She's wondering how she can leave without being noticed when Doctor Morris comes up to her.

"How are you doing, Lisa?" he says, offering her a sandwich from the tray he's balancing precariously in his left hand.

"I'm . . . well, thanks."

"Were you close? I mean, I know you helped him out, but were you friends?"

"Yes, we were. He was a very nice man, easy to talk to."

"It's upsetting finding someone like that."

"Yes." She's already stuck for something to say and pretends to sip her tea, which is still too hot and burns her lip, while he puts the tray of sandwiches down on the table behind them. She watches his slim back as he moves. He's wearing a silver grey jacket and his hair touches the collar of his shirt at the nape of his neck. Next to him she feels plain and dowdy.

He turns back to her. "It may be an idea to see someone to talk it through with, if you're finding it difficult. I can recommend a local psychotherapist, if you think you might need one."

"Oh — no, it's okay." She responds a bit too quickly and he looks at her enquiringly. "Actually, I'm already seeing someone for something else."

He takes it in his stride, as if it's completely normal to be in therapy — which, to a doctor, it probably is. She stammers, embarrassed. "But thank you, it's kind of you to think of it."

"No problem, it's what I do. But I do know, even if you feel all right at first, it might hit you later, so do look after yourself, won't you?"

She nods, unable to speak.

"Do you live alone?" They both look at Riley and he laughs. "Of course you don't, you have him. He's lovely." He bends to stroke the dog's head. "But, anyone else to look after you?"

"I'm fine, really — I'm used to it. And there's Jessica, over there."

"Ah yes, we met briefly at the village fete." He looks over at Jessica, who's still deep in conversation with Oscar and his wife, then glances at his watch and jumps.

"I have to go. Sorry. Please excuse me — and look after yourself. Go and see your therapist."

"I will."

"And you have my card if you need to talk." He smiles at her and he's gone.

She grabs Riley's lead and slips back home, unnoticed.

* * *

John's death has triggered a new sense of hopelessness, a despondency that she can't seem to shake. In the days following his funeral she lies in bed for long hours, dozing or staring into space, barely able to move. She's aware of the phone ringing and once or twice Riley jumps up when the doorbell goes, but she doesn't move. The picture of Ali is still by her bed, together with the silver box, and she puts them close so they're the first thing she sees when she opens her eyes.

She doesn't even want to talk to her mum and she knows her voice will give her away. She waits until a time when she's likely to be out with her friends and leaves a message with the radio on in the background to give the impression that everything is normal. She tries to sound cheerful, saying how busy she is with work and sorry not to have called before.

She comes across Doctor Morris' card in the kitchen and ponders it, remembering his words. But calling him is out of the question. Everything's pointless, a struggle, not worth the effort. She eats cereal and biscuits and it's only when these run out that she drags herself into some clothes and gives her patient dog a short walk to the shop.

Riley's joy at being out at last triggers her guilt, though, and she changes course for the lake, hoping there's no-one around. But Jessica's the first person she sees and it's too late to turn away.

"Lisa — how are you? I've been calling. Did you go away? Everything all right?"

"Yes, sorry . . . I've been ill."

"Well you look terrible. Have you seen the doc?"

"No. It's nothing, really. I'm just a bit . . . low."

"It doesn't look like nothing to me. Come to mine, I'm going to give you a coffee and something to eat. You look as if you're fading away!"

Reluctantly she allows herself to be ushered towards Jessica's house, where she cuts big chucks of fresh bread and makes cheese and tomato sandwiches. Lisa nibbles distractedly, to be polite, though she couldn't feel less like eating.

"Is it because of John? Finding him like that must have been pretty awful for you."

"No. Well, yes — in a way. Actually it wasn't finding him, it's more that — well, too much bad has happened and it all seems so pointless." To her horror, her eyes fill with tears. She can't contain them and they pour down her face, dripping from her jaw onto the table in front of her. She makes no effort to wipe them.

Jessica sits down in front of her. "Lisa, you must see someone. What about the psycho?"

Lisa shakes her head. "I cancelled. I just couldn't."

"Rearrange it. I'll drive you there. It's important and you need someone to help you. Do you have the number with you? We'll do it now."

In the end Lisa allows herself to be led back home to make the call. Jessica sits with her as she dials Graham's number and leaves a message for him to call with the next available appointment. Jessica is adamant that she'll drop everything and they should go as soon as possible, and insists she leaves

Jessica's mobile number as an alternative, just in case. Then they go together to the shop, both dogs following, to buy supplies for Lisa's empty food cupboards. Lisa allows herself be led and cajoled and when they return to the house, laden with carrier bags, they seem to have enough to feed a family of four for the next month.

"I'll never get through all this," she says, staring at it all helplessly.

"Most of it will keep. Tins, packets, some fresh for this week. No wonder you've been ill, you eat like a mouse. I'm going to cook some stuff to put in the fridge and the freezer. Then you've got no excuse."

So while Jessica buzzes around the kitchen, Lisa sits and listens to her chat, letting it wash over her. When the phone rings, she starts nervously and spills her tea. Graham's measured voice greets her.

"I've been wondering about you. Did you get my messages? You've missed three weeks now." Three weeks? Has she lost track so badly?

"Sorry, I — well, I need to fix an appointment."

"Tomorrow morning any good?" Jessica nods, hearing the question from where she's standing, and they fix a time.

"Good," says Jessica as Lisa sits down. "That's a good start."

* * *

The picture on the wall behind Graham looks different today, the smudges hiding their secrets, no longer meaning anything.

"I'm sorry I missed my appointments."

"I was concerned, Lisa, but I'm glad you came today. Did something happen?"

"Yes. John, my next-door neighbour — the one who gave me his dog — he died. I found him."

"I'm sorry to hear that. It must have been difficult for you."

"It wasn't, actually, not really. I went in to see him and he was sitting quietly in his normal place. It wasn't horrible. But I was a bit shocked. And I'm sad. Just really sad. I liked him."

"Of course. What did you do?"

"Called the doctor — he sorted it all out. I went to the funeral, too."

"How was that for you?"

"I was in a bit of a daze and I thought about Ali all the time."

"But you did feel strong enough to go. Did you get a flashback, or panic?"

"No, but I couldn't really focus on what was happening."

"And how are you feeling now?"

There's a long pause while she searches for something to say. "I've been very . . . flat. Nothing seems important anymore." She looks away, not wanting to see his reaction.

"A lot has happened to you. Some people spend their whole lives and never see a dead person, let alone find the body. You've had a lot to deal with and it's not surprising you feel as you do."

"Yes, but . . ." She hesitates, not sure what she's trying to say. "I was just beginning to think, hope, that I was coming through it."

"That's good. What gave you hope again?"

"I was starting to feel I had the strength go out, do more, and have friends. And now I'm back to where I was."

"Which is?

"Frightened, alone, feeling hopeless. Unable to deal with life."

He writes something down while she picks at her fingers. Then he looks up again.

"Do you remember when you first came here, I asked you what you want?"

"Yes."

"Has that changed now?"

"I don't think so."

"Tell me again."

"I want a normal life, with friends and family and not to be scared any more. I don't want to be defined by what happened. As it stands, I'm still Lisa, whose best friend was murdered in front of her. I want to be able to live without the nightmares and the flashbacks and the fear of men and crowds and loud noises." It's a long speech, and when she stops it's as if all her energy has evaporated with her words.

He's silent for a few moments, looking down at his notes. "Have you thought any more about going to see Fergus?"

* * *

Another flashback. And the reason for her sense of shame becomes clearer.

This time, she's at home, flicking through the TV channels looking for something worth watching. A brief image of a panel show appears, four people standing nervously, their fingers on the buttons — and she's back in the flat with Ali and Fergus.

Lisa had never taken drugs before, though she knew plenty of people who had, or did, both at school and at work. She'd just not been in that kind of crowd. But when Fergus offered them a spliff one evening when they'd got back worse for wear from the pub, she thought nothing of it — after all, it was pretty mild stuff and they were all adults. They were watching some mad quiz show on the TV and it seemed to fit that they all went a little crazy too, sitting there in a row, Lisa, then Fergus, then Ali. The happy threesome.

Then they opened another bottle of wine. They played charades and laughed until they cried at their inept efforts to understand each other. They lost interest in the TV and played loud music, dancing round the flat. Fergus kissed each of them, and then both — and it seemed so natural when they staggered through to Ali's bedroom, hanging on to each other, that they should end up together on the bed.

She woke suddenly, her head thumping, nausea threatening. She couldn't work out where she was. It was still dark and her first instinct was to reach for the glass of water she always left by the bed. But she was on the wrong side, and when she reached out she touched warm skin and jerked into shocked wakefulness. She sat up in a hurry, her forehead crackling with pain, the sheet falling from her shoulders. She realised with horror that she was naked. This was Ali's room — and Ali was next to her, still asleep. With this realisation came the horrible, dream-like understanding of what they'd done. Both of them. They'd abandoned all modesty, ripped their clothes off, and skin-on-skin, arm on leg, hand on breast, on buttock, on engorged penis, they'd indulged themselves and each other, the three of them, for what seemed like hours.

As quietly and gently as she could, she climbed out of the bed and searched around for any piece of clothing she could find. Finding her jeans and a top — Ali's, not hers. She crept barefoot into the silent sitting room, then into her own bedroom. There was no sign of Fergus. She checked the bathroom and the kitchen. He'd gone. With relief she sat on the edge of the sofa in the sitting room, staring without seeing at the empty glasses and bottles in front of her. Discarded roaches sat like grubs in the ashtray and flakes of crisps littered the floor, but she couldn't move to collect them up. She was rigid with shame. What did we do? Why did we let it get so out of hand? She'd never behaved badly in her life, and now she'd done something so awful she could hardly think of it without cringing. Her mum — she banished the thought of her mum. It didn't bear thinking about.

In the shower she scrubbed herself from top to bottom until her skin glowed red and raw. She plunged her fingers down her throat; nothing came up but bile, acidic and pungent. Revolted, she brushed her teeth, rinsing, gargling, forcing great gobs of toothpaste around her mouth until it stung. When she opened the bathroom door and stepped into the sitting room, Ali was lying on the sofa in her dressing gown looking at her, clutching a cushion to her stomach. They stared at each other for a moment before Lisa sat down.

"How the fuck did that happen?" Ali said, her voice low and gravelly.

"I don't know. I feel really, really bad."

"Save us all from drink and drugs. I feel like crap too."

"I'm sorry, Ali. God, I wish we hadn't done that. The three of us. What were we thinking?"

"I'm sorry too — mostly for being such an idiot on a work night. Lord, how am I going to get through the day feeling like this?"

"I never thought I'd do anything like that." Lisa was close to tears.

"Wait, are you upset?" Ali sat up, put her arm around Lisa's shoulders.

Lisa nodded, unable to speak.

"Listen, people do that all the time," Ali said. "I had a friend at college who had regular threesomes . . . usually her and two blokes, it has to be said. But there's no need to feel so bad."

"But . . . I've never . . . I don't . . . you, and me . . . and Fergus." She drops her face into her hands with shame.

"Look, it's okay, Lisa. It's okay — really. We haven't hurt anyone, and nobody needs to know if you don't want them to."

Lisa was taken aback and not a little impressed at Ali's response to their unplanned night of passion together. This was something she hadn't known about her friend before. "Well," she said, grimacing. "No way I'm doing that again." Then, when Ali said nothing: "You're not . . . ?"

"Not what?"

"Not, well, into that?"

Ali laughed. "Your face is a picture. Don't worry, three's still a crowd for me." She groaned. "I've got to go and shower. And change the bed." She jumped up, grabbing some empty glasses and heading for the kitchen. "Are you going to work?"

"I suppose so. I feel like shit, but it's my own bloody fault."

"Me too." Ali sat down again, as if the journey to the kitchen was a step too far.

"What are we going to do about Fergus?" Lisa said.

"What do you mean?"

"Well, there's no way I'm going to feel comfortable with him now."

"I don't know. Avoid him for a while?"

Lisa rubbed at her forehead with both hands to ease the pain. "I wouldn't know what to say if I saw him again." She pauses to think. "This changes everything, doesn't it?"

"With him, maybe."

"Not with us?" Lisa shot a look at Ali, the thought piercing through the fog in her brain. The idea that a stupid mistake like this might spoil a lifelong, trusting friendship was unbearable.

"Don't be daft. Water under the bridge. Forget it — put it down to experience. We don't need to make it mean anything. But it might change things with Fergus."

"I suppose so."

"It depends what he expects to happen now."

"Oh my God. Do you think . . . ?"

"Probably not. But if you're worried about it, we need to make it clear. So he doesn't get any ideas . . . text him."

"Let's do it now."

* * *

Hi Fergus, hope you're okay. Last night was wild, wasn't it? Just so you know, never again. Just not our thing (normally!) A and L x

They didn't hear back from him. No text, no phone calls, nothing. Ali was surprised — she hadn't expected him to blank them — but Lisa was relieved, though nervous, wary when they were out. Not long afterwards, she bumped into a couple of people from the pub on her way back from work and asked after him, keeping her voice casual, she hoped normal. He was working on the other side of London, on a big housing project, living and working away from home.

Lisa did as Ali suggested and put it behind her. All down to experience. No need for anyone else to know. They avoided the pub for a while and it was months before they saw Fergus again.

* * *

"You're very quiet. Was it very hard?" Lisa was lost in her own thoughts on their way home, Jessica's question catching her off guard.

"Yes, it was. Every time's hard. And I don't know if it's helping. I haven't slit my wrists yet, so maybe it is." Jessica shoots her a glance.

"Sick joke," Lisa says. "Sorry."

"Well at least it was an effort. But don't scare me like that." There's a pause as she negotiates a roundabout. "Has it ever got that bad?"

"Not really. I've been very down, but not to that point. I suppose all my energy has gone into trying to live a normal life, rather than give up. I suppose some part of me was settling into a routine of sorts. Now that John is gone it's shaken me."

"I think you've done incredibly well, with all the horrible things that have happened to you. I would have been absolutely floored."

"No you wouldn't — you're far too practical. Look how you've got yourself together since you broke up with Mike."

"You can't compare that with what you've been through. But it has given me a very tiny insight into how it must be for you."

"Yes, well, I've got a long way to go yet."

"You know you can always call me, don't you? I hate to think of you trying to deal with it all on your own."

"Thanks. But when I feel like this, I can't bring myself to do anything about it. I disappear into a pit of sadness . . . it's like wading through mud. So it's not that I don't feel I can call you, it's more that I just can't."

"Well I won't let it happen again. I'm going to keep an eye on you."

Lisa smiles weakly. "Good luck with that, then."

There's a pause while she looks without seeing at the cars whipping past on the other side of the road.

"Actually, we've just been talking about something which might help. Or it could make things worse, I suppose." She's voicing her own fears — of course she has no evidence either way. "I need to do some research and think about it before I decide what to do."

"What's that?"

"Restorative justice. I read an article about it in the paper."

"What is it then?"

"It's when the criminal comes face-to-face with the victim. It's to help both sides really. For me, it would be a chance to go and talk to Fergus in prison, under very controlled circumstances of course. There are just so many questions and I can't help feeling like he has the answers."

"Wow. That's pretty big."

"I'm stuck, Jessica. I'm obsessed with remembering what happened. I can't stop thinking about it. He might be able to fill in the gaps."

"Really? Does Graham think it could help?"

"He seems open to the idea. For some people it does help and it can be life-changing. It's supposed to give the victim a chance to recover some sense of control."

"Do you think you can do it? You still seem pretty fragile."

"I don't know," Lisa says. "It takes a long time to set up, I think. And I'm not sure I'm brave enough. But I might find out what really happened."

"Sounds like a bit of a risk."

"Well, I wouldn't be on my own. I need to find out much more before I decide if I can face it."

"Worth investigating, I suppose."

"I'm going to check it out and then decide. I won't rush into anything. I promise."

She leans back in the seat, stretches her legs and closes her eyes, thinking about Fergus and the possibility of seeing him again.

* * *

She calls the policewoman who'd visited her in hospital. "I'm interested in restorative justice and how it works. I'm not saying I want to get in contact yet. I just want to talk to somebody about the process, find out what happens. Can you help me?"

"I'm sure I can," the policewoman replies. "The Probation Service has proper facilitators, you need to talk to one of them. I'll get them to call you. They should be able to answer all your questions about what happens."

"So it wouldn't be you?"

"No, I'm not qualified to do it. There are people trained to facilitate the meetings. You'd get one assigned to your case, someone with the right kind of experience. She or he would set up contact with the offender and manage all the communication, if you decide to go ahead. But it's best if you ask them all your questions rather than me — they're much more familiar with the process."

No harm at the first stage, then. Doesn't mean I have to do it.

"Could you ask someone to contact me then, please? Just to talk it through. I don't want to start anything yet."

"Of course, I understand. It may take a few weeks, just to warn you, but don't worry, I'll make sure somebody gets in touch."

"Thank you."

"Good luck with the restorative justice. I'm sure it's worth you looking at it."

She's already nervous and she's barely started yet. She types restorative justice into a search engine and reads, the tension tightening her shoulders. She finds people who've suffered burglary, muggings and rape. Skimming over the details of the crimes she focuses on what the victims have to say about the face-to-face meetings. On the whole, they seem to react positively, saying they're glad they went through it. The process seems measured and controlled, the victim able at any stage to back out without repercussions.

Of course, there are no stories about the ones that didn't work.

* * *

"I'm dying to tell you something," Jessica announces.

"Good or bad?"

"Oh, good, definitely. For me, anyway, and I hope for you. That's if it comes off."

"What, then?"

She leans forward, conspiratorially. "I'm going to buy John's house."

"Really? What? How come?"

"Well, at the funeral I got chatting to Oscar and his wife and he told me that he's the executor of the will. He's John's only remaining relative, you know. He's going to have to come back over from Spain to clear out the house and put it on the market. He said that they've got no interest in holding onto it. And then I suddenly thought — why don't I buy it? I'll have the money from my half of the house and my parents have offered to help. John's house is much smaller than mine, so it should be affordable — well, I hope so, anyway."

"Jessica, that would be brilliant," she says, taken aback, trying to match Jessica's enthusiasm while still absorbing the idea.

"Wouldn't it? I could really keep an eye on you then." Jessica laughs. "Your face is a picture. Oh, don't worry. Mike's not coming back, he won't bother us now."

Her eyes have betrayed her. But she wasn't thinking of Mike. While she loves the idea of having Jessica nearby, she's protective of her small haven, the quiet life she's worked so hard to establish.

"It's not that." She tries to find the words to express it without offending Jessica. But Jessica is ahead of her.

"If you're worried about your privacy, don't. I promise not to overdo it," Jessica says. "Don't forget I'll be working for my living, with a bit of luck. Anyway it's early days — I might not get it."

"Did Oscar say he'd let you know?"

"Yes, we exchanged numbers. It would be a win-win, if it works, because he can save on agents' fees and it will have landed in my lap at just the right moment, as long as he doesn't want a ridiculous amount for it."

"It's going to need some work, it's pretty old-fashioned and run down."

"That's perfect for me, it makes it more affordable and I can do it exactly the way I want. It's not too big. And the dogs can play together if we leave that hole in the fence . . ."

Lisa can't help smiling. "Jessica, it's a perfect plan — I mean it. When will you know?"

"Well, he thinks it'll take a while to sort the probate out. He's coming back in a few weeks' time and then we can discuss price and so on."

CHAPTER EIGHT

The call comes when she's least expecting it. She has to run for the phone from the front door, bringing mud and rain with her into the sitting room.

"Hello, is that Lisa? My name's Sarah Turner, I'm a facilitator for the National Probation Service. I understand you're interested in knowing more about restorative justice and how it might work for you. Is now a good time to talk?"

She scrambles for her notebook under the pile of papers on the table and sits down, grasping the handset with rigid fingers.

"I've got a ton of questions," she says as she sits down, oblivious to the trickle of water pooling on the floor beneath her chair.

"I'm sure you have," Sarah replies. "I understand you're at the initial stages, is that correct?"

"It is. I'm not sure if it's something I want to do at all," Lisa says. "I need to talk through the process with you, if that's all right."

"Of course. It's best to meet in person to go through all your concerns and questions properly. Then if you do go ahead, you can decide if I'm the right person to help you. Can I suggest a couple of options?"

Lisa's disappointed. It's already three weeks since she'd spoken to Sally, the policewoman, and she was hoping to get some answers. But she can see the sense in a face-to-face meeting. She settles for the next available appointment, in a week's time. Sarah offers to come to Lisa's house.

"Actually, could we meet at my mother's house?" The question is out before she knows it. "Could she be involved? She's been through a lot with this herself."

"That's a very good idea," Sarah replies. "I'll see you then."

She hadn't intended to tell her mum yet. But having her there will calm her nerves. And they can talk it over afterwards and decide between them whether or not to go ahead.

She hopes the whole idea won't be upsetting for her mother. She's quite likely to think it's completely mad and try to persuade Lisa not to do it. But it seems to be the only way to know for sure.

* * *

"Mum? It's me."

"I know, dear. How are you? You sound excited."

"I need to talk to you about something important, are you busy?"

"Just waiting for supper to cook. I've got twenty minutes or so. What is it?" A note of concern creeps into her voice.

"Nothing to worry about. It's just, you know I've been trying to remember what really happened in the flat when we were attacked?"

"Oh, Lisa . . ."

"Bear with me, Mum. I was doing some research online and I found an article about restorative justice. Have you heard of it?"

"I think so, but I don't know what it is."

"It's when the victim of a crime meets the offender, face-to-face."

"What on earth for?"

"To talk about how the crime has affected them. So the criminal gets to understand how much hurt and pain they've caused. It could be a crucial part of my recovery."

"My goodness. You're not thinking . . . ?"

"I'm just going to find out how it works. I haven't decided anything — until I know what happens, I'm not going to decide one way or the other. The thing is, I've been talking to someone who knows all about it. She can answer all my questions, well, all our questions."

"All our questions?"

"Her name is Sarah and I've arranged to meet her at yours next week. I hope you don't mind. She thought it was a good idea that you get involved too. And I'd really like you to be there."

"I don't know, Lisa." Her mum sounds worried. "Are you sure you want to do this?"

"We're just finding out what it's about. I want to know what happens if I do go to meet him."

"But why, Lisa? It's not going to change anything."

"That's just the point, Mum. It does change things for people. It helps the victim regain control. It could help me a lot. And I've been worrying about what happens when he comes out. This might help me come to terms with it. I'm not committing to anything, but if it helps, it's got to be worth doing. Please Mum, say you'll help."

"All right, if I can help, I will. But, please be careful. You don't want to make things worse."

* * *

The reaction from Jessica is quite different.

"Good idea," she says. "Just deciding to learn about it will make you feel you're getting somewhere. Do you think you might get to the truth of what happened? If you decide to meet him, that is." They're trudging round the park on their normal route, a soft drizzle glistening in their hair.

"That's what I'm hoping. I need to know if my memory of that night is real, or some concoction of my sleep-deprived brain. There may be things that happened that I'm still not remembering. And I've got to ask why he did it. I still don't understand what got into him."

"You may never know, I suppose. But at least you'll have tried."

* * *

Sarah arrives with a pile of files and leaflets. They sit round the tiny kitchen table so that Lisa can take notes more easily. She feels stupidly nervous.

"So," Sarah begins. "With restorative justice you need to understand what it can do for you, and think about whether it's something you really want to do. It can take months to set up and there are various stages, so there's no pressure on you. Shall I start by explaining what it is?"

"That would be good," Lisa says. Chloe nods.

"Restorative justice gives victims the chance to meet or communicate with their offenders to explain the real impact of the crime. The idea is that it empowers victims by giving them a voice. It also holds offenders to account for what they have done and helps them to take responsibility and make amends."

"How successful is it, generally?" Lisa says.

"Most of our victims are positive about the results. They feel it helps them to get their lives back."

"And does it ever go badly wrong?"

"Like what, for example?"

"Well, if they get violent, or someone gets hurt?" It's weighing on Lisa's mind that if Fergus were to make an aggressive move, she'd have a panic attack and all the courage, all the effort that she knows it will take to get her there, will be wasted.

"It's unlikely, to be honest, because it doesn't do them any good, but there's always a guard right there. We look out for any sign of threatening behaviour way before the actual meeting. However, anger can be part of the process. And it's more likely to come from the victim's side."

Lisa shivers. "Does it ever go wrong for the victim? Like, if they learn something about the crime that they don't want to know?"

"Not in my experience. Do you think that might apply to you?"

"It might, I suppose. I have no memory of parts of that evening — and there may be more things I've blocked out."

"What's more common is that the victim doesn't get any sense of remorse from the offender. That can be pretty disappointing. But every case is different and it very much depends on your expectations."

It takes nearly two hours to run through all their questions and by the end Lisa's head is hurting and she has pages of notes. When Sarah has gone, they make sandwiches and carry on talking. They draw up a list of pros and cons in Lisa's notebook. The pros seem to outweigh the cons, in terms of their potential impact. Though she thinks the cons could be pretty bad.

Despite everything in her that instinctively shrinks from the idea of facing up to Fergus, she feels strangely drawn to it. If there are answers to her questions, he's the only person who has them.

* * *

"Have you made the decision?" Graham asks at their next session.

"I've decided to go to the next stage. We've decided. Mum and I."

"What's the next stage?"

"They'll find out if Fergus is willing to meet. Then, if he is, we'll exchange information about what we want to say and ask. It's all pretty controlled, and it won't happen quickly even if I decide straight away."

"Do you think you'll go the whole way?"

"I think so. I'm not a hundred percent, but I think I've got to."

"Why have you got to?"

"Because it's the one thing I haven't done yet to help myself. It could give me the answers I need, and then I can finally get on with my life."

"What if it doesn't?"

"If it doesn't, at least I will have done my best for Ali, to find out why he did it."

"And for you?"

"I want to know if he remembers."

"Remembers what, exactly?"

"What actually happened. With Ali."

"And if he doesn't remember, or won't say?" A note of caution creeps into Graham's voice.

"I'll have to be ready for that."

"If you decide to go ahead with the meeting, make sure you see me first. You'll need to be prepared."

* * *

Their faces go pale with shock when she tells them.

At first she was going to call to explain the reasons for her decision, but it seemed wrong. They're victims, too. She owes them the courtesy of being there in person. So she finds herself sitting in her usual place on the sofa telling them why she's decided to meet Fergus in prison.

"But what for, Lisa?" Diana says, the worry lines on her forehead deepening. "What good can it possibly do?"

She's been through it enough times with Graham to know why she's doing it. She explains in as few words as possible that she feels stuck, unable to move on because she's fearful of everything. The discussion with Sarah has convinced her that the opportunity to face Fergus has the potential to empower her again and could answer some of the questions that torment her. She tells them that she needs to know what happened to Ali.

"And I also need to do this, for me," she says. "I'm going to be very frightened no doubt, but I'm hoping it'll be worth it. It seems to work for a lot of people."

"Restorative justice — I've never heard of it," Geoffrey says, shaking his head. "I mean, I've heard about criminals learning to take responsibility for what they've done, as part of their rehabilitation. But I thought it was all to stop them reoffending. I've not heard of that sort of thing to help the victim."

"It's quite a new thing. So it's good the opportunity's there."

"Are you sure you actually want to see him face-to-face? Couldn't you ask your questions by email or something? It would be far less frightening," Diana says. Her face is still pale and she picks at the hem of her cardigan. She looks older today, aged by her grief.

"It wouldn't be the same, it really wouldn't. The face-to-face contact is important. Apparently you get signals from their body language as well as what they say and how they say it. It's set up that way for good reasons. Of course I'm scared of seeing him, even being in the same room, but the whole thing's carefully managed. I won't be on my own with him at any point. There'll be at least three other people in the room including a guard."

"Who else will be there?" Geoffrey says.

"The facilitator, a woman called Sarah. I've already met her, with Mum. She looks after the whole process. I can take someone as a supporter and so can Fergus. Then there's his probation officer and a guard or two, either in the room or just outside."

"A supporter?" Diana asked. "Why does he get a supporter?"

"It's not supposed to be confrontational or intimidating for either of us, so each person gets the same. And we sit round in a circle, which sounds weird to me, I'd rather have a table between us, but apparently it's not good to have a barrier." She'd been particularly concerned about this when they saw Sarah. She'd asked if it was possible to do it differently. But she was told the circle is tried and tested.

"It all sounds very modern to me," Geoffrey says, scratching his head and smoothing down his sparse grey hair.

"I suppose if you feel you must do it, and if you think it'll help . . . Who are you taking with you?"

"Mum's going to come with me. We've talked about it a lot. She didn't want to, at first, but now she understands it a bit better, she's all right with it."

"That's brave of her," Diana says. "When will it be?"

"Oh, quite a while yet, I should think. A couple of months, maybe more. There's a lot of negotiating to do — we give him our questions, and he gives us his, if he has any. He might refuse to do it, anyway. He hasn't been asked yet."

"And if you change your mind in the meantime?"

"I can pull out at any stage, even at the last minute. And I can always try again. Look, I know this is all a bit of a shock for you," Lisa says. "But I really feel I need to give it a go. If it works for me, perhaps it could help you and Connor too?"

"Gosh, I'm not sure it's for us, really," Diana waves her hand as if to brush away the thought.

"Let's see how Lisa gets on," Geoffrey says. "She can try it out for us — if it works for her, perhaps we'll think about it." For the first time since she arrived, there's a note of humour in his voice. "The poor chap won't know what's happening if we turn up mob-handed."

"I don't think we could do that. But maybe you'll decide to do it too, sometime in the future, when you've had a chance to think about it."

"Well, I think you're very brave, Lisa," Diana says. "Very brave indeed."

* * *

Her insides have turned to mush. She takes painful gulps of air, too fast.

Graham is taking her back to the night when Ali died.

I can't do this.

"Try to relax. Take your time."

Relax? No chance.

He waits.

She takes a few minutes, wrestling with her emotions, slowing her breathing. Eventually, with some force of will, she nods silently, unwilling to trust her voice.

"Can you remember what happened next?"

She cradles her stomach to soothe the turmoil.

"He came towards the door. I'd gone to open it and I had my arm out to wave him through. He suddenly reached out, slammed the door shut and grabbed my arm, holding it really tight. It hurt. He wouldn't let go. I was yelling at him and Ali was shouting."

"Where was Ali at this point?"

"In front of me, between us and the window."

"Go on."

"He let go of my arm and grabbed me by the hair. He pulled my head back. Then I realised there was a knife at my neck." The pressure is threatening over her eyes. With the knuckles, she massages her forehead until the skin stings, her eyes squeezed shut in concentration. She swallows hard.

"Ali screamed at him to stop. I could feel his breath on my neck, smell the whisky. The knife was cutting in. It didn't hurt, which was odd, but I could feel the blood trickling. I was terrified, so scared that he'd cut my throat, I was shaking and my legs were giving way. I . . . I thought that was going to be it." The tears prick at her eyelashes, and she shakes her head impatiently, not wanting to give way.

"Was he shouting too?"

"Yes, I think so. There was such a lot happening. He was shouting, Ali was screaming."

"You're doing really well, Lisa. What was he saying?"

She shakes her head, eyes squeezed shut, her thoughts in a tangle, her head hurting with the effort of trying to remember.

"Was he shouting at you, or her?"

An ocean of blood rushes to her head. "Say that again?"

"Was he shouting at you, or her?"

The fleeting memory she's been searching for lands like a raptor dropping on its prey. Her hands fly to her open mouth. She looks directly into Graham's questioning eyes, seeking sanctuary. She can't speak. She closes her mouth and her eyes.

What did I do?

* * *

"Come on, Lisa, you decide . . . who's it going to be. You, or her?" The voice rasped in her ear, his lips touching her flinching skin. The hard edge of the knife was against her throat as she trembled, trying desperately to keep her balance, her neck arched painfully backwards. She knew she should say something, calm him down, but nothing came out of her mouth. Something warm was running down her neck. Ali was screaming, pleading with him.

"Shit, Fergus, stop, oh my God. Stop! What are you doing? Fergus!"

"Shut up," he yelled at Ali, turning away from Lisa for a second. She almost lost her balance, his fist in her hair tightened. The knife pressed deeper.

"You or her!" he yelled again and she flinched. She wanted to struggle, kick him, make something happen to stop him, but her limbs were frozen.

She took no decision. It came out unbidden, a low whisper, pure reflex, like an electric shock. "Her." Ali screamed again, a howl of horror, her voice breaking with the effort. "Fergus!" His grip on her hair slackened just a fraction as he turned away — and in that moment she was free, her arms flailing, trying to grab the hand with the knife.

But something strange was happening. She was falling, her body collapsing like a rag doll. Sinking to the floor, hands at her throat, she observed the lower half of the room in a haze — the legs of the coffee table, the bottom half of the sofa, dust and clumps of fluff underneath. Must give it a clean tomorrow . . .

His feet, in slow motion, brown leather loafers flexing, heading towards the window.

* * *

There's no question in her mind that it happened. At last she understands what's been sitting at the back of her mind, trying to surface, ever since her memory started to trickle back. And as she sits there in Graham's room, the horror of what she did hits her, her chest enclosed in an iron grip, her head bursting with the knowledge.

Thoughts race through her head, questions leaping. Did I know this all along? Did my memory shrink from the shocking truth, refuse to recognise it, hide it away until now? Did I knowingly block it?

How can I face Ali's family now? How can I face my mum? How can I face myself? I can't recover from this. I'm a monster. There is no life for me. How can I forget what I've done, now?

A deep chasm of despair opens up and she drifts towards it, helpless.

"Her." That one little word, is at the heart of everything.

She made the choice.

* * *

Graham draws it out of her. He's patient and gentle. He has to be. The final piece of the jigsaw, the realisation that she'd chosen to save herself over Ali, has shocked her. Her body is numb.

She can barely speak. When she opens her mouth, a sob escapes. He provides tissues, waits while she calms herself and wipes away her tears.

"I chose. He wanted me to choose between Ali and me, and I chose her. It's my fault she died. Connor was right all along. I did save myself over Ali. Oh, God . . ."

He continues to wait, as if nothing has changed.

The pain in her chest has spread. She tries to breathe deeply, but it hurts too much. She's overwhelmed by a feeling of utter exhaustion, as if all her energy has seeped out of her. She swallows a few times, wipes away the tears that continue to fall. But he's still waiting.

"Is it worth carrying on with this?" she says.

"Carrying on with what?"

"With the therapy, with trying to deal with the guilt."

"Why do you ask?"

"Because now I know it was my fault that Ali died, there's absolutely nothing I can do about it."

"On the contrary. You don't know it was your fault and there's a lot we can do. I'd like to explore that moment — when he gave you the choice. If you think you can."

She feels too weak to object, though she knows it's hopeless.

"What happened after you fell to the floor?"

"I'm not sure. I was in shock, I think."

"You must have been very afraid. He was holding you by the hair, with a knife cutting into your throat."

"Yes, I was terrified. I just wanted him to get off me, to let me go."

"At that moment, when he was holding you, what did you think he meant?"

"I had no idea what he meant. It didn't occur to me that he might want to kill us. It was all so sudden."

There's a long pause as if he's waiting for her to give him more.

"So when you answered him, what was going through your mind?"

"I just said it — I didn't mean him to kill Ali!" It's an anguished shout. She regrets it straight away but Graham doesn't react.

"Of course you didn't. So what did you think might happen?"

"I suppose I thought he might let go and I might be able to kick him, or grab his arm. Or just get away. I'd have said anything to get him off."

"So it was a primal, instinctive reaction. You just wanted him to let you go." It wasn't a question.

"I suppose so."

"And when he did release you, what did you do?"

"I tried to grab him — I wanted to, but my body wouldn't move. I was already blacking out. I was bleeding. It all gets a bit hazy after that. But as I collapsed, I saw him moving towards the window where Ali was. I watched his feet."

There's a pause. Lisa stares into Graham's face, looking for disapproval, shock, disgust. But his eyes, fixed on hers, show none of that. After a moment he leans back in his chair.

"In replying to him, by saying the word 'her' what were you doing?"

For a moment she's not sure what he's getting at. "It was a reflex — a gut reaction. I had to say something, he was waiting."

"You reacted by?"

"By answering."

He stays quiet, looking into her eyes, as if waiting for more.

"By choosing."

"So you chose to say 'her', rather than 'me'."

"Yes." Her whole body aches.

"What did you mean when you chose to say 'her'?"

"Hurt Ali, not me," she whispers.

"Did you really mean that?"

"No, no, of course I didn't mean it. I didn't want him to hurt Ali, but I was so scared. I was clutching at straws, I'd have said anything, I don't know what I meant."

"Did you know what his next move would be?"

"It was just a reaction, there was no logic."

"It's all right, Lisa. There was no intention on your part — so what did it mean?"

She's still not sure what he's getting at. Then she feels a whisper of recognition and something unfolds in her mind.

* * *

"It was a reaction to him yelling at me." She says the words slowly, deliberately. "I had to say something. He wanted an answer. I didn't know what he would do."

"So how do you feel, understanding that?"

She's unable to answer for a while. He waits.

"Oh God, I don't know. Why didn't I say 'me'?"

"Why didn't you?"

"Because he already had me, I was helpless, bleeding, I couldn't do anything. And at least if I said 'her', he might let me go. It's strange, though. A part of me feels relieved. Now that I know. I did choose, but I didn't know what it meant." She searches for disbelief in Graham's eyes, but finds only expectation, interest.

"So by saying 'her' in response, you were hoping he'd let you go?" He sits back in his chair, as if to emphasise the point.

"Well, yes."

"Can you hold on to that, do you think?" She's quiet for a while, thinking it through. It's all so new, shocking and yet so obvious.

"I don't know. Maybe. As long as nobody else knows."

"Would it bother you if other people knew?"

"I'd hate people to misunderstand. It would be easy for them to think I made a conscious choice, that I wanted to save myself and purposely put Ali in danger. I don't think I could bear that."

"Nobody will know, unless you tell them."

Another realisation pricks at her. "Oh God, what if I'd remembered before the court case?"

"Would it have made a difference to the outcome?"

"I don't know. I suppose not. He would still have had to plead guilty."

"The only difference is that other people would know what a horrible thing he forced you to do. Anyway, you didn't remember."

She sits thinking about this for a moment.

"He could say it's my fault Ali died, I suppose. It won't change his situation. He'd still be guilty of manslaughter and GBH. But what if he tells people?"

"Are you frightened he'd tell someone in particular?"

"I don't know. Ali's family, maybe."

"What would he get out of it? He'll just look even more guilty because he forced you, at knifepoint, to choose."

"He could do it to be vindictive. They might blame me if they knew."

"He could, but there'd be nothing in it for him. What's he got against you? It wasn't your fault he went to prison. He managed that all by himself."

* * *

What she hasn't told Graham, or anyone else, is that she's remembered the night they spent with Fergus and the nature of their relationship, both before and after that. That twinge of recollection which bothered her over weeks and months is now a memory — and it's accompanied by deep shame.

She agonised over withholding it, but now she's convinced herself that it's irrelevant, it doesn't make any difference to the outcome. The police don't need to know. Graham doesn't need to know. The true cause of her psychological state is Ali's death, not that mad, stupid night. And her mum doesn't need to know. Does she? What if Fergus lets it slip — would anyone believe him now? They'd think it's all made up, wouldn't they? The idea that she's let her mum down badly, after everything that's happened, intensifies her shame. But the idea of telling her is worse. Unthinkable. She just has to hope that Fergus won't use it against her.

* * *

The only time she and Ali had argued was about Fergus.

Because it hadn't ended with the text. Yes, he'd worked away from home for a while — more than six months, as it happened. But when he returned, he'd appeared again at the pub and Ali had bumped into him on a night when Lisa was working late. They'd kissed and made up, sat in a quiet corner and agreed to be friends.

Ali dropped this casually into conversation soon afterwards. Lisa was horrified. She wanted no reminders of that night, nothing to do with Fergus or his drugs. She'd yelled at Ali, accused her of being thoughtless, of forgetting how upset and ashamed she was. Ali, always the more laid-back of the two, had stuck to her guns, argued that Fergus meant them no harm, wasn't pushing them to do anything, just wanted to clear the air. In the end, they'd agreed that Ali would see Fergus if she wanted to. She would tell him that Lisa was too embarrassed about what they'd done and preferred not to see him.

As time passed Lisa became more optimistic. They started going to the pub again, and sometimes Fergus would be there. She would tolerate his presence, be polite, civil. If he joined their group, she would be careful not to end up next to him and avoided him if she could. He seemed to accept the situation and left her alone. There was only one moment that unnerved her. He was at the bar with some friends, the whisky flowing, and she noticed him looking at her, an odd expression on his face. She looked away, pretending not to have seen him. When she glanced back, he was laughing with the group, his back turned.

* * *

She sits on a hard plastic chair in the corridor, trying not to pick at her fingers. She bites her lip instead, so hard she can taste the blood. Chloe sits close, their arms touching, Sarah on her other side. They've travelled here together on a long, uncomfortable journey from home, arriving at last late in the morning, but in plenty of time for the meeting. The prison is a sinister building that squats in the countryside of northern England. It couldn't look more like a prison, grim and menacing.

More than once on the journey, listening to the rhythm of the train on its tracks, Lisa asked herself what the hell she was doing, putting herself in the most confrontational, stressful position she could possibly think of. But she made it, and now she's here, she's not going to turn back.

She'd expected Fergus to be reluctant to face her, but he'd agreed straight away. There followed a long-drawn-out exchange of questions by post and email, handled by Sarah at one end and Fergus' representative at the other. Once she'd committed to it, she was determined to make it work.

She's spent a lot of time with Graham, working through her fears, finding ways to calm the demons. She's rehearsed the questions and imagined the scene over and over, hoping that familiarity and visualisation will calm her.

Her stomach refuses to settle. All through the three-hour journey she tried to ignore the cramps and the sickness that threatened to overwhelm her. When they arrived at the prison gates half an hour early, she was so near to panicking she nearly turned and ran. It was only because of her mum that she carried on.

The mass of grey stone and curling razor wire on the outside walls were deeply intimidating. At the entrance their bags were searched, and Sarah surrendered her mobile phone. Lisa hung on to Chloe's arm as they followed a guard through a labyrinth of corridors, their painted walls reflecting the hard fluorescent light. Closed doors lined each side, their dark secrets hidden from view, and unpleasant smells hung in the air: cabbage, sweat and a faint whiff of disinfectant.

The group stopped at a sign marked Chaplaincy, and the guard motioned them to the chairs lining the corridor. He disappeared through a glass door.

They wait in silence, shifting nervously on the hard seats.

She just wants to get it over with. She starts to pick at her fingers, where the skin beside her nails is already torn and inflamed. The glass door swishes, the guard reappears with a key and opens the door opposite them. Sarah leads the way into a large square room, cold and bare but for a small circle of six chairs. A small window, high on one wall, frames the grey sky outside.

They sit facing the door, where the prison officer stands. Sarah, Lisa, Chloe in a short row. Lisa takes her mum's hand, which curls over hers.

"They've gone to fetch him now," Sarah says.

* * *

The minute the door opens, the room is infused with tension. Lisa shrinks into her chair, feeling its power.

Two men lead the way and Fergus follows, head down. There's a general shuffling and scraping of chairs as they sit.

Lisa can't take her eyes off him as he takes his place in the circle. He's small and thin, his face pale, his hair cropped to a fuzz. She looks at his feet, remembering the brown leather loafers, but he's wearing scuffed trainers. He seems ordinary, scared even. The thought calms her a little as she waits for Sarah to start.

After a brief introduction when she names each person and their role in the meeting, Sarah outlines the format. They start with the questions they've all seen in advance. They speak when they're invited to by Sarah, in turns. Afterwards there'll be tea and biscuits. They don't have to stay for that part if they don't wish to. They all nod in silence, except Fergus.

"Let's start with you, Fergus," Sarah says. "How would you describe what happened that evening in June last year?"

His eyes flash onto Sarah's face, then flick down again. He sits slumped, arms folded, says nothing. Lisa holds her breath. Oh God, what if he refuses to speak?

"In your own words, Fergus. Take your time." Sarah says. They all focus on him.

He clears his throat, shifting in his seat. When he finally speaks, his voice is quiet, monotone, his eyes almost closed.

"I met up with the crowd at the pub. I'd had a lot of stuff, drugs, and nearly a bottle of whisky before I went. The work had dried up and I'd had a bad day. I'd been drinking since lunchtime."

"What happened at the pub?"

"Not much. When the girls left, I followed them to the flat. I asked to use the toilet and they let me up."

"So, you went to the toilet — and then?"

"I wanted to stay, just for a while. I wanted company. They were drinking coffee . . ." He pauses and glances at Sarah, as if for approval.

"Go on," she says.

"I dunno. I said something stupid — about a three-some." He finally glances at Lisa. She holds her breath as he looks down again.

"They asked me to leave and, I dunno, I just lost it. I just wanted to talk, wanted a bit of company — and they were trying to chuck me out. I was mad with them. So I went to the kitchen and took a knife." He stops again and leans forward, elbows on knees, head hanging. "I was totally out of my head. I lost control." His voice drops to a hoarse whisper.

Lisa's rigid, her eyes glued to his face.

"And then?" Sarah says.

"And then, something happened to me, I dunno what, but I was so angry, it just took over. I grabbed hold of Lisa. There was lots of screaming. It was so loud, I was confused, my head was gone." He stops and looks at Sarah again. "I wanted to stop the screaming. That's all. I didn't mean . . . I just wanted to stop the screaming."

"What happened next?"

"I can't remember anything after grabbing Lisa, and the screaming. The next thing I knew, they were locking me up."

Lisa is incredulous. She studies his face. He must have remembered more than that, surely.

Sarah nods. "Thank you Fergus. Lisa, do you want to ask something?"

Lisa stares at him, willing him to make eye contact. "Do you remember what you did with the knife?"

He stares at the ground.

"No."

"But you do remember grabbing me."

"Yes."

"What were you going to do with the knife?"

"I said, I dunno." The probation officer shoots a look at him, a silent reproval. He sits back.

"You had the knife to my neck. Look." She pulls the scarf away from her throat and lifts her chin so that the light falls on the scar, the blood-red slash across her white skin. "That's why Ali was screaming. You don't remember that?"

He looks up, but not into her face. To Sarah, he says, his tone still unemotional. "I don't remember that."

"You cut me, there was blood everywhere. Ali was trying to stop you. I don't believe you don't remember."

"I don't remember." His tone is flat, stubborn.

"So do you remember what happened to Ali?" Lisa says, persisting, anger beginning to rise.

"No. Nothing else." He still doesn't look at her. Why doesn't he look at me? He's holding something back. She wants to shake him, hit him, kick the truth out of him. She looks at Sarah again, who nods her permission.

"You don't remember how Ali came to fall out of the window?"

"No, I don't." It's a flat response, a little louder than before. He's trying to shut me down, she thinks. Her mum's hand is on her arm now, a gentle restraint. She ignores it, the blood rising. She needs to control her voice. She doesn't want him to hear the emotion. But he's got to know what he's done — to Ali, to her, to all of them.

She pauses for a moment to steady her breathing. She tries a different tack, her words slow and clear. "So do you remember what you said to me?" A slight movement from her mum on her right. They hadn't discussed this.

He looks at her then, a hint of uncertainty, his eyes meeting hers for a brief moment before he looks away, then at Sarah. She nods, as if to allow the question.

"There was a lot of shouting and screaming, that's all I know." His tone is dismissive now.

She wants to scream at him. The fear has gone and she feels nothing but anger. All the tension of the past months mounting, a volcano on the brink.

"Come on, Fergus, you must remember — what did you say to me?" Her voice has risen, a sharp edge to it, and both Sarah and her mum turn to look at her, startled. Her mum tugs at her arm as if to say, but she has to do this.

"I don't know," Fergus says. "What do you want from me? I don't know what I said to you."

"You said," she says, leaning forward, enunciating each word with precision. He lifts his eyes at the cold fury in her voice. "You said, 'Who's it going to be, Lisa? You, or her?'"

She pauses as realisation dawns on him, the colour draining from his face, his eyes wide open with what looks like fear. There's a sharp intake of breath from her mum, but she can't stop now, she has to get it all out. A slight shake of his head, a denial, makes her yet more determined. His eyes are fastened to hers as if by some invisible thread. She won't let go. He has to know.

"You gave me the choice. You had a knife to my throat, and you . . . you made me choose."

* * *

Her heavy words fall into the room. There's a long silence while everyone absorbs what she's said. She can feel their eyes on her, but she holds Fergus in her power now and she won't let go.

He swallows noisily and sits straight in his chair. He unclenches his hands, places them flat on his thighs.

He flashes a look at Sarah. "She's lying. I never said that." He drops his gaze to the floor but his voice carries round the room, echoing in Lisa's head.

Her body tightens with fury and she almost rises from her chair. Sarah holds her hand out, palm down, a gesture that makes Lisa sit back, biting her lip.

"Do you remember what you did say?" Sarah says.

"No. I already said, I can't remember. But I never said that, I wouldn't have said that."

Sarah's hand drops and Lisa jumps up from her chair, her hands balled into tight fists. "But you did, Fergus. You made me choose. You were holding me by the hair. The knife was cutting into my throat, I was bleeding. You made me choose." From the corner of her eye she sees the others flinch at the venom in her voice.

Sarah leans forward. "Lisa, please sit down."

She sits, her body stiff. "You made me choose, Fergus."

"I didn't! What do you want from me?" His voice rises and Sarah leans forward as if to contain him. Everybody waits.

Is he really going to deny it? How can he? Will they let him get away with it? "I want you to recognise — what you did to us."

There's a long pause. They all look at Fergus. He stares in silence at his hands, elbows on his thighs, head down. Then, slowly, he lifts his arms, curls them up and back and holds his head in a tight embrace, shielding his face. The supporter on his left puts a hand on his shoulder.

His voice is low and shaky. "I didn't know what I was doing. I didn't mean . . . I'm sorry."

"So you do remember?"

"I'm not sure, it's all a haze, I was out of my head. I just wanted the screaming to stop, that's all it was. That's all I remember."

"Just because you can't remember, it doesn't excuse you, and it doesn't make it go away," she says in a rush, the words tumbling over each other. "It was horrific, what you did, and what you made me do."

"What do you want me to say?" he says again, but this time all the confrontation in his voice has gone.

"You cut my throat, you caused the death of my best friend. And you — you made me betray her."

"I'm sorry. I really am. I don't know what else to say."

His voice doesn't sound sorry. It's not enough. She wants him to feel her pain.

"What you can explain is why. Why me, why us? We hadn't done anything to hurt you."

His eyes flick back to hers and he shakes his head. "I wasn't myself. The drugs . . ."

"You were supposed to be our friend." She spits it out. "We were close . . ." Realising what she's saying, she stops, her heart pounding, she's almost let it slip out. Wide-eyed, she looks at him and sees a flash of understanding.

"I know, we were. But I lost it, completely. Something happened to me — the drugs, the drink. Some kind of mad, jealous rage. I really fucked up. I'm sorry, Lisa. I was your friend and I'm sorry for everything."

She holds his gaze, searching for the lie. But all she can see is need. Is he looking for forgiveness? A strange mixture of emotions grip her — grief, anger, sympathy? There was a time when she'd liked him, laughed with him, trusted him, even. Sitting there facing her he looks young and vulnerable. Her fear falls away. He's just a lad who's been overtaken by events, no more. His life has been wrecked, too — it's his own fault, and he knows it. He's not evil, he's sad. The whole bloody thing is sad. Her eyes well up and she fights to keep the tears at bay.

There's a long pause, then Sarah sits straight in her chair and everyone changes position in their seats, as if a gust of wind has touched the room.

"Lisa, perhaps you could describe to us how you've been affected by the events of that evening."

Lisa takes a moment, steeling herself.

"My life is completely different. I get flashbacks and nightmares. I haven't slept properly since that day. I'm too frightened to go out to work. I'm scared of everything: men, loud noises, public places, strangers. I've been on medication for depression ever since."

That's the speech over with, then — the one she's rehearsed. She soldiers on with the rest, unable to stop.

"When I remembered — that I made the choice — I was completely devastated. I felt like I'd killed Ali myself. I didn't think that even my meagre subsistence was even worth living." Chloe grips her hand tightly and she daren't look at her because she knows there'll be tears on her face and she can't bear to see them.

There's a long silence while her words seem to echo around the bare room.

"How do you feel about that, Fergus?" Sarah says.

"I wish it never happened," he says with a look of sheer desperation. "I regret it every day. I never meant to hurt anybody. I'm ashamed of what I made you do, and I'm so sorry."

* * *

They excuse themselves from tea and biscuits after the meeting. It strikes Lisa as a bizarre idea, to be sharing a civilised snack with Ali's killer, after all that's been said and done. She's overwhelmed with exhaustion. Enough is enough, I've said what I came to say. I know all there is to know, now.

Sarah winds up the formal part of the meeting. She asks for a measurable outcome — a promise from Fergus to his victim. Lisa and her mum have discussed this in advance. They want him to get clean. If drugs really have played their part then he needs to give them up if he's going to change.

He agrees to rehabilitation and therapy. Lisa offers him no option. His remorse seems genuine, though, and she can't ask for more. When he leaves the room, flanked by his probation officer and a guard, he shuffles and dawdles like a small child.

She just wants to get away, calm her roller coaster emotions and absorb the events of the day in her own environment. She needs Riley, his constant warmth, his soft coat.

* * *

The train clacks and rumbles towards home.

She collapses in a heap of fatigue at a window seat, staring unseeing at the ground racing by. The cold of the prison has touched her bones and she's chilled to the core. Her mind's frozen, too.

Chloe falls asleep straight away, her head lolling. Lisa knows she has some explaining to do, but there will be plenty of time to talk later. Sarah sits opposite Lisa, making notes.

After an hour or so her mum wakes up and Sarah orders hot drinks for them all. When they arrive, she looks at Lisa. "How do you think that went?"

She attempts to kick-start her brain.

"I'm still trying to decide. It was really hard seeing him again," she says. "At first, I thought he was going to be resistant and deny it all, and I didn't want him to get away with it. I started to get really angry."

"It's understandable," Sarah says.

"But I believe him. I don't think he can remember what happened. And at the end he seemed genuinely sorry for what he did."

"Were you frightened of him?"

"I was at first. But at the end, he seemed ordinary. And scared, too. I almost felt sorry for him." She sighs. "It's all so sad."

Her mum nods. "I didn't know you'd remembered more. Why didn't you tell me, darling?"

"It was only a few days ago. I'm sorry, I'm still coming to terms with it myself. I don't want anyone to blame me for Ali's death. I didn't mean for him to hurt her."

Tears stream down Chloe's face as she leans over and hugs Lisa. They break apart and rest their foreheads together.

"What a terrible thing for you to deal with." Sarah's eyes are full of sympathy. "Are you getting some support?"

Lisa turns towards her. "A lot of therapy."

"Do you think today's meeting will help?"

"I need to think about it for a while, absorb it properly. He doesn't remember what happened and I still don't know why he did it. I suppose I'll never know what came over him. Will I feel any sense of resolution? I don't know."

"Sometimes there's no logical reason for someone behaving like that, particularly when drugs are involved. You just happened to be there."

"So it's all down to bad luck?"

"Maybe."

Lisa thinks about that for a while, the countryside passing in a blur of green and grey. The train rolls and sways with a comforting, hypnotic rhythm and she closes her eyes. Perhaps she should stop asking why and how. Perhaps it's all down to fate, or luck, or randomness. But it's the betrayal that she needs to come to terms with.

* * *

It takes a long time for her to regroup after the prison visit. When she gets back home, it feels like she's been away for weeks and the house has that odd feeling of neglect that follows a long holiday.

In many ways seeing him again was cathartic. She's no longer frightened of him, she knows she feels sorry for him, even though she doesn't want to admit it. She hadn't foreseen that.

He'd gone to the flat in a drugged state, not meaning to attack them, hurt or kill them. She's pretty certain of that. When he did attack them, it was because he'd lost his mind on drugs, and in the end he just wanted to stop the screaming. There was no other reason.

And he doesn't remember the moment when Ali fell.

They would never know what really happened, whether she was pushed, or fell by accident, or even jumped, as he'd claimed at the beginning. Whatever happened, she fell and died, and there was nothing they could do about it. Whatever Lisa had said in reply to Fergus, that's the fact of the matter.

I didn't mean him to harm Ali. I didn't know what he would do. If she says it often enough, perhaps she'll end up believing it.

* * *

"You look different," Graham says. It's the first time she's seen him since the prison visit. It's getting on for two weeks now.

"I feel different," she says.

"In what way?"

"Fergus seems less important. I'm not as frightened of him."

He nods. "Well, that's good. What do you mean, less important?"

"He didn't remember what he made me do — I had to tell him. So I felt more in control than him. And he had no excuses for what he did, only the drugs."

"Does that make you feel better about what he made you do?"

"I still wish I'd chosen myself instead of Ali, if that's what you mean. But I don't know if it would have made any difference. Anything could have happened, no matter what I said."

"So do you think you played a part in Ali's death?"

"Yes, indirectly."

He nods, a minuscule movement of his head.

"Does that bother you, that you'll never know?"

"Yes and no. I don't know. I'm hoping I can come to terms with it."

Another tiny nod. "Will you tell anyone else about it?"

"I'm not sure, now. If it's less important to me, it matters less if people know. It depends who it is and why they need to know, I suppose. I'm still not sure what to tell Ali's family. I don't know how they would react and whether they need any more horrible detail than they've already had."

"Does your mum know?"

"She was there when I confronted him, so yes. It was a shock for her, though, she knew nothing about it."

"How was she after the meeting?"

"She wanted to know why I hadn't told her, of course. But when we talked about it, she understood why. It was because I felt so ashamed. And horribly guilty. I couldn't tell anybody."

"And is that how you're feeling now?"

"It's only been a couple of weeks."

He shifts in his chair, crosses his legs the other way. Today his socks are matching. He looks more rested, the lines on his forehead softening into his fringe.

"How are the nightmares? Flashbacks?"

"I've not had any flashbacks since we saw him. Bit early to tell, probably. The nightmares have lessened too. I'd call it disturbed sleep, but not every night. I've slept much better in the last few days."

"That must be a huge relief for you."

"It is. Waking up not feeling desperate, even once a week, is a massive improvement. If I can sleep better, maybe gradually I can get back to who I am."

"Do you want to go back to how you were, before the attack?"

"I meant . . . finding out who I am now. It's hard to find the right words. But I don't want to focus on myself any more. I need to think about other things, other people, rather than myself and what happened to me."

"Do you think that will help?"

"Definitely. I've thought about little else for nearly two years. Quite apart from the lack of sleep, it was pretty awful being me."

* * *

She doesn't want to be ungenerous or self-pitying. She tries to block the feelings whenever they strike, which is usually when she thinks about other people's good fortune. There are plenty of people who seem to sail through life with nothing getting in their way, only happy times and success punctuating their voyage.

She discusses these feelings with Graham.

"I don't want to end up a sad, bitter person because of what happened to me. I don't want my life to be formed or overtaken by it. I know it sounds childish, but it feels really unfair. Why couldn't I have a normal life?"

"Who do you know who has had a normal life?"

"Well, there are lots of people."

"Like?"

"Well . . ." She looks at Graham, who waits for her reply.

"Your mum?"

"Not my mum, because of losing Dad so young."

"Jessica, then."

"Yes, except her husband beat her up."

"Who else?"

"I can't think. I'm sure I know plenty, but I can't think of them."

"Do you see what I'm getting at? Things happen to everybody. Other people's traumas may not seem as bad as what happened to you, but for them, those things are probably pretty awful."

"I suppose so."

"And they're affected in various ways. And maybe they change because of what happened to them. But it doesn't mean that changing is a bad thing. Or that people lose control of what they want and how they live the rest of their lives."

"Yes. I mean no. I think I get what you're saying."

CHAPTER NINE

There's a tumble of letters and leaflets on the mat by the front door. Most of it is junk mail, but there's one envelope, thick and white, that catches her attention. Her name and address are typed and she doesn't recognise the name on the franked stamp at the top.

It takes her a while to read the letter, though it isn't long.

In formal legal language, it informs her that Mr John Grey, recently deceased, has left £50,000 in his will to Ms Lisa Fulbrook.

Unbelieving, she re-reads it until the words and the numbers jump out at her in a bewildering jumble. When Riley's bark at the back door announces his desire to come in, she leaps up from the table with a sudden burst of nervous energy, her slippers sliding on the tiled floor.

To give herself time to absorb the incredible news, she makes up the log burner in the sitting room, waits for a flame to take hold, then plops herself down on the sofa and picks up the letter again.

"Well, I'll be. Bloody hell." Riley looks up at her as she lets her body fall backwards, lifting her feet into the air.

"Fifty thousand pounds, Riley! John's left us fifty grand!" He wags his tail and lands his front paws next to her. She hugs him until he wriggles, kissing the top of his soft, shiny head. He licks her ear in response, infected by her excitement.

Lisa has never had much money in her adult life and she can't remember the family having much, either. Chloe had always worked part-time and survived on that income and a small widow's pension, while Lisa's pay has never allowed her to do more than foot the bills and put food on the table. She'd received a small sum in compensation for her injury but it's pretty much all gone on therapy.

She's never imagined having this much money. It's so unexpected she can hardly bring herself to believe it. Warning herself not to get too excited in case it really isn't true, she reads the letter yet again. It invites her to call the lawyer's office for further details.

She can't believe it. All she did was look after Riley, which wasn't hard — quite the contrary. She did a bit of shopping for John and helped him out when he was ill, but fifty thousand pounds? It's a huge reward for so little. She wonders if his nephew, Oscar, is annoyed that she's been given such a substantial amount.

Glancing at the clock, she sees that there's a whole hour and a half to kill before she can call the lawyers, so she runs upstairs, throws on her clothes and leaves for a walk in a daze.

* * *

> Dear Lisa,
> Sorry to be formal, but dealing with lawyers and such like in the process of executing Uncle John's will has become a bit of a habit!
> John has written you a letter, which the lawyers will hand over when you meet them. I haven't read it, nor has anyone else, and I don't know its contents. However I do know that he left you a not inconsiderable sum in his will.
> I want you to know that as far as me and my family are concerned, it was absolutely up to him what

he did with his money. I also want to reassure you that with the house and the rest of his investments, we've done extremely well out of being his only surviving relatives! It was a great surprise to us that a modest man like John had built up such a large pot of money, despite having no immediate family to leave it to. I'm very happy for you, and of course for Riley, who I know will benefit at least as much as you do from this gift.

John was a lovely man, humble and unassuming. He never expected anything of anybody. He was extremely grateful that you took Riley on and were able to look after him properly. He was also appreciative of your help with the small tasks that you so willingly undertook. He told me about his birthday tea — and he was most touched that you visited him in hospital when he was unwell.

Thank you so much for befriending him and for helping him in his last days. Thank Riley, too, from us, for being a friend and a comfort to him after Elsie died.

Please accept the money he has willed to you. I'm sure he wanted to offer you a reward for your kindness and to thank you properly. Please do with the money as you wish, and enjoy it!

With all our best wishes,

Oscar.

PS. I understand you're good friends with Jessica, who's buying the house. Good to know it'll be in safe hands. O.

Dear Lisa,

I hope I haven't shocked you with my gift and that you accept it in the spirit with which it is given. As you know, Oscar and his family are my only living relatives and I've left them with plenty to keep them comfortable.

You and Riley were good friends to me in the last year or so and I wanted to give you something to show my appreciation. I can't take it with me, after all.

I know very little about you but it seems to me you've had a difficult time and are trying to recover quietly on your own. Perhaps this gift will help in a small way to make your life — and Riley's, of course — a little more secure. Actually I hope you'll use part of it to have some fun, maybe take a holiday or buy yourself a car. Please treat yourself! It would be nice to know I've brought a little light into your life, as you did into mine.

With very best wishes,

John

* * *

"Fifty thousand quid??" Jessica's voice is rising to a squeak. "Five-oh, thousand pounds?"

Lisa laughs. "Yes, five-oh. Four huge zeros. Not enough to make me an oligarch, but much more than I thought I'd ever have. And I wasn't expecting anything."

"Where are we going, then?"

"What?"

"Where are we going? You must have a holiday, after all you've been through. Go on, it'll do you the world of good."

"A holiday?" Despite John's suggestion, she really hasn't entertained the thought. She imagined putting the money away, investing it, getting a pension, securing some kind of income for her future. God, that's boring.

"Yes, for God's sake! You know, when you travel to a lovely place and have a fantastic time seeing a new country or a new place, eating nice food and relaxing? Lisa?"

"Yes — sorry. The concept is just so alien to me. I haven't had a proper holiday in so long."

"Come on, Lisa! It'll be the best thing for you. You don't have to spend it all, you know. I'll come with you — I need a break, too, and I certainly will in a few months' time when I've moved house. How about May or June, when it's getting warm. We could go abroad, maybe to the coast somewhere . . ."

"Abroad? I don't know. I'm not very adventurous, you know."

Jessica is jumping with anticipation. "But you can be now!"

Her enthusiasm is infectious. She's laughing and bouncing about with excitement.

"Maybe we could have a look — but let me get used to the idea first. We can research it together. What about the dogs?"

"True. I hate the idea of kennels. We'll just have to find somewhere that will take them, too."

* * *

They sit overlooking the seafront on the pavement of a quiet café, cups of strong coffee in front of them, talking. It's been a beautiful day, and they've walked for hours along the coastal path, finishing back in the village tired and tingling from the breeze and the sun's rays. The dogs, after a long drink of water, have settled down at their feet, dozing in the warmth of the early evening.

In the event, their conversation simply takes a turn, as conversations sometimes do, and Lisa finds herself telling Jessica what really happened to her that summer of 2013.

"I've remembered it all now," she says. Jessica looks up from her coffee.

"You have?"

"Yes. It's bizarre. For a long time my mind blocked it out, because it was too awful to contemplate."

"I've heard that happens sometimes."

Lisa looks at the view in front of them. Waves breaking on the sand, the northern Spanish coast, blue sky beyond. A small white yacht making its way slowly across the horizon.

The simple metal table between them with its napkin holder and old-fashioned cruet stand, the smell of garlic rising from the kitchen.

"Yes. But this was more than just trying to remember. I had terrible feelings of guilt and responsibility."

"What for? He was the one who killed Ali."

"Partly because I lived and Ali died. It's called survivor guilt. Psychospeak."

"So you feel bad because you lived? That sounds unfair."

"Yes, because I lived, but it was more than that. I just felt, even though I couldn't remember, that it was all my fault. And when Connor accused me of saving myself and not Ali, I became convinced that I'd done something terrible. It was haunting me."

"The whole thing was horrific — it's not surprising you felt like that." Jessica shakes her head, as if to dispel the image.

"Yes, but what I'm trying to say is — it was actually true. It wasn't just me feeling guilty because I survived when my friend didn't. It was more than that."

"What was it then?"

She hesitates, her heart pounding. "He gave me a choice, Jessica."

Jessica's eyes widen and she puts her cup down. "What do you mean?"

"He gave me a choice — me or Ali. And I had to choose."

Jessica lets out a whistle of air through her teeth. Lisa can smell the bitter tang of coffee on her breath.

"Oh Lisa. Oh my God. You chose."

"Yes." She looks into Jessica's eyes and sees only shock and concern, no hint of withdrawal.

"No wonder you were so traumatised."

"Yes, it explains a lot, doesn't it?"

Jessica frowns, her forehead crinkling. "Well, maybe. But, what did he mean? What was he going to do?"

"That's just it. I have no idea. I had no idea then, either."

"Didn't it come out in court, when he was convicted?"

"At the time of the court case, I was in hospital. I couldn't remember much at all. It seems he didn't remember, either. He was very drunk and sky high on drugs as well. There was no mention of it in his statement, no evidence, nothing to explain what he really intended to do. And when we met at the prison, he said he remembered nothing after grabbing me. Not cutting me with the knife, not pushing Ali. Nothing."

Jessica blows another whistle, frowning with concentration. "But, hang on, you didn't know what he meant and neither did he — so surely you can't blame yourself?"

"He obviously wasn't intending to offer us a bunch of roses. He meant us real harm, Jessica, and I directed him away from myself, towards Ali."

"But he had you by the hair, didn't he have a knife at your throat?"

"I just wanted to get free, to try to stop him — that was my only chance. But it was all in the heat of the moment. I said it without thinking."

"So you still blame yourself? Despite the knife?"

"I blamed myself at first, when I remembered. He gave me a choice and I chose to protect myself rather than my best friend. "

"But you thought he was going to kill you, for God's sake. All you wanted was to get him to let you go. I'd have said anything."

"You can see why it was so cathartic for me when I remembered. It was mind-blowing. I thought I was going to explode. Fortunately, I was with Graham when the memory came back."

"Wow. I mean, I understood before, but obviously it was even worse than I knew. I'm so sorry, Lisa."

"I haven't told anyone else. Except Graham, of course. And my mum had to know, because I confronted Fergus with it at the prison."

"And he said he hadn't remembered?"

"He said not. He was stunned when I told him."

"Ashamed, I hope," Jessica says.

"I think so. Hard to tell, but he seemed remorseful."

"And you don't want anybody else to know what he made you do?"

"I'm pretty sure they wouldn't understand. Nobody else needs to know."

"I won't tell a soul. It's not my story to tell. I promise."

"I know — that's why I told you. You've been so good to me. You must know you've helped me enormously. To recover, that is." The tears are threatening, annoyingly, when she's got through the worst of it without breaking down. "I just wanted you to understand. And to say thank you."

"Don't thank me. I'm just glad you're feeling better. And I'm glad you told me."

"I hope it's not too much of a burden, knowing."

"Why would it be? It's not my burden."

The tears trickle down. "Thanks, Jessica."

* * *

Everything seems different as she walks up the path to her front door. Things look cleaner, brighter, and there's a fragrance in the air that she's not noticed before. It's mid-May. In her absence the trees have sprouted fresh leaves, their soft green shoots reaching upwards like infant children to their mothers. Some of the gardens along the street are already in bloom, making her own frontage, and John's — now Jessica's — seem bare and colourless.

Inside, she dumps her bag at the bottom of the stairs and throws open windows and doors. She wanders outside, where the grass has grown long and the creeper which climbs up the back of the cottage criss-crosses the kitchen window with new leaves and burgeoning flower buds.

The holiday has given her a new perspective. It's not simply the result of being away somewhere new and unfamiliar that has made the difference. The ability to escape from that moment almost two years ago eluded her for so long that now that she's free of it, she sees everything in a new light. Familiar things have changed shape, and colour, and density, before her.

In Spain she'd been able, for a few hours at a time, not to forget, exactly, but to compartmentalise — to put the terrible memories into a part of her mind which she could choose not to access for a while. It's as if her mind is organised in soft, swirling layers, in order of importance from outside in. The present, the top layer, has taken over and flourished, fed by new experiences and senses, while that defining event in her past, with its dark nightmares and flashbacks, has shifted to a lower layer, diminished and weakened through neglect.

She takes a deep breath in. Feeling as though, for the first time in so long, she finally can.

* * *

The door opens and Connor's face appears, high in the doorway. He smiles and the tension in her shoulders eases.

It's June again, a few weeks since the meeting with Fergus. She'd talked to Ali's family on the phone shortly afterwards, trying not to dwell on his lack of memory about how Ali died. She knew it would be disappointing for them, though in some ways she felt it was better not to know. She emphasised his remorse and his promise to give up drugs, which seemed to give them some comfort.

She's thought long and hard about whether to tell them what Fergus made her do, but in the end has made no decision. She may tell them one day. Anyway, two years after the event is still too soon. She doesn't feel bad about leaving it, or guilty, she simply wants to wait a while for everyone to recover, to gain their strength. Then she might think about it again. They've all had enough pain and grief in the last two years and she doesn't want to give them more.

Today's visit is about the future, she hopes, rather than the past. She feels close to them, after all the pain the two families have shared. And Ali would want her to stay that way.

"Hi Lisa — come in, we're all in the sitting room, go through." Connor waves her through the hallway to the open door. Diana greets her with a hug, holding her close, and Geoffrey with a warm, dry kiss on both cheeks. The tray of tea and biscuits is already on the table in front of the sofa and as Lisa sits down, Diana pours into flowered china cups. She looks up at Lisa and smiles.

"You look so well!"

"I feel well. I've had a holiday — my first proper holiday abroad, ever, really. I went to northern Spain with a friend and our dogs."

"How lovely. It must have suited you." There's a slight pause as they look at her expectantly, she's unsure how to respond.

"It did. I'm feeling better — generally."

Diana squeezes her hand. "I'm so glad. You've had such a difficult time of it."

"You too. It's hard not to dwell on what happened."

"We try to remember her as she was, rather than how she ended her life. She'll always be young and beautiful, and alive, to us."

"Yes." She looks down at her tea, stirring it thoughtfully, watching the little bubbles bursting as they trace slow, fluid circles.

"It's hard to believe it's two years," said Geoffrey. "It seems no time at all to us."

It feels like ten years to me, she thinks.

"And Connor, how are you doing?" she says, to lighten the mood, hoping for positive news.

"Better — I've got a new job in a software company in town. They're all quite young, and doing really well. I like them and the work's interesting. I'm lucky."

She's been worried about seeing him again, but there's none of the coldness about him from last time.

"Brilliant. I'm glad for you. Actually, I've got a new job too! Helping to run a florist at the local garden centre, part-time."

"Lisa, that's great," Diana says.

"It is great, actually. Not too stressful, and I'm really enjoying it — especially doing the displays and the arrangements. It's brought out my creative side."

"We're so pleased for you."

When she leaves, they all hug her warmly, including Connor.

* * *

"Hello, Ali," she says quietly. A soft breeze lifts a curl on her forehead and touches the flowers in her hand. A robin flits from stone to stone, eyeing the intruder in his territory. The gravestone no longer looks shiny and new, but seems to have settled into its environment, comfortable in the company of others.

There's no-one else around as Lisa sinks onto one knee at the grave and places the flowers in front of the stone. It's as if Ali is there in person. Lisa can feel her comforting presence all around.

Memories of their teenage years together flit through her mind, like images in a slideshow. Both in badly fitting school uniform, walking home, dawdling after lessons. Laughing together until they cried at some comment that wasn't even funny. Trying on each other's clothes, experimenting with makeup, doing each other's hair before going out on a Friday night. Then at the flat in the city, the excitement of making their own way in life.

She stops herself there. She blocks the bad memories, at least some of the time. But today, on the second anniversary, she wants to remember Ali properly, recall those good memories and forget the circumstances of her death.

She stands and looks around. Diana, Geoffrey and Connor are coming towards her. She waves and goes to greet them.

* * *

She sits in the back garden with Riley, a book on her knees. It's late summer, a Saturday and she has the weekend off, for once, so she's making the most of it.

The garden has benefited from her new experience with plants and flowers, and the borders burst with colour. Geraniums in pots line the back wall of the house and there are alliums and agapanthus in bloom alongside exotic grasses and shrubs. Many of the plants have been rescued from the nursery, too small or unpromising to sell, and nurtured back to health on her kitchen windowsill or in the shed.

Her gardening skills are blossoming together with her back yard. She's not sure where this might lead, but she's found work she enjoys, which she can learn from. There's minimal stress. She's grown in confidence dealing with the public and her displays and floral designs have earned many compliments along with the respect of her employers. It's even taken over from the editing work, which had shrunk to a trickle, too small to survive on. She'd taken a deep breath and told them she was changing direction and would no longer be available for that kind of work. She's even contemplating taking a floristry course, moving it all a step further.

Jessica, too, has benefited from this new-found source of know-how and has redesigned her own garden into a contemporary haven, complete with water feature and deck, all provided and set up by the nurserymen. They've fixed the fence, but instead of mending the hole where Riley squeezed through, they've left a proper gap in both fence and flower beds and created a gravel path between the two gardens so that both dogs and owners can move easily from one to the other.

Sitting there in the warmth of the afternoon, she starts to drift. The book lies untouched on her lap.

This is so different. I'm so different, now.

She remembers her first days at the cottage, when she was frightened of everything and consumed by guilt. Withdrawal from the world had been her way of escaping. That self-imposed solitude had focused her inwards, collapsing her like a burst balloon and threatening to leave her damaged and irreparable. She'd acted in self-defence, removing herself from the world she knew, not trusting it any more. She'd been trying to escape the hurt and the horror it had unexpectedly thrust upon her, to avoid even the possibility of further pain, and that meant people.

Two years to go.

At one point the thought would have terrified her. Now she looks on it as a day that she'll face and deal with. He's just a man who did something terrible, once, in the past.

Does she still feel guilty? Yes, sometimes. But she knows, really knows now, that there was nothing she could have done to help Ali, even if she hadn't been forced to make the choice. Lisa might have died, or both of them, or neither of them. And any other outcome than the actual one would have led to life progressing down quite another path.

Riley's tail starts to wag and his ears twitch. A voice from the house calls. "Hello?" With a scrabble of paws, Riley's gone, through the open back door. He reappears with the intruder behind him.

"You left the front door on the latch. You should be careful, you never know who might walk in."

"I knew you were coming. Anyway Riley would bark if it's someone he doesn't know."

He walks over to Lisa. He looks tired.

"Are you done, doc? No more callouts?"

"I'm done. Off duty. Time to relax with you." He settles into the chair next to her and stretches his legs.

THE END

ACKNOWLEDGEMENTS

This book started with a germ of an idea while I was out on my daily dog walk, and grew from there. So I must acknowledge my two good-natured terriers, Cookie and Tipsy, who walk me every day and keep me sane.

Many thanks to my good friends Joy Ferguson and Her Honour Judge Katharine Marshall for their invaluable advice; to Lee Knight and Sharon Bloom, my early readers.

I'm grateful to Fiona Turner from the Restorative Justice Council and to Kostas Panagiotou from Victim Support for their time and their openness.

Heartfelt thanks to the wonderful Faber Academy and my tutors Louise Doughty, Erica Wagner and Shelley Weiner, as well as my writer colleagues on the six-month course, who have been so supportive.

Also thank you to Marlow Book Club, Tugboats, Scribblers, the marvellous VGs and to my family — all of whom knew I could do this even when I didn't.

ALSO BY SUSANNA BEARD

WHAT HAPPENED THAT NIGHT
THE GIRL ON THE BEACH
THE PERFECT LIFE
THE LOST BROTHER

Thank you for reading this book. If you enjoyed it please leave a review on Amazon or Goodreads. We love to hear from our readers. If there is anything we missed or you have a question about then please get in touch: feedback@joffebooks.com

Join our mailing list to get new releases and great deals every week from one of the UK's leading independent publishers.

www.joffebooks.com

Printed in Great Britain
by Amazon

78766667R00146